Praise for *All the Peopl*

'This well-paced, brilliantly written, black satire is laugh-out-loud funny, a fantastic piece of comic writing that will have you hoping that this is just the first of a whole shelf full of books from Lynch' *Sunday Tribune*

'I have rarely laughed and smiled from cover to cover with a new novel. But Declan Lynch's work will afford readers happy hours of laughter and I told you sos . . . An obligatory read' *Evening Herald*

'A soot-black, booze-sodden comedy of horrors, a satire on men who sell their souls to lousy television and bad music in the mistaken belief that they can live happily on the proceeds' *Sunday Times*

'Just raucously, spontaneously funny; bellylaugh funny' Gerry Stembridge

'A piece of cross-genre jet black writing. Music, murder, mystery, drugged-up, drunken dark delights spin through this book . . . it's a damned good yarn' *Big Issue*

'A very funny, dark and intriguing read' *Hello!*

Declan Lynch writes for the largest selling newspaper in Ireland, the *Sunday Independent*. He is the author of *All the People All the Time*.

Do Nothing Till
You Hear From Me

Declan Lynch

POCKET BOOKS

TOWNHOUSE

First published in Great Britain and Ireland by Pocket/TownHouse, 2003
An imprint of Simon & Schuster UK Ltd, and TownHouse Ltd, Dublin

Simon & Schuster UK is a Viacom company

1 3 5 7 9 10 8 6 4 2

Simon & Schuster UK Ltd
Africa House
64–78 Kingsway
London WC2B 6AH

Simon & Schuster Australia
Sydney

TownHouse Ltd
Trinity House
Charleston Road
Ranelagh
Dublin 6
Ireland

A CIP catalogue record for this book is available from the British Library

ISBN 1 903650 57 7

Typeset by SX composing DTP, Rayleigh, Essex
printed and bound in Great Britain by
Cox & Wyman Ltd, Reading, Berkshire

Do Nothing Till
You Hear From Me

Chapter 1

It was something that Dwight Yorke said. They were chatting in the executive lounge at Old Trafford, and Dwight mentioned that he had three cars to suit his different moods, a Mercedes for when he's doing business, a Range Rover for everyday use and a Ferrari for fun.

So when Freddie Dowd gets back to Dublin, he buys a Mercedes, a Range Rover and a Ferrari just to get the fever out of his blood.

And still, none of them feels quite right for what he has to do today. Dwight never mentioned what a man should drive if he has to visit his estranged wife in a clinic where she is being treated for alcoholism and drug addiction. Dwight said nothing about that.

He goes for the Merc. Freddie Dowd, here on business.

It has been six months since he got lucky, six wild months climaxing in the buying of the three cars like Dwight Yorke. But this day will try his soul. Luckily, despite it all, Freddie Dowd has a soul. He had it when he had nothing else, through the dark years when he knows that they were all laughing at him, mocking his latest effort

1

to crack it, to run that gig, to manage that torch singer, to discover that actress, to make that movie, to bring something to the party.

Laughing at him, too, because he looked all wrong, a little guy with big afro hair and big ideas, and a serene little smile on his lips, he who had so little to be serene about. The little guy that everyone loves in a Woody Allen movie, but that they cross the road to avoid on Baggot Street. Because in the Woody Allen movie they know that the guy is actually Woody Allen, the toast of Manhattan. In the Freddie Dowd movie . . . well, it's just some hippie from Dún Laoghaire who went on one too many missions in the acid wars, the sort of guy who is liable to get up and dance on his own in the pub if he likes the band.

He even has a slightly embarrassing walk, almost robotic, very still from the waist up, very quick on his feet, like he is being drawn trance-like to some holy spot known only to himself, drawn by the strange music which only he can hear. Some sixties eastern shit, with bongos.

But in the Freddie Dowd movie that Freddie Dowd sees it is the glorious summer of 1968 and Van Morrison has just released *Astral Weeks*. And Van hooks up with Freddie and Van sees clearly that Freddie is the only one who knows just how great Van Morrison is, how stupefyingly great. And from that day to this, Freddie would protect Van in the one way that Van needs protecting – from interviewers asking him personal questions.

He would sit in on all those interviews and if Van started hating the general drift, Freddie would break in and say 'later for the garbage', the catchphrase he has borrowed from the Man. And if Van couldn't take it any more,

Freddie would explain to the journalist that the man is not being difficult, it's just when you are as ridiculously great as Van, it doesn't really matter whether you can rabbit all nice and polite with the *New Musical Express*. Later for the garbage.

Not that the Freddie Dowd movie ever gets made. He just talks about it, how you can make great music and great money the way that Van did it. Two weeks to record *Astral Weeks* in New York City, two shimmering weeks and a thousand years before we will truly know the consequences.

In real time of course, Freddie never did hook up with Van, but listening to *Astral Weeks* got him into jazz, and jazz above all else keeps him sane, he reckons. He talks a lot about jazz these days, how jazz has this inherent greatness which would be obvious to everyone if the industry just got the finger out and pushed these cats like Miles and Bird and 'Trane who left all this great shit behind them, great shit just lying there in the back catalogues, nothing required but some cool artwork and a sense of right and wrong.

And when he talks jazz, when he talks about selling jazz for actual money, they humour him, and he says he only has to be right once, and they know that it won't happen, and they thank Christ their heads are not so full of shit, and they thank Christ they don't look like that.

And along with his big bad hair and his eyes blazing with hope in his latest discovery, and that look of inexplicable inner contentment, Freddie Dowd has this soft little voice, almost inaudible at times, meaning that sometimes he has to repeat things, he has to say all his shit twice.

He's keeping that voice now, just as he's keeping the big

bad hair and the mysterious smile, now that he's got lucky, now that he was right just the one time. He feels the need to keep looking like that, and sounding like that, just to let it be known that he finally cracked it and it didn't freak him out, that a guy could make big money and still not get an executive haircut, sitting in the barber's chair in The Shelbourne with some stockbroker cat getting a hot towel in the next chair, inviting him upstairs for the Full Irish and a rap about his property portfolio. Later, much later for the garbage. But it also reminds him of who he is, and what his soul is made of, and that he still has a soul like he always hoped he would have, when he got to the land of dreams.

He checks to see that it's still there most days, but especially today. Driving to the Stepaside Addiction Centre in his sky-blue Mercedes, way out beyond the southern suburbs of Dublin, he checks it again. He still has a soul, he reasons, because he hit paydirt without even trying. What he did, he did as a wage-slave during one of those weird times, putting on the suit with the skinny leather tie and hacking nine-to-five in advertising to stop the fuzz from coming in the windows, knocking out this jingle for a TV ad campaign, a jingle for the phone company. The title was a steal from Duke Ellington, 'Do Nothing Till You Hear From Me'. But nobody spotted it, because nobody knows things like that any more. He did not ask Paddy Lamb, the manager of the boyband Fellaz, to remember it and to make the boys do a version of it that became number one in every country in the world where people have money. Freddie Dowd, official loser of the Borough of Dún Laoghaire, did not ask for this. He owes nothing to no one and no great crimes were committed in claiming the loot, just a

4

misdemeanour really, a dodgy little number that he knocked out during his lunch break.

He particularly owes nothing to his wife Dorothy McIlroy, who has been living with a rich man and, occasionally, sending money to their daughter Nadine, which Nadine sends back by return of post. He still lives where he and Nadine have lived for seventeen years, a basement flat in Dún Laoghaire that will do them fine until the big moolah comes through.

He sees a sign for Stepaside and he feels a surge of the old fear. He can't do this. And he can't not do it either. The counsellors insist it will be good for him, and good for Nadine if she can possibly make it. They say that the victims of addiction are like the addicts, never fully healed until they go back in there and confront it.

Confronting Dorothy. He shivers. They say it's the most harrowing thing that happens at the Stepaside Centre, this confronting. But Dorothy tells him she's big enough to take it. Freddie agonizes about it, having gone to such lengths to avoid her over the years, refusing money when he needed it so, so bad, letting her pay Nadine's school fees but no more, determined not to draw her on him again, not to be lured back into the madness.

Dorothy phones him up one day like he always knew she would, like he always feared she would, looking to sit down with him and have an actual conversation, not the usual flurry of chat that happens when they meet by accident on the street. And yet, amid all the panic, there is some twisted need inside him to go to her. Some inability to refuse her when she is at rock bottom. Maybe for the good times.

He lowers the electronic window thinking that the cold

air will keep him alert, cruising up the avenue to the dreary old mansion where some ambassador used to live, drearier still this morning in the January fog which is doing his head in with its shades of Hammer Horror, like some half-dead old geezer will answer the door and tell him there's no one in and no one has lived here for twenty years and then he will hear a voice from inside saying, 'Who is it Charles?'

He is afraid for himself, and he is afraid for Nadine. She is seventeen tomorrow. The most she will do in the circumstances is write a letter two pages long, concluding with this sentence: *My mother is a drunken twat.* The idea is, you show this to the counsellors to give them a bit of background, and eventually they give the letter to the addict after about five weeks out of the six, when they're beginning to see the light.

Freddie is driving up to the front steps when he sees her off to the right of the big house, or rather he hears her first and then he sees her. She is laughing her head off, at him. It's the Dorothy laugh, no question, still sounding like she has just heard the dirtiest joke ever. It takes him all the way back to a vision of her at a party, drinking whiskey and belting out this dirty, dirty laugh at something he was saying, a real live New Yorker that Freddie Dowd brought over to Dublin to read her poems, a 'punk poet' as they billed her, and he's rapping and she's laughing, laughing at his jokes. He tries to remember what he was saying to make her laugh so hard, but all he recalls is she was definitely laughing with him and not at him. He could tell.

The man standing beside her right now, he is a funny, funny man. The man is trying to light Dorothy's cigarette, but she keeps spluttering, still creased by the sight of

Freddie Dowd at the wheel of a Mercedes Benz. The man with Dorothy is Gerry 'Bricks' Melvin, a sax player. And a wizard. And a wild, wild cat. All of these things, often in the course of the same night, often during one of those nights on the Leeson Street strip a long time ago.

Freddie gets out of the Merc. He tosses the keys and catches them cleanly, to show that the wheels are all his. They're all laughing now, the three of them reunited like this in a place like this, all sober, and apparently intending to stay that way, so early in the day. Their destinies seem to be intertwined in drink or in rehab, Gerry arriving in last night a few hours after Dorothy.

'See you later, chief,' says Bricks Melvin. He hops away apologetically, a big, elegant, sad-eyed man with a droopy moustache, a younger Einstein. He hops away too quickly for Freddie, who immediately feels exposed to the full attention of Dorothy.

Bricks saunters off into the fog. Dorothy takes Freddie by the hand, still speechless with mirth. She leads him down the side steps into a basement canteen, thronged with about thirty clients, alcoholics, drug addicts, compulsive gamblers, and those who have come to confront them. Only that the visitors are wearing overcoats, you could hardly tell which is which.

'Sorry, babe,' she says. 'It's just the sight of you behind the wheel.'

'It's my car,' he says.

And she laughs again.

He has no sure way of knowing how Dorothy will react to anything he says, whether she will laugh like a drain or stab him in the neck with a broken bottle. Today it seems

7

she is being Dorothy at her most together, a fantastic lady all electrified, radiant with positive energy. If Freddie didn't know better, he'd say it was this honeymoon period they talk about when someone goes off the sauce. But he knows better.

He squeezes into a seat at the edge of a table full of the flushed-looking family of some young guy wearing a baseball cap, some fucked-up child, one of the E generation. They sound like they're from the country. It is still a surprise to Freddie that people down the country do drugs.

Dorothy is getting decaffeinated coffee from the machine. Above her is a board stretching around the walls on which is written in gold paint the Twelve Steps of Alcoholics Anonymous. The steps mention God a lot. He wonders if Dorothy has got God.

Freddie watches her filling the coffees. He eyes her up and down. She would be thirty-five now, but even in these blue overalls she's wearing she could still pass for twenty-five, maybe on account of the life of luxury she fell into, probably because she is permanently wired. Freddie imagines that other men must be as intimidated as he was by the first sight of her, the crewcut, the leather, the body-piercing, which she seems to have abandoned for today at least, and the general vibe of Art. She tells people first thing that she's a performance poet, and most of them skulk away after the opening exchanges, their heads full of disquieting images of Warhol and Patti Smith and Lou Reed and punk rock. But a few heroes like Freddie Dowd stay in there just to listen to the soft Manhattan music in her voice, and they soon see how warm and generous and smart and funny she really is, and they fall in love with her.

And pretty soon after that, they start to think that maybe they had it right in the first place. Pretty soon they want to run away. But not Freddie. Because he knew straight away that this was maybe his one shot, and he was right. He knew that no normal Irish woman would ever sleep with a man like him, who looked like he did, and did what he did. Whereas to your New York punk poet, it was no crime for a guy to look a bit cosmic, to bang on about all sorts of projects and ambitions, even if most of it was obvious bollocks. It was no crime at all to your Manhattan avant-garde type. But in Dublin, before all the optimism took hold, it was a crime punishable by no money and no sex, and that sound of chuckling as you left the room.

Dorothy had none of that meanness in her. But then he remembers the moment about a week after they met, when they were lying on the grass in St Stephen's Green, and she had a bottle of Smirnoff in her, and Freddie spoke ill of the film *Gandhi*. He said it was overly long. Dorothy let it rest for a minute or so, and then said, with a venom which chills Freddie even after all this time, 'Some of the greatest men have been mocked for their beliefs.' She went on to lacerate him for having the gall to badmouth a spiritual giant like Mahatma Gandhi – Freddie who brought punk poets over from New York so he could get them drunk and fuck them and, by the way, it's totally unprofessional to fuck the talent, and that's it, over, finito, asshole.

They had another drink to make up, and another to fall out again, and when eventually they were back on civil terms, after a hideous night of public shouting drenched in booze, after a row that took them through a dozen pubs and three nightclubs and down to an early-morning pub on the quays, Freddie realized that this lady was bringing much, much more to the party than the high, wild and handsome spirit of rock'n'roll, New York style.

She later confessed that she was furious because Freddie was looking at other women. He was chuffed at the notion of anyone feeling possessive about him, and he didn't deny it. He had been squinting at other ladies, now that he was at last having regular sex. They all looked so placid, so undemanding, compared to Dorothy, so right for him, who hated confrontation so much, who hated even raising his voice, so right, like they wanted to take him home and knit him jumpers in bright fantastic colours, and none of this help-me-make-it-through-the-night routine.

He thought he might get around to these ladies eventually when he was free, but he never did. And that was nearly twenty years ago. Dorothy brings the coffees. Freddie goes to take a sip, but the instant he lifts the cup, he realizes his hand is trembling, so he puts it down again on the wild off-chance that Dorothy mightn't have clocked it.

Dorothy starts up one of her mid-range, earthy chuckles. 'You've had it pal,' she says. 'You're freaked out.' She offers him a cigarette, a Dunhill.

'Gave them up,' he says.

'You're a fucking pro.'

'Couldn't afford it.'

They laugh.

'This place is tough,' he says, looking up at the Twelve Steps.

'Tougher still for a rich bitch,' she says.

She's rich all right, due to living for the last five years

with Richard Madigan, a big-time accountant with artistic tendencies. But she is no rich bitch by any normal definition. She still has the implacable stare of some lost fifth member of The Clash, and her skin is as bad as ever when you get up close, like she never fully snapped out of some marathon sulk, which to Freddie only adds to her sullen magnetism. He will bet money that old Richard offered many times to have the zits removed by some vastly expensive and painless method, only to be met with a contemptuous refusal, Dorothy spurning such dishonest bourgeois crap.

Freddie knows her enough to know that she really wasn't after Richard Madigan's money, that the notion of it is ridiculous. Rather, she loved the man, fiercely, slavishly, transcendentally, and so she spent every hour of every day of five years driving him progressively crazy until it was reliably reported that he flew one day to the Cayman Islands to stash away some loot on behalf of some of Dublin's most prestigious business leaders, and then threw himself from the twelfth floor of the five-star Capricorn Hotel, leaving a note on the pillow of the four-poster in his suite which said that he loved her madly, and he was leaving everything to her.

But he couldn't face another day.

And maybe he had a few money worries too.

'Listen babe,' she says, taking his hand again. 'I want to send Nadine some dough for her birthday.'

Freddie thinks of the letter that Nadine has written.

'That's not really the most fantastic idea,' he begins.

But Dorothy cuts across him. 'I'm not talking a huge amount of money,' she says. 'Richard fucked up.'

Freddie flinches. 'Shit,' he says.

'I could spare maybe a hundred grand?' she says.

'Oh, shit,' he says.

'Price of a rabbit-hutch in Ringsend babe,' she says. 'Nothing more.'

'No need,' he says. 'Really, there's no need.'

'I need a new start,' she says. 'I need to get back to the streets.'

'No need,' he says. 'I . . . I have money.'

'Shush now,' she says. 'I'm here to get well.'

Freddie tries again. 'Dorothy, I want you to listen to me. I said, I have money. That Mercedes is really mine.'

'You're shitting me,' she says.

'I wrote a song for . . . a boyband . . . for Fellaz.'

'Never heard of them.'

'"Do Nothing Till You Hear From Me"?'

He finds himself humming the intro. Dorothy joins him, recognizing it from somewhere.

'I can explain,' he says.

Dorothy is suddenly deflated. 'You don't need me any more,' she says.

'You're here to get well,' he says.

They sit in a circle in group therapy, six clients and six friends or relatives who are meant to be brutally honest in confronting them. Freddie is given to understand by the two counsellors present, a young gunslinger with big red hair and a middle-aged teacher-type lady, two women with a high reputation for cracking some of the hardest nuts on the block, that they will break Dorothy down and then build her up again. He marvels at their ambition.

But then Dorothy is already introducing herself to the group with, 'I'm Dorothy and I'm an alcoholic.'

And then there is a silence.

The silence goes on, and Freddie's discomfort deepens. Dorothy sits directly opposite him. He remembers that underneath the boiler suit, her arms are covered in tattoos. He has a sudden surge of compassion for her. This woman has sat down with Allen Ginsberg, he thinks. She shouldn't have to listen to this shit, and he shouldn't be the bourgeois bastard laying it on her. But then the counsellor with the big red hair nods to him and he breaks the silence.

'I'm here for Dorothy,' he says. His voice sounds hushed even in this quiet room.

Dorothy leans back like the smallest noise from him is unbearable. He is aware of people straining to hear him, but he is incapable of raising his voice above a certain volume, like he has been living for years in a house in which someone is dying.

'I'm here for myself,' he says. 'But if I am being totally honest, I am here for our daughter, Nadine.' And because I'm afraid not to be here, he thinks. But no matter. 'Nadine is very angry with Dorothy,' he says. 'She was angry for a long time that Dorothy didn't want to see her. And then she was angry that Dorothy *did* want to see her. You know?'

Dorothy nods quickly, appearing to accept this. Freddie finds the nerve to go on.

'It freaks me to see Nadine so angry,' he says. 'It freaks me that whatever is wrong with Dorothy, and whatever is wrong with me, too, might be passed on to Nadine. Somehow.'

The young counsellor breaks in.

'And how does that make you feel?' she says.

13

He checks to see if Dorothy is ready to pounce, but she just nods again. Anyway, she will be prevented from pouncing. It is part of the therapy that the addicts have to put up with everything that is thrown at them, in spite of their overwhelming urge to bite back.

'How does that make you feel?' the counsellor tries again.

'Freaked,' he says.

The counsellor digs in.

'Any other feelings?' she says, making major eye-contact. And for a strange moment Freddie finds refuge in those caring blue eyes, maybe even a glimmer of hope that he might hook up with this counsellor lady with the big red hair and something about her telling Freddie that when she has done with the old head-shrinking manoeuvres for the day, she might like nothing better than to give Freddie Dowd an uncomplicated sexual experience and maybe knit him a jumper in bright fantastic colours. That old feeling that only Dorothy can stir. Dorothy, who is leaning forward now, like she is hearing his bad thoughts.

'I don't think feelings are the problem here, you know?' he says. 'I don't think that Dorothy has ever had a problem with feelings. I would say that Dorothy has too many feelings, you know?'

No one seems inclined to stop him, so he goes on. He is in that place where he can hear the strange music.

'It surprised me to hear Dorothy introducing herself as an alcoholic,' he says. 'I know it sounds a bit old fashioned, but I never felt that Dorothy was an alcoholic in the normal sense. Not completely. I just think that Dorothy . . . I just think she's a bit . . . moody.'

Dorothy nods again, slowly this time, solemnly.

Freddie was on the brink of saying she was a bit unstable, but something in those pale green eyes told him to go with moody. It feels liberating to Freddie to be saying these things at all, and to say them to Dorothy's face too. Maybe it's the money, giving him strength.

He goes on. 'Dorothy wasn't the most fantastic mother. I think she'd agree with that. I'd say from day one, she had no maternal instincts at all. But that's cool. She was . . . how can I describe it? She was . . . an artist. She just hated living out in Dún Laoghaire with a husband and a small child. She felt trapped. She couldn't write poems any more. And maybe the drinking got worse as a result.'

Freddie senses the counsellor's unease, and he knows that he's pulling his punches somewhat, but he genuinely believes that, yes, Dorothy is of course an alcoholic and a drug addict, but she has about a thousand other exotic tendencies as well for which booze and drugs offer no explanation.

And then Dorothy gets up and leaves the room, like this has nothing to do with her.

Afterwards, back down in the canteen, Freddie is told that she is in her room and she won't come out. Bricks Melvin comes over to him, full of positive vibes that this time around he will crack it. And Freddie gives him his phone number, suggesting that when Bricks gets out of here, he might teach Nadine a few scales on the sax, or whatever.

Then Freddie drives home in his sky-blue Mercedes, shattered.

Around ten o'clock that night at the Stepaside Centre,

Dorothy comes down to reception. She says she is angry about the quality of the food.

An hour later the nurse at reception goes upstairs to check on Dorothy, but she is not in her room. The window is open. The nurse shines her torch on the tarmac below, on the body of Dorothy McIlroy.

Chapter 2

She walks Dún Laoghaire pier most days. Freddie picks out a CD for her, and puts it into her Discman, without her knowing what it is until she switches it on outside the People's Park. He slips it into the machine with that little smile that says, later for the garbage.

Today Freddie gives her jazz. She's not ready for it. Who is ready for this stuff? I mean who could honestly say that they like jazz? Miles Davis, he sucks. He is just taking the piss. John Coltrane? 'A Love Supreme'? More like, John Coltrane, 'A Man Taking the Piss'.

And still Freddie says, hang on in there, you will get it if you hang on in there. Like, a normal father would expect you to get good marks in your exams and go to university and so forth, but Freddie just asks that you read good books and listen to jazz, which is actually a big thing to ask. Maybe too big.

I mean, he must have noticed that the only thing these jazz greats do any more is die. Nearly every week he comes back from the library with a photocopy of an article about some jazz great who's just died. He gives her the photocopy and then while she's reading about this jazz great and all the other jazz greats he played with forty years ago, Freddie plays some sounds, turning it down to explain how they were all on heroin at the time. He just puts it out there, not saying if it was good or bad that they took heroin. Bad, by the sound of it.

She would say this to Freddie, except she reckons he can't take it today. Not with Dorothy doing herself in. She will tell him later on. She will say she hung on in there, and she still doesn't get it, and she's not the only one. Ah, forget it, he loves these guys. He will just shake his head like you said something hilarious, and he will go, 'Hang on in there, you will get it if you just hang on in there.'

But you might be mad by then, Nadine will say. Mad as fuck, mad as Dorothy. Which is a sore point because Freddie doesn't think Dorothy was mad, not really. He thinks it's society's way of putting people in a box.

Freddie wanted to take her out to some Louis Stewart gig tonight for her seventeenth, Louis plucking jazz guitar, but that's not really on now. She wonders if it crossed Dorothy's mind at all, just before she threw herself out the window, that this wasn't exactly the ideal time for it.

Tonight, maybe the flat is the best place to be. Freddie still looks a bit of a plonker when he's out in public, with his fuzz. And he used to have loads of weird stories, but now he keeps telling the same one over and over, how he stole the title of a Duke Ellington song called 'Do Nothing Till You Hear From Me' when he wrote a jingle for the phone company, and then Paddy Lamb the boy-band manager got Fellaz to do it, and no one knew about the Duke being caught up in it and all.

They'll know soon enough, if Freddie keeps telling them. Poor Freddie. He screwed up big on Dorothy. He just couldn't resist it, the big sap. He really believed that she was making an effort. Then he turns his back on her for five minutes and she's out the window.

Nadine has the pier almost to herself today, thanks to the vicious cold. It must be nearly a mile out and back, long enough anyway to work up these speeches in her head that she never has the heart to lay on Freddie when she gets home. She reckons this is why they get on so well. They're soft, the two of them. A pair of wusses. They never fight about anything serious.

Nadine knocks off the jazz. She's got a Billy Joel album stashed deep in the pocket of her leather coat, but she has never sunk so low as to put it on. It was given to her last summer, by Trayton. It's the only thing he gave her, apart from this smell that still clings to her somehow. She started walking the pier trying to get rid of it, thinking the air would blow away this scent, this waft that was his gift to her. One Billy Joel album, and that waft, and his New York City phone number that eventually put her through to some old man in Tennessee.

And every day her head starts to fill up with this wild shit like, what if Trayton, the fucker, made a genuine mistake when he gave that number to Freddie down at the hotel with the taxi waiting, what if he felt hassled by the taxi and forgot his own phone number, or maybe forgot just one digit on the bit of notepaper he stuffed into Freddie's top pocket, because she didn't have a pocket for him to stuff it in?

Freddie had no number to give him in exchange, because

Freddie had no phone because he had no money. So what if Trayton made a genuine mistake and is himself walking up and down some pier in New Jersey or somewhere thinking he can't go on living for sixty or seventy years knowing it will never get any better than last summer, you just know these things deep down.

But most days, deep down, Nadine reckons there was no horrible mistake, that she got turned over, and that's the end of it.

Freddie, of course, was deeply shocked by the Billy Joel album, calling it a very ugly scene. He bought the coat for her, to console her, and so she wouldn't get frozen on her walks. Full-length black leather, a bit of a Nazi job, but great pockets for filling with jazz CDs that no one ever hears.

Freddie let her leave school too, because she was so fucking miserable. And anyway, with all the money coming in you wouldn't need an education. Not a formal one anyway. You would just need to listen all day to Freddie shite-ing on and on about jazz.

Trayton. His first name was Trayton, or so he said.

Halfway up the pier Nadine steps on to the bandstand and off the other side, a superstition. She remembers that Dorothy put on some performance here on a Sunday afternoon, some sort of mime. She remembers being very ashamed.

She felt something in a general sort of way when Freddie sat her down and told her that Dorothy was gone. She felt sorry that her mother was dead, because you only have one mother and all. But she felt sort of relieved, too, that Dorothy wasn't around any more.

And that's all the emotion she has on that subject, because she can smell him again, that fucker Trayton. Six months after it, she can still smell him. She is not imagining it, she can actually smell him still, a real waft of some American soap or oil or spray or scent or cologne or lotion or fragrance or some fucking juice that seeped out of his skin and into hers. Even the lousy weather can't blow it away when it hits her like this, taking her back to when they walked here in the heat, knowing they would have all afternoon up there on the third floor of the Royal Marine Hotel, on the big bed in his father's room.

And after that, and all the stuff they said drinking beer and smoking American cigarettes on Kilbrittan beach in the evening, it makes her so sick that she was such a sap, walking up and down this pier in January with nothing except this animal mist that he left on her to torture her, and this Billy Joel greatest hits album that he bought her because Billy is his main man.

And then, oh Jesus, she told him stuff after a load of beer up there on Kilbrittan beach, really embarrassing shit about the great books she has read, harping on in her little high-pitched voice about her all-time favourite *Catch-22*. And this seemed to kind of put the wind up him because he started shite-ing on about how she is far too great looking to be reading books, how you never see great-looking women reading books, and maybe there's a reason for that, the reason being, they get books written about them, mostly by strange little guys. It was like he sussed the bit of madness in her, and he wouldn't have it. Because the really amazing thing about Trayton is that he doesn't like mad women. As far as Nadine can see, Trayton is the only man alive who

21

doesn't go straight for the mad ones. He explained that most folks are a bit crazy in some respect, but it can be cured by doing the right things. The problem is, most guys don't want things to change because it's so much easier to fuck crazy women straight off, and too late they realize they're with a wrong one, and they can't get out of it.

She tried to explain this to her friend Regina, how Trayton actually made you feel totally together, totally right in the head when you were with him, just totally. And Regina would drink to that, a double.

Then his scent hits her again, reminding her that, like a sap, Nadine had to push it on Kilbrittan beach, babbling on in her high-pitched little voice about how wrong he was, how *Catch-22* was the coolest book ever written. But he wouldn't buy that either because he got stuck on her legs, like a woman with good legs just had to find something better to do with her life than bury herself in a goddamn book. And Nadine thought she had him there because she is doubtful about her legs, considering them long enough but not exactly a brilliant shape. But like Regina says, they'll do for around here.

She owes Regina for taking her out on the town for about six months solid to get over it, six months being pawed by sick old men in Rojack's nightclub, after which she knew she'd never get over it but at least she knew a bit about real life, the sort of really bad experiences you need when you're young if you want to avoid turning out like Freddie, who knows nothing about real life except what he hears through the magic horn of Miles Davis. And baby, that ain't much.

Jesus, if Freddie had any idea of the places she's been and

the badness she's seen since last summer, his fuzz would turn white in a minute. Freddie thinks she goes to trendy places where you drink coffee all night, not knowing that Regina brings her to be pawed by these old men in Rojack's, while Regina gets hugely twisted.

And all this walking up the pier, there's badness in that too, Regina telling her that the best revenge is to fuck with the heads of all men, to watch the poor sick bastards with their eyes out on sticks when you walk the walk. It got a bit sad with Regina in the end, because Regina was turning thirty and doing so much crying into her nightclub wine you'd think she was the one who got turned over, the way she kept asking Nadine to tell her again about Trayton, tell her again how he was going to be an engineer and build a house for the two of them with his own hands, a house with no books in it. And how he told her that her life was one sweet moment, tell her again about that fantastic explosion in her belly when they got it together on the big bed in his father's room, tell her, tell her tell her while they shout for another bottle of nightclub wine or maybe have one sent over to the table by some sick man in a suit. Which Nadine could handle because, apart from the books and the jazz, the one thing Freddie taught her was how to drink, so she wouldn't end up like Dorothy.

Just look at it, he would say, just look at it.

And this would come in handy when Regina would get legless, like the time she got this serious dose of the hiccups and she threw her head back with her mouth open while the barman poured wine down her throat from a samovar-thing, with the crowd on the dance floor cheering.

Regina's away now, promoted to the London office of

23

the bank, from where she fucked off to Amsterdam and hasn't been heard from since. Either she's gone totally on the drink or totally off it, but anyway she fucked off the way everyone in Nadine's life seems to fuck off. Everyone except Freddie.

But then Nadine sometimes figures she's had all the people she needs in her life, without leaving Dún Laoghaire. She's read all the books and heard all the albums, she has seen the madhouse van coming and going, and now she just wants to be with Trayton, living a normal life in a normal house with a normal American. For Dorothy.

It's what she wouldn't have wanted.

But listen, Dorothy was a rock next to Trayton. Dorothy wanted to take her to New York too, and she meant it all except, being Dorothy, she went out the window.

Two weeks ago, Dorothy was standing at the end of the pier. Nadine felt a bolt of panic to see her standing there. She can't just turn around and march back down the pier. She hopes for a few daft seconds that Dorothy might not recognize her, with the scarf covering most of her face. But then Nadine is about six feet tall and she looks even taller in the leather coat and she has long black hair that you can't really miss blowing wild, and Dorothy is sort of her mother. And Dorothy is giving her a big smile.

Nadine keeps walking towards her. There's no escape, not like bumping into her on the DART and getting off at the next stop.

Dorothy is wearing a fawn coat and no nose-jewellery, a conservative look if you ignore the crewcut and the Doc Martens.

Nadine takes out a packet of ten Rothmans and roots deep in her pockets for a lighter. Dorothy offers a lit cigarette, and Nadine lights her Rothmans from it.

Dorothy is still smiling.

'I'd smoke in the middle of a hurricane, honey,' she says.

'Yeah,' says Nadine.

'Can I walk with you?'

Nadine shrugs. They start back towards Dún Laoghaire, Dorothy all composed, Nadine feeling that it will take another seventeen years to get to the other end of the pier.

'You know what, Nadine?'

'What?'

'You're beautiful.'

'Sorry about . . .'

'Richard.'

'Richard.'

'I'll tell you the truth, Nadine, I feel like I'm free again. I feel fifteen years younger, back on the streets. It's like the man said, when you ain't got nothing, you got nothing to lose.'

'Sorry anyway, OK?'

'I'm going into rehab, honey. I'm gonna make you proud of me.'

Nadine is forcing the pace. They reach the bandstand. Dorothy offers her another cigarette but she refuses, avoiding eye contact.

'I'm an alcoholic,' Dorothy says, 'but today, I'm a happy alcoholic.'

Dorothy laughs, a big belly-laugh. Nadine lets out a snigger. It's almost impossible not to respond to Dorothy's laugh.

'I want you to come to New York,' Dorothy says.

Nadine lets out a full laugh at this. Dorothy tries again.

'I don't mean now, I just mean some time.'

'Getting dark,' Nadine says.

Two weeks ago, she had seen Dorothy for the last time, and this was the last thing she said to her: 'Getting dark.' They were near the entrance to the pier. The light was giving up on that dirty January day. It was starting to drizzle. She recalls that, for one desperate moment, she thought Dorothy was going to hug her. So she skipped on to the pavement and started towards the car ferry. The traffic was crawling now along the seafront. She slipped through the cars to the other side of the road. Dorothy stayed where she was.

'New York!' Dorothy shouted.

Nadine laughed again. She turned quickly up Marine Road past the Royal Marine Hotel and on through the main street in the direction of home, the basement of 21, Waterloo Terrace. Which Freddie is thinking of buying, along with number 22 and maybe number 23, while he's hot. Or maybe he'll go for one of the penthouse apartments down by the seafront, for the view.

He really doesn't know what to do with himself, does Freddie.

Two weeks ago, and now Dorothy is gone. Nadine reckons she should be feeling worse about it, but she is feeling the cold now, irritating her back. It gets like this sometimes, this withered patch about the size of a CD, just below her right shoulder. It happened in the car when Dorothy went apeshit during a row with Freddie, and drove straight into the railings down there at the end of the main street, outside the People's Park. There was an engine fire and Nadine in the back seat got burned.

She was five then, but she still dreams of being trapped in the back of a burning car.

She thinks, New York my ass.

Chapter 3

Gerry 'Bricks' Melvin is eating dessert on his second day of treatment at the Stepaside Addiction Centre, when the thought occurs to him that this is the best time of year for trying to get off the sauce. With the cold and the rain and the inclement conditions all round, what else would you be doing? It's not like you can sit out in a beer garden sipping cool lagers. It's not like some summer festival down the country, doing the gig, then getting hammered all night with the local woollybacks.

No, you're better off in a joint like this, getting your shit together. And just when he is settling on this thought, just when he is about to share it with the kid in the baseball cap across the table from him, to boost his morale, this good thought starts turning bad on him.

By the same token, he can't help thinking, there is really nothing in this world to beat hot whiskeys in front of a big fire up in Brabazon's of Howth, a storm battering the windows, and then back to Barney McKenna's for a blast on the old horn. Yes, for the drinker the winter season has its compensations. Which is why he downed a bottle of vodka yesterday, to clear his head one last time, and to put one over on the Gestapo.

And while punters who don't know their stuff would be wondering why a man aiming to give up the drink would be smuggling vodka in his overnight bag, to the *cognoscenti* it makes sense, the ritual of the last bottle, the danger of your whole system collapsing if you just stop dead. Even if there are classier places to do it than the toilet cubicle, trousers around the ankles in case the Gestapo get curious and break the door down, as they well might in a house full of certified loopers.

And then a nervous dash across the basement hall to dump the empty bottle wrapped up in a laundry bag in the kitchen rubbish, to cheat the inquisition. And a very close call when the nurse looked into the kitchen and Bricks bullshitted that he was on breakfast duty, sussing out where the sausages were to save time in the morning.

One night, a long time ago, he improvised a response to a Dexter Gordon solo at the Montreux Festival. Now he is doing his best work matching wits with a nurse who has probably been to see Garth Brooks nine times, and who is giving him grief about fucking sausages.

Then there's the trifle, in a metallic bowl. This trifle that he is eating has no sherry in it, but it makes him think sherry. And for Bricks Melvin, thinking is next to doing. It's the trifle all right. The trifle in a metallic bowl. It's the trifle that is doing his head in. He's not thinking sherry any more, he's thinking prison, he's thinking funny-farm, he's thinking orphanage, the gulag. Every institution that Bricks Melvin has been in has given him the odd bowl of trifle in a metallic bowl in exchange for abusing him. The deal is, they torture you, they ruin your life, and you get to eat trifle.

The difference is that this here is an institution that Bricks Melvin signed himself into. There's no denying it, he checked in here a free man of his own volition, and there's nothing to stop him checking out. He felt over the Christmas that the time had come, that he needed to give it one good shot in a setup like this, after breaking his jaw last year when he fell against the door of a taxi. A bad break for a horn player. But he was soon back in Brabazon's with his jaw all wired up, sucking wine through a straw.

And in appreciation of this, he is telling himself to cut it out and finish his tea and do the washing-up the same as these other poor fucks in this canteen, when the rage starts up in him again. He starts to think that the bastards have buggered him up so completely, they don't even have to come looking for him any more. He arrives on their doorstep with his bag packed, in his good suit, asking to be let in, and paying a couple of grand for the privilege.

This is how it happens for Bricks Melvin, days and weeks and months of peace, or something like it, and then this rage, this boiling anger. And nothing to cure it now, his last bottle of vodka gone. He clenches his whole body, for fear that he will lose it completely and start breaking things. He gets up from the table and puts his bowl on the draining board. Then he walks slowly and stiffly up a couple of flights of stairs to the dormitory which he is sharing with three others. Something tells him that, at the age of forty-five, this will be his last dormitory.

There is not much packing to do, because he hadn't properly unpacked. Maybe he knew deep down that he wouldn't take to this regime, the way they put a bomb under your personality, the way they keep an eye on you all the time, disturbing you when you're trying to read the paper, always barging in, invading your privacy.

This is what he was talking about with Dorothy, when she broke his balls about the vodka. This is what he was talking about, this thing he sussed in group therapy, that it was all wrong to be invading a person's privacy in this way, that his feelings were his own bastard business. Bricks Melvin's feelings can't be put into words, they can hardly even be put into music. Like he told Dorothy, he never stayed long in AA because of all the chat about how you feel. Dorothy is from America, they like all that shit in America. Bricks Melvin is a sideman, a horn player, a man from nowhere, and going nowhere. Whatever he feels, he puts it into his playing. Feelings are high things, and you don't want scattering them around on punters in the AA rooms. This is known to every serious player. The big mistake he made was thinking there was something wrong with that. Thinking that if he checked in here to kick the habit, and the lifestyle, he might be able to hack it better in the world.

Dorothy too was trying to take it away from him, this thing that he has. Telling him he can't get sober and stay a player. Telling him there is another life for him out there beyond his wildest dreams, not because this programme is easy, but because it is hard. Telling him he has to stop being Bricks Melvin, the player, because that guy is dead inside, he feels nothing any more except a few blue moods that he lifted from Dizzy Gillespie.

And then she was dead.

So much for the psychobabble.

31

It's a bit blurred after that, because the vodka has this habit of blowing huge holes in his head. The truth is, he felt nothing all night and the next day. He woke up with the nurse shining a torch in his face, his morning call for a few words with the cops, just another drunk in residence with not much to say except that Dorothy was a sad case, mentioning that he knew her when she did a bit of mime, at which point he could see the cops losing their appetite for the chase.

He reckoned he would rest up here for six weeks and go straight out again on the drink. Out that front door and directly down to the nearest pub, with about fifty square meals inside him to soak up the sauce. He would play for the money and drink, play and drink, because no music worth a shit was ever played on fizzy water, but on booze and badness.

He talked a pack of lies all day about Dorothy in group therapy, and he could feel it doing him good. For a few moments he got gung-ho again about the programme, the Twelve Steps up there on the wall, and then the thing with the trifle kicked in, and the hole opened up again. He has to get out now, before he loses control. He has to get out before they fuck with his head. He has to beat the house just one time.

He goes to his bedside locker and throws a couple of books he brought with him into his travel bag. They don't let you read books in this place, they've got about a hundred rules against privacy. And Bricks Melvin will not, for any reason, give up his privacy. He just can't do it. Bricks Melvin can handle his feelings, he just can't handle institutions, even ones that he picks out himself from a colour brochure.

Maybe he can't get a proper gig at this time, but he can still play jazz when the time comes. They're not getting this thing that he has. They can keep the two grand, but they're not getting this thing that he has. He will be able to walk out the front door, he reckons, not like some poor fuck who ran across the fields last night, like he was breaking out of Colditz. All right, he will be able to walk out the front door pretty fast, hoping there's no one down at the desk to give him any more shit.

He needs to do this right. He takes his good black suit down from the wardrobe and changes into it, stuffing his casual gear into a travel bag. He puts on the black ankle-length overcoat that he bought with his last cheque, a few grand built up week after lousy week for playing in the pit at the bastard panto. *Aladdin* is paying for all this. And now they'll say it's all been a waste of time, that he didn't have the chops for it. They can say that, but they're still not getting this thing that he has.

Bricks Melvin looks at himself in the wardrobe mirror. Everyone in here says he has a look of Einstein, the cool genius look but, in Bricks's honest opinion, he doesn't look nearly as mad as Einstein. And besides, Einstein's hair was all white and Bricks Melvin's hair is all black. Little differences like that. It's probably just the moustache. He'll shave it off first thing. You don't want to be too recognizable in this town. He picks a crumb of trifle out of it. If they'd given him ice-cream, maybe he'd still be here.

He grabs his overnight bag and walks calmly down the stairs to reception. Mary the night nurse is at her station.

'Hello, Gerry,' she says.

'Goodbye, Mary,' he says. 'I'm cured.'

Chapter 4

It is two days since Dorothy died. Freddie figures he ought to have some words of wisdom with Nadine, but it's obvious she doesn't want to know. So he's been business-like, like you have to be when the Reaper is about, and maybe the two of them will do the grieving thing eventually, when it sinks in.

Nadine was so cool about it, like it was only a change of plan and nothing permanent, like the Reaper didn't impress her at all. Freddie himself was freaked out, but he can't dress in black yet without feeling some twisted sense of relief. It looks like he'll be the chief mourner. They'll be releasing the body in a few weeks, if no one on the American side or no one belonging to Richard Madigan claims it.

Freddie goes to a kitchen cupboard and takes down the birthday cake. From where Nadine is on the higher level of the flat, he is just out of view. He opens the packet of candles. He quickly arranges seventeen of them and lights them. Seventeen. Like, ten was ridiculous, fourteen was, like, help me out here, but seventeen is just crazy, crazy shit.

He switches off the main light and carries the cake to the kitchen table. Then he puts on the music, a piece by Duke Ellington and his orchestra.

Nadine drags herself up from the beanbag where she is reading *Zen and the Art of Motorcycle Maintenance*, prescribed last week by Freddie. Here she comes, nearly full-grown but not quite in Freddie's eyes, not quite because there is still something of the child in her, something in the way she moves, man, that tells Freddie she is still his Nadine, and nobody else's. Here she comes now, serious-looking, like Dylan's sad-eyed lady. But when she smiles it's like the heavens open, as Van would have it, kind of an all-American-I'd-like-to-teach-the-world-to-sing smile that maybe she got from the sweetest part of Dorothy, this smile that she switches on when all seems lost. Because she can't help it, because it comes from that place in Nadine where no man has come, a place that is for ever young.

'Let's do this,' he says, cutting a quarter of the cake.

Here it comes now, that smile. Yes, Nadine is about three-quarters grown up, but Freddie guesses there's maybe just a quarter of her that remains free of the bad shit that settles in all our souls when at last we make the beast-with-two-backs, when finally we get what we want so bad, and we know it will never be enough.

Freddie steers Nadine to the table in the candlelight. The atmosphere seems right for both a birthday and a bereavement, a party or a séance.

'Nice,' she says. 'That music . . .'

'That's Duke Ellington. It's called "Sophisticated Lady".'

'Nice,' she says.

'We owe a lot to the Duke. I mean, just the two of us.'

'I know,' she says.

And Freddie does his riff again about how it was done, about the crime behind the fortune, how the title of his big hit is a steal from Ellington, a number called 'Do Nothing Till You Hear From Me' that he borrowed when he did a jingle for the phone company, thinking that no one would notice. And nobody did. And then Fellaz took it up and did boffo business in two hundred countries around the world and still no one is any the wiser.

'No one knows shit like that any more,' Freddie says.

He throws a can of Miller from the fridge. Nadine catches it.

'Maybe they never did,' she says.

Freddie cuts her a large slice of cake.

'Lager and walnut cake,' he says.

'Sophisticated lady,' she says.

Freddie puts the track on again. It sounds very old and romantic, like something heard over the wireless in a James Cagney movie.

'You really like this number?' he says.

'It's OK,' she says. 'It's got . . . it's got . . . a tune.'

Freddie has this weird urge to ask Nadine to dance, but then the thought brings him down, seeing himself as the father dancing with his daughter at her wedding to some unsuitable dude. And anyway no dance will bond them closer than they are now, in this candlelight situation, bonded too on this day by their Levi jackets and jeans, though of course Nadine in her immaculate way looks a bit like the Corr sister who was thrown out of the group for being too good-looking, while Freddie in his rags looks a bit like Mr Wavy Gravy on the morning after Woodstock.

Freddie slips out the kitchen door and into the hall. He is back straight away with a set of keys that he puts on the table in front of Nadine. She lights a Rothmans.

'With a little help from the Duke,' he says, 'I've bought one of those new penthouses facing out to the sea. For you.'

Nadine touches the keys in amazement.

Freddie puts another set of keys next to them.

'And this is the apartment next door to it,' he says. 'For Freddie.'

Nadine takes a swig of Miller. Freddie savours these wide-eyed moments. As she plays with the keys, he notices she's not wearing one of her many nail varnishes, maybe as a mark of respect to Dorothy, who warned her against all cosmetics. Then again she's wearing a major amount of face-paint and eye-shadow and such, and she's even dyed her black hair blacker, so hell, maybe she's wearing some invisible flesh-coloured varnish. Maybe Freddie should keep talking property.

'I'll have a bed instead of a couch,' he says. 'And a bedroom. A bedroom with a view. It's not built yet, not fully . . .'

'Are we really, actually rich?' she says, still staring at the keys in the candlelight.

'It's hard to believe,' he says.

'Well, are we?'

'I think so. We have three flash motors outside.'

'True.'

'So?' he prompts.

'We're loaded?'

'Absolutely . . . effectively.'

'Effectively.'

'Well it's like with the cars. I'm still borrowing the money against the overall. I'm on the phone to Paddy Lamb every other day. He says it's cool.'

'It's cool?'

'I figure that every day I wait, the price of stuff is going up. And anyway . . . to tell the truth, I need to get it out of my system.'

Nadine plays with the keys.

'Is it out yet?'

Freddie laughs.

'It's out,' he says.

Money has magic, he reckons, the breadheads are not all wrong. It can turn him into a sugar daddy after seventeen years of waiting for the repo man, and it can even get him into gala occasions with this angel across the table, because it is completely OK for a rich guy to come up the red carpet looking like Freddie, a guy big enough not to give a shit about how he looks, though it is totally unacceptable for the penniless version of Freddie Dowd to even think about it. Yeah, money has magic. It can't turn him into Leo Di Caprio, but that's all right. There will be no makeover, no Armani suits. Being an odd little geezer in an old Levi jacket and jeans is something to hold on to in this life. It's what he knows.

'The Ferrari?' she says. She turns an invisible steering wheel.

'No way,' he says.

'Way,' she says.

'I'd never forgive myself,' he says.

He opens a can of beer.

'The Range Rover?' she says.

'I wish you wouldn't,' he says.

'You teach me. You're a good driver.'

'No way would you take my advice.'

'Would.'

'Since when?'

'Since now. I'm seventeen. So . . . advise me.'

'My advice?' he says. He senses a challenge in her voice, some need for words of wisdom. He directs her to the sofa with an exaggerated formality. She sits on the sofa and Freddie paces up and down in a parody of the dutiful father.

'All right . . .' he says, taking this chance to say a few things that he kind of needs to say, but which are not too heavy-duty for the occasion.

'All right. Never let your daughter leave school . . . unless you've written a worldwide smash hit.'

'Go on,' she says.

'And . . . don't give your daughter any jazz records because she'll only pretend to listen to them.'

'Uh-huh.'

'I suppose . . . never visit your wife in rehab and refuse her offer of money.'

'You did that?' she says.

'Afraid so.'

'Go on,' she says.

'And when your daughter is eighteen, she can use the Range Rover.'

'Seventeen-and-a-half,' she says.

'And three-quarters,' he says.

She grunts. She looks away from him, shades of Dylan's sad-eyed lady returning.

39

And never have a daughter in the first place, he thinks, because she'll grow up, and meet someone like you.

Bricks Melvin arrives into Brabazon's of Howth with his travel bag and his saxophone case. He walks briskly to the bar, looking neither left nor right, giving the impression of a working musician having a quick snort on his way to a gig.

In truth he has just been made homeless. While Bricks was trying to get his shit together out in Stepaside, the landlord saw his chance and changed the lock. He left the saxophone case outside the door, and an unframed picture of Bricks with Ella Fitzgerald. So it's time to move on again.

Bricks stands at the bar and orders a brandy. The lounge is nearly empty but seats are not for him. He always stands in bars.

The first sip is something holy and righteous. It is the answer to everything.

When he was a child, Bricks Melvin played in the orphanage band so they wouldn't hit him. When he was older, he played for love. But when he became a man, he played for brandy. He rolls a cigarette. It is perfectly clear to him now. He will keep on doing what he has been doing, playing bog-standard gigs for money, to buy brandy. This thing that he has, this wild thing, this jazz, there's no call for it. All that matters is that he knows it's still there if he needs it.

He spends about four slow brandies thinking in this hard-headed way, feeling practical and wise in the ways of the world. He is flicking through the phone book looking for a hotel out this direction like any sensible person, when he remembers he has Freddie Dowd's phone number, over in Dún Laoghaire on the other side of the bay. He orders another large brandy. He grips the counter with both hands, to steady himself. He needs to swallow another little piece of his pride tonight. With all Freddie's troubles, tonight the jazzman needs to hit on him for a place to stay because it's out of the question to be spending money on hotels that could be spent on brandy. It hurts, it always hurts, even after twenty-five years not making the rent, looking like a man of style, scavenging like some wild dog. But it has to be done. It's either rent or brandy, and there's no contest any more. All the way out in the taxi from Stepaside he was thinking about the first brandy of the evening, knowing at last and for all time that he could never give up such a pleasure. He had settled this matter with himself and with the world, and it seemed like something to celebrate, a fresh start.

The therapy gang had done the trick in ways they could never have foreseen. At last, the penny had dropped for Bricks Melvin. There was no past, and there was no future. It was one day at a time from now on. He would stay in the moment, and if he could possibly manage it, he would drink Hennessy brandy in the moment.

He needs to sit. The punters are coming in, crowding him at the bar. He hates physical contact with punters, even when they brush past him in a pub. He doesn't shake hands with punters, he doesn't high-five them and he definitely doesn't hug them. And punters means everyone.

He lugs his bag and his axe and his brandy into the corner. He gets a packet of Major out of the machine because at this moment, he needs to smoke them faster than he can roll them.

Freddie Dowd is not exactly a buddy but he's a genuine enough guy. A genuine loser, like Bricks Melvin. There was no agenda with Freddie Dowd, he was what he appeared to be all the time, a total failure. Now it seems he's got a day-job at last, chauffeuring some geezer who probably can't read or write but who never wasted his precious time trying to bring a bit of art to the punters. Dorothy laughed, how she laughed when she saw Freddie behind the wheel, but it was a sad scene too. Sad to see a failure finally admitting that he's a failure. If Bricks had the choice, he would prefer to be taking advantage of some corporate fuck, or someone who was getting all the breaks, instead of someone as poor as himself. But the choice now is between Freddie Dowd, one of the few guys who gives him respect any more, and Dollymount Strand in January.

He doesn't use public transport so it will have to be a taxi, a drive along the coast from Howth to Dún Laoghaire, in a cab probably driven by some guy who was once a member of the next U2. Then a sit-down with Freddie Dowd and maybe a rap about Dorothy, and how he's getting over it. And, in the morning, a clean slate.

He picks up the payphone and psyches himself into it.

'Freddie? It's Bricks Melvin.'

'Hiya, Bricks.'

'About Dorothy . . .'

'I know, man. I understand.'

'She'll be missed.'

'She was one of a kind, man'

'I'm a bit embarrassed here.'

'Where are you, man?'

'I broke out.'

'Eh . . . drinking?'

'I just checked out of Stepaside. And then I get up home and I guess it's, like, Houston, we have a problem.'

'I hear you, man. Get a cab over here. We'll organize something.'

'You're a gentleman.'

'Pleasure.'

'Listen, Freddie. I didn't make it at Stepaside. But I have to tell you something.'

'It's all right, Bricks. You gave it a shot man.'

'I have to tell you . . . the one thing a man needs more than anything else is his privacy.'

Nadine takes a swig of Miller.

'More good news?' she says.

Freddie looks like he's all wound up. He slumps down into the couch.

'Yeah, I guess it is.'

'Good news, man?' she says.

Freddie throws the cordless phone at her.

'You gave it a good shot, man,' she says.

Freddie lunges for her and she squirms away from him. He chases her around the kitchen table. She ducks and weaves, laughing and shrieking, just the width of the table keeping her from capture. They both seem to have the same idea simultaneously, but Nadine gets to the cake first.

She plays it just right. The cake is still in its box, the better for throwing. That look in her eyes tells Freddie that if she has to, she will use it. Freddie groans with frustration. He holds his hands up in surrender.

'I'll let you go this time,' he says.

They walk back warily to the main room. Nadine sinks back into her beanbag, facing Freddie on the couch.

'Look, I can't help it,' he says. 'I just love those guys.'

'Bricks Melvin?'

'He'll have to stay here for a night or two.'

'All right.'

'I'll try, OK? I'll try not to say it.'

'Say what?'

'Man.'

'Just pretend . . . pretend that jazz sucks.'

'I can't pretend. I love these guys.'

She has another go. 'Just pretend . . . it's guys out of their heads on gear. That's what I do.'

'Does it work?'

'Perfectly.'

'I guess I'm just in awe of someone like Bricks Melvin.'

'You're a sap.'

'It's not just that. It's more than that. I love guys like Bricks Melvin, because they are really brilliant at what they do. And there aren't many guys who are really brilliant at what they do.'

'Another drunk?' she says.

'Doesn't matter. Doesn't matter a bit. That's what I'm trying to tell you, Nadine. It doesn't matter how messed up he is, he's so good at what he does, you have to forgive him everything. And I mean everything.'

'So . . . if Dorothy wrote great poems, it'd be all right?'

'She wrote some pretty good ones.'

'So?'

'So . . . what do I know from poetry?'

Freddie gets up and goes over to the table.

'I hear you,' she says.

Freddie starts to cut the cake.

'I hear you, man,' she says, deadpan.

Freddie walks to the bin, like he hasn't felt the needle at all. He dumps the cake in the bin. He disappears into the hall for a moment and comes back holding the Billy Joel CD.

'Don't move,' he says.

He takes out the disc and bends it until it seems sure to break.

'Break it,' she says. 'It's nothing to me.'

The doorbell rings.

Freddie throws the disc to Nadine like a frisbee. For one scary split second there, she thought they were fighting about something serious.

Nadine opens the door to Bricks Melvin and he knows straight away that the last thing he wants to say to her is the speech he's been composing in detail in the taxi on the way over, the grovelling speech of the wandering minstrel. It's not just that he bottles it, he doesn't even see it as the decent thing any more. It's not the brandy wearing off, it's a sure sense that it wouldn't be right to grovel before this marvellous creature, at least not tonight. Maybe not tomorrow night either. Because he knows this face. Those high cheekbones do it for him, maybe a Latin hint with the eyes which are so exquisitely drawn, then the fine mouth which won't easily crack a smile but which is not unkind, and the interesting pallor. And the way she moves now, leading him through the hall, she's giving out this stuff, just the way she is made, sending a thousand volts of sweet recognition straight through the jazzman.

Because it's as simple as this. Back when he played for love, he had a woman in mind who was perfect for him. It's a thing that players do, play like they're dug into some woman just beyond reach like the girl from Ipanema, imagining that. If she existed in real life, these men wouldn't have to conjure her up with their music. But Bricks Melvin is pretty sure that if she existed in real life, she would look exactly like Nadine Dowd.

By midnight, Freddie has it figured. The three of them are sitting around the kitchen table talking and having a laugh, though mainly it is Bricks talking and Nadine having a laugh. Freddie is dreaming, imagining some sort of future for Bricks that doesn't involve crashing on other people's floors. He's a funny, funny man, is Bricks. When he is calm, like he is tonight, just rambling on and rolling cigarettes and sipping a can of beer, it is a beautiful thing to be in his company. There's an elegance about him that reminds Freddie of some riverboat gambler, some dude called Doc with a superior sense of style born out of some inner strength, some certainty in his talent. Freddie can look back on a few nights like this, stretching back ten or even fifteen years, and feel privileged that he knows Bricks Melvin, and proud to share the pleasure with Nadine.

He can also look back on a few nights when being with Bricks was a very ugly scene. But he was always able to swallow it, on general principles.

There was just one time when Bricks went totally over the line, a scene that still gives Freddie the shits, when this Leeson Street bouncer went down an alley with Bricks to sort out a few musical differences, and Bricks turned the tables and took the guy out with a few kicks in the balls, and then took to using the guy's head as a fucking football while Freddie stood there, petrified by this show of cold brutality on Bricks's part, this pure psychotic reaction, until there seemed no way the guy could survive such a kicking, at which point Freddie just ran away. Maybe the guy lived, maybe he died. Freddie never mentioned it again to Bricks, because he just couldn't handle it.

But he could handle a lot, like being on the strip with Bricks and ending up in some brawl on the dance floor for reasons he couldn't rightly understand. He could handle walking down Grafton Street in the early hours and running into Bricks, sick with booze, and Bricks asking him for twenty lids with his moustache caked with blood and vomit. He could deal with that, by just giving him the twenty lids. For being a genius.

The difference tonight is that Freddie Dowd has serious money. He is a fucking breadhead, man, in a position to do something meaningful for Bricks Melvin. And he can hardly wait to start.

'I want to get personal, Bricks,' he says.

Bricks passes a roll-up to Nadine. It's just a small thing, Freddie reckons, but she looks so comfortable tonight smoking, sometimes with the lit cigarette turned into her palm, kind-of an earthy vibe, boss of the smoking scene like some country cousin.

'Get personal, Bricks?' Freddie says again.

'Sure,' Bricks says.

'I want to know what's so wrong with the Stepaside Centre?'

47

Bricks lights Nadine's roll-up and one of his own, drawing deeply on the cigarette as he formulates a response.

'I guess what's wrong with it is . . . some of us are just not ready for it,' Bricks says.

'Right.'

'And it's full of drunks.'

'Right.'

'I'm not being funny here,' Bricks says. 'Who's the first person I see? It's Dorothy.'

'Just a coincidence,' Freddie says.

'No coincidence. It's a place for drunks, right? And most drunks who are at it long enough, they get to know one another,' Bricks says.

'My theory, Bricks, is that Dorothy wasn't really an alcoholic,' Freddie says.

'Now you're being funny here,' Bricks says.

'I'm serious. I think it was just an excuse,' Freddie says.

'In her case, it was a bloody good excuse,' Bricks says.

'Anyway, I still don't get it,' Freddie says. 'Why would you go to all the trouble of getting in there, only to leave like that?'

'It's hard to explain to a normal person.'

'Right, man.'

'Maybe I went in there, just so I could say it didn't work.'

'You just weren't ready?'

'If I had any chance at all, it went the minute Dorothy . . . checked out,' Bricks says, his voice going quiet.

'But you sounded so up, when you were talking to me,' Freddie says.

'I was up. For that particular five minutes, I was up. When she checked in, Dorothy was up. We drunks are always having these . . . spasms of hope. But the minute you left . . .'

Freddie takes another can from the fridge and places it in front of Bricks.

'What about you now, man?' Freddie says. 'Will you do the AA thing?'

Bricks opens the can, and takes a sip. He is still quiet, not remotely drunk.

'I'm in a place now, where Bricks Melvin just needs some privacy.'

'Right,' says Freddie.

'They've done their best,' Bricks says.

'They try to break you down,' Freddie says.

'They can't break me down,' Bricks says.

'No.'

'Well, they can. But they can't build me up again.'

'Right.'

'Invasion of privacy.'

'The thing that makes you tick.'

'Exactly,' Bricks says. 'They look for the thing that makes you tick, the fucks. What makes you tick, makes you drink.'

'So when the drinking stops, so does the. . . the ticking?' Freddie says.

Bricks agrees vigorously.

'When they get in there, to your private mind . . . the fucks . . . the fucks . . . the fucks . . .' Bricks sounds like a stuck record. Then he's flowing again. 'It's like that story about the guy holding the palm of his hand over a flame,' he says. 'And no one knows how he can stand it. They think it must be a trick. And the guy says, the trick is, not minding it. It's the same with Bricks Melvin drinking. Sometimes it's going to hurt. Sometimes it's going to hurt like hell. The trick is, not minding it.'

'Cheers, man,' Freddie says.

'I've got a gig. Paddy Lamb always has a gig for me,' Bricks says.

'It's not really you, Bricks,' says Freddie.

'It pays,' Bricks says. 'It's me.'

'I've got to tell you about Paddy Lamb,' says Freddie. 'I've got some dealings with him myself.'

'Like . . . you're doing a bit of driving for him?'

'How's that, man?'

'The cars outside. You driving him?'

Nadine is giving Freddie the eye, like she wants the sleeping arrangements to be sorted. And Freddie decides this is not the right time to confess that he has become a millionaire while Bricks Melvin is still crashing on people's floors. It would destroy this lovely buzz.

Freddie can't face it tonight.

'Later for the garbage,' he whispers.

But big ideas are forming in his head, put there by the magic of money. Ideas that involve Bricks playing jazz for a living, and not whoring himself any more, just for a gig. It's not much, really, to give a man a job doing what he does. But it seems so hard to pitch it without coming across a bit preachy.

It's two in the morning. It will be Freddie on his usual sofa in the main room, and Bricks in a sleeping bag on the couch. Nadine disappears into the bedroom with no goodbyes.

'Seventeen,' Freddie says.

'She's gone to bed?'

50

'They don't talk much any more.'

'You've made it nice here,' Bricks says. 'A lot of books, a lot of music . . . kinda sparse.'

'Kinda can't afford much clutter, man,' Freddie laughs.

'And Nadine. Kinda sparse on the old conversation?' Bricks says.

'Listen, I'm rapping with some buddy in Bewley's about politics and whatever, it's all rabbit, rabbit, rabbit, and Nadine is sitting there totally quiet, probably thinking, who are these sad motherfucking assholes, and why don't they just shut the fuck up?' Freddie says.

'They're different,' Bricks says.

Bricks closes his eyes and tries to get comfortable on the couch.

Freddie has one last urge to talk about the money he is about to receive, and all the things he will do for the good of mankind and the salvation of his soul.

The beer is making his mind race. He fancies sitting up talking about those mad nights on the strip with Dorothy. Something about this arrangement brings it all back, people crashing on couches and floors, beer and smokes and talk. Something about this arrangement brings a different feel to the flat, like one more person changes the whole chemistry of the place. Like everything suddenly feels very temporary, and they'll all be gone their separate ways tomorrow.

He sees Nadine's packet of ten Rothmans on the kitchen table and he must have one. A cigarette. He wants one of Nadine's cigarettes. For the first time in ages, he really craves a smoke. He gets up and takes a Rothmans out of the packet and lights it. The first pull sends his head spinning.

'You want to hear some music?' he says.

Bricks grunts in the negative.

Freddie opens another beer.

Chapter 5

Paddy Lamb loves what LJ Carew does. She is doing it now, interviewing him for her TV show, *LJ Today*. They are chums and they let it show, face to face on a big leather couch in Paddy's office on Merrion Square.

'I love what you do,' he says.

'Thank you, Paddy.'

'I mean it, LJ. I love what you do.'

'Let's talk about Paddy Lamb.'

'Who?'

'Let's talk about you.'

'Paddy Lamb doesn't matter.'

'Yeah, yeah.'

'Well, it's true. All I do as a manager, if you like, is encourage the talent.'

'Some say you only love them for their money.'

'Who says that, LJ?'

'Cynical people.'

'You think I only love you for your money?'

'Don't know about that.'

'I . . . love . . . what . . . you . . . do. I mean it. And when I say it to the boys, I mean it. And when I said it to Placido Domingo last week, I meant it. And anyone who really and truly understands this business, they know what I mean.'

'Do you hate anyone?'

'OK, straight up, I'm not a huge fan of the Andy Williams comeback.'

'There you go.'

'I think a man of his age, taking on that schedule, is asking for major trouble.'

'I'll tell him that when he's over here next week.'

'But I can't help loving him, for doing it.'

Freddie is watching them. He left Bricks Melvin conked out in the sleeping bag to keep this lunchtime appointment with the heavy hitters. He has strong and long-standing opinions about Paddy Lamb and LJ Carew, but getting physically close to them, watching them as humans with no critical distance, seeing what they put into it in this hot room with a camera crew working them like lab rats, he is kind of impressed.

Paddy Lamb is bred in the purple, but in a rough-hewn sort of way. He is one of that breed who got called Paddy by his English public schoolmates, the wild Irishman in their eyes, a big-house smoothie in the more jaundiced view of the actual Irish.

Paddy in his own way is a hugely successful crossover act, with an exquisite style of speech that is somehow not plummy, but calm and precise like there's a showbiz lawyer measuring each beat. Silky-sounding but with the look of a countryman, brawny as he walks his seven hundred progressively farmed acres.

The word is that Paddy Lamb really does love what LJ

Carew does, all the time, but she is strangely aloof. It is baffling the gossip columnists who are sure that a working-class gal like LJ couldn't possibly refuse a gent like Paddy, or his mansion up on Kilbrittan Hill.

Freddie wonders, Does LJ Carew have any idea what they say about her? He imagines that she must not, or else she simply could not cope. She could not be giving out that constant blast on the celebrity hunting-horn if she had a trace of negative feeling in her body. She just yammers away, talking up every piece of showbiz shit like it was gold. She can't possibly know the story doing the rounds about how a Sunday paper photographed her in her superbly renovated Ringsend cottage, and they wanted her to pose with a book, and there was nothing to read apart from the instruction manual for her new Mitsubishi Black Diamond widescreen television. So they snapped her reading that, in German.

She can't possibly know how they laugh at her stunningly obvious string of boyfriends, the rally-driver, the Premiership footballer, the celebrity chef and that essential beauty-and-the-beast phase with a big, fat, ugly property developer worth about two hundred million at a conservative estimate. Or two hundred million in debt, at an equally conservative estimate. They say that not even LJ could get a clear picture on that, so she left him.

Freddie watches Paddy Lamb and LJ Carew coming down from another session under the lights, and he understands for a few moments what Paddy means about loving the lot of them, every last poor demented freak who puts himself up there to be showered with sarcasm from the safe heights where the hepcats live.

But then, just when Paddy's voodoo is working on him, Freddie remembers Bricks Melvin. These are not victimless crimes, he thinks. When Paddy Lamb is launching another chart-buster, and when LJ Carew hypes it like it was gold, somehow the world seems a little less welcoming to musicians of quality and distinction. Somehow the size of their failure and their disappointment seems more immense. And now is not the time for Freddie to be forgetting this, now that he's taking the showbiz shilling. Now is not the time to be losing his mind to the razzle dazzle.

Paddy is calling to him from across the room.

'Come and join us, Freddie,' he says. 'Special friend.'

Paddy has his arm around LJ's shoulder. Freddie, stepping through the TV equipment, looks at the two of them canoodling like Lulu back in the sixties thrown together with some hilarious viscount. LJ is all funky and feisty, her act is that of the sexy little blonde with the big, big personality, and if there's any difference between her act and her life, no one can see it. Beside her, silver-tongued Paddy looks like some jovial aristocrat stroking the maid. Which is fine sport all round, but unlikely to lead up the aisle of Westminster Abbey.

'LJ Carew,' says Paddy, 'meet Freddie Dowd. A very talented man and a very nice man.'

Freddie sits down opposite them. LJ Carew gives him a big grin and a little wave.

'I know you,' she says. 'I know you to see.'

'I know you to see as well,' Freddie says.

'Touché,' Paddy says, guffawing.

'I was brought up in Dún Laoghaire,' she says. 'I used to see you with your little girl.'

'Nadine.'

'Sorry?' she says.

'Speak up, Freddie,' says Paddy. 'Freddie is very soft-spoken. Very middle class.'

Paddy gets up to usher out the camera crew. Freddie offers LJ Carew a Rothman from a new pack of twenty. As she leans over to take a light, he again sees the sexy little blonde with the big, big personality, a celeb, a star, a bunch of showbiz clichés and nothing to do with him.

'Nadine,' he repeats, louder. 'Her name is Nadine.'

'You used to walk up and down the pier all the time,' says LJ. 'And I mean, all the time.'

'I couldn't think of anything else to do,' he says.

'I remember you were very . . . very striking,' she says.

'You mean ugly,' he says.

'No, striking,' she says.

Freddie reckons the difference between ugly and striking is a couple of million quid.

'Nadine is very tall now,' he says.

'Christ she was just a baby,' LJ says. 'Mind you I was only . . . what? . . . ten?'

'In that case, I was only about twenty,' Freddie says.

LJ puts out her cigarette.

'I'm giving them up,' she says. 'I'm just freaked out meeting the famous Freddie Dowd.'

Paddy is back again. He throws himself down on the couch, and loosens the top button of his denim shirt. Sandy-haired and brown after a week in the Caribbean, he looks like a man who can't stop laughing at some outrageous stroke of good fortune. He fondles and scratches

57

his chest hair in a way that is so totally unfashionable, it seems to Freddie beyond cool.

'Catching up?' Paddy says.

'I remember everything,' LJ says.

Paddy puts his arm around LJ again.

'This lady remembers everything except the bad things.'

Paddy slides a Chinese menu over to Freddie.

'If it's acceptable to you, Freddie, we'll get something delivered. It's just I don't see enough of LJ, and seeing as she's here . . .'

Freddie is on the back foot. The original idea was a restaurant, to check in on the business side, hence his choice of the Mercedes for the drive from Dún Laoghaire to Paddy's grand offices on Merrion Square, where Paddy can point to the statue of Oscar Wilde in the park below and insist that old Oscar would be gagging for the boybands.

'Whatever you like,' Freddie says.

'Good man,' Paddy says, ringing the Chinese on his mobile.

'What are you having?' LJ says.

Freddie looks at the menu, thinking he'd like to have a straight answer from Paddy about the money.

'Duck à l'orange,' he says.

He hands the menu to LJ. She takes her time.

'Kung po mixed vegetables,' she says.

Paddy repeats the orders over the phone.

'How long have you got, Freddie?' he says.

Freddie laughs. 'An hour?' he says.

'I can tell you what you need to know right now,' says Paddy. 'And then we can enjoy our lunch.'

'I'm just checking in really,' says Freddie.

'Don't worry about it, Freddie. That's the only thing I would say to you, even if we sat down all afternoon crunching the numbers. Don't worry about it.'

Freddie lights another cigarette. 'No sweat,' he says.

'It would only bore the arse off you, my friend.'

'Sure.'

'The accountant is off in London for the week, but if there was anything new . . .'

'Let's just have lunch,' Freddie says.

Late in the afternoon, driving home in the sky-blue Mercedes, Freddie is buzzing after a few bottles of Paddy Lamb's champagne. He must be about twenty times over the legal limit, but the Merc nearly drives itself. His head is full of Paddy's polish, and some of it is starting to make perfect sense.

'You are one of us now,' said Paddy. And it felt fine. It felt like he could have it every way, like he could be one of them and still have a soul. He always felt more accepted anyway by outsiders like Paddy Lamb or Dorothy, Bohemian types who have knocked around a bit and who see him as just a middle-class guy with a few lifestyle quirks, and not some fuck-off freak.

Outsiders like LJ too, who improves all the time with the champagne, who sees him as striking, striking she said, and she said it most sincerely, striking and not simply strange.

He is grateful for the money and for the attitude. And in the light of all that Dom Perignon, it now seems completely uncool that he came in today expecting to crunch numbers all afternoon with a dude like Paddy Lamb.

'It's not the civil service,' Paddy said. 'In this business

you live like a gypsy. You don't get a neat little cheque at the end of the month. Your arse is always out the window.'

Paddy talked again about Andy Williams. 'The guy just can't help it,' he says. 'He's one of us, looking for the love he never had. So he hears that he's happening again, and instead of relaxing beside the pool and taking the money, he's over to the Chris Evans show, right? With these huge big teeth smiling away, and the rest of him falling apart in front of us. The guy is in major trouble. And why? Why does he put himself through this thing that no ordinary person could tolerate? Why does he do all this when there's no money angle to it, except to put some lawyer's daughter through college?'

Paddy took down another bottle of champagne, to hide his emotion.

'For Andy,' he said, 'it's about who he is, and what he is, after the lawyers have had their piece. Andy and LJ and you, my friend Freddie Dowd, and Paddy Lamb, we're all gypsies.'

There was a lot of emotion in that room, a lot of bonding between Paddy Lamb and LJ Carew and the guy that they look up to, Freddie Dowd. That's how Paddy put it.

'We are in there having fun, drinking with Liza Minelli,' he said. 'But we look up to guys like you, Freddie. Guys with a bit of integrity. Guys who've been hammering away at the coalface for a long, long time. We are down here and guys like you are way up there.'

Way up there, getting big respect from Paddy Lamb and LJ Carew, who remembers everything except the bad things. LJ Carew who kept touching him and who wants to interview him tomorrow.

'Just be yourself,' she said.

At this time, in a nearby corner of the Lamb empire, Bricks Melvin is taking his saxophone out of its case. He has turned up on time for his gig at the Tara Street studios. He has also impressed the boss man, Tim Foley, by arriving with Nadine.

Foley is a fresh kid wearing an Eminem vest who seems too young to be running anything, especially an old-style hack job like this. He is amazed that Bricks has never been on the DART before.

'I don't like public transport,' Bricks says.

'Unless you happen to be with a beautiful lady,' Foley says.

'Nadine showed me the ropes, very kindly,' Bricks says.

He takes out a new reed, and wets it with his lips.

Nadine is sitting at the grand piano, watching him.

'Coffee, Nadine?' Foley says.

'No, thanks,' Nadine says.

'Gum?' he says, holding up a Wrigley's.

She takes it. 'Smoke?' she says.

'Sorry,' Foley says.

'This won't take long,' Bricks says.

'As long as it takes,' Foley says.

The deal is, Bricks will play 'Stranger on the Shore' and 'Yesterday', and it will go out under the name of the waxen-faced Johnny Shine, the wrinkliest act in Paddy Lamb's stable, whose Golden Notes series of instrumentals is a big seller among the Irish in Britain. Shine is a reasonable player, but you won't find him doing seventy-eight takes in the studio. He will blow his best for one hard session, but as he says himself, he is no fanatic. So he skips off to buy another pub, or to work on his golf handicap, leaving a few imperfect performances behind him. And then Tim Foley calls Paddy Lamb and Paddy recommends a musician, some worthy cause. And then it's just a question of signing the confidentiality agreement.

Tim Foley hands the sheet of paper to Bricks Melvin. Bricks leans against the grand piano. He straps on his saxophone as he reads the document in detail. He unbuttons his ankle-length overcoat, but he does not take it off.

'Can I take your coat?' Foley says.

'That's OK,' Bricks says, continuing to read.

'Nadine?' Foley says.

Nadine unbuttons her leather coat.

'OK,' she says.

Bricks told her to keep her coat on in this place. He didn't say why.

'Who's engineering the session?' Bricks says, without looking up.

'I guess I am,' Foley says.

'OK,' Bricks says.

Foley offers another stick of gum to Nadine. 'It's a nuisance, this confidentiality agreement,' he says. 'Whaddya think, Bricks?' There is a note of impatience in Foley's voice.

Bricks takes a Parker pen out of his inside pocket. He rests the sheet on the grand piano, and signs it.

'Some guy told the papers once,' Foley says. 'Paddy freaked.'

Bricks gives him the signed sheet. He puts the Parker back in his inside pocket.

'Believe me,' he says. 'I wouldn't tell my own mother.'

Chapter 6

Paddy Lamb recommended it, his usual at the Bandillero. Corned beef and cabbage and a bottle of Wolf Blass. He and LJ Carew are sitting in Paddy's usual red leather booth, underneath a signed photograph of Liam Neeson. It's the speciality of the house, signed photographs of the stars. It's early in the evening, and Paddy is starting to look like a countryman who has been out in the fields all day, high in the colour after his champagne afternoon with LJ Carew and Freddie Dowd.

'Two million?' LJ says.

'Higher,' Paddy says.

'That's a lot.'

'No kidding,' he says

'About two point five?'

'Point seven.'

'Sterling?' LJ says.

'Sterling,' Paddy says.

'I'm impressed.'

'Lucky old Freddie,' he says.

'You're keeping it safe for him?'

'I hid it.'

'Oh,' LJ says.

'I hid it first in the Isle of Man. And then I hid it in the Cayman Islands. And after that . . .'

'After that, what?'

'How much do you want to know?' Paddy asks.

'Come on, Paddy. You love this.'

'People give me total control,' he says. 'Royalties, everything. It all works out in the end.'

'It didn't work out for The Cisco Kidz,' she says.

'We settled. Amicably.'

'Poor kids. When they know what's happened to them, they'll have Alzheimer's.'

'I've got a touch of it already,' Paddy says.

He pours two glasses of Wolf Blass. The waiter brings two plates of corned beef and cabbage. The piano player starts up for the evening.

'Bewitched, bothered and bewildered,' Paddy says. 'He's on the screws tonight.'

'Go easy on Freddie Dowd,' says LJ. 'If anyone ever deserved a break . . .'

Paddy considers this, chewing a mouthful of corned beef.

'I'll tell you how it is, LJ,' he says. 'I always said if I ever amounted to anything in this business I would do two things. I would return people's calls – it's always some arsehole that never returns your call, the top guy always returns your call – and the second thing is, I would blame no one but myself if I ever got ripped off. Good luck.'

Paddy raises his glass of wine to Bricks Melvin, who raises one in return from the other side of the room.

LJ Carew turns around to see Bricks smiling and raising his glass.

'Mad bastard,' she says.

'That's Freddie Dowd's girl with him,' says Paddy. 'Lovely.'

'Two million quid's worth,' says LJ.

'Two point seven,' says Paddy.

Paddy calls for another bottle of Wolf Blass to be brought to Bricks Melvin's table.

'Nadine,' says LJ. 'Nice name.'

Paddy raises another glass to Bricks Melvin, and blows an imaginary saxophone.

'Nice people,' Paddy says.

'The strangest people are getting rich, Paddy,' she says. 'And the strangest people are getting poor.'

Paddy signals to the waiter to come to him.

'It's all about confidence now,' he says. 'I said to The Cisco Kidz, there's only one thing worse than losing money. And that's the whole town knowing that you lost money. You know that this town is full of blokes who nearly invested in Riverdance, but didn't.'

'I know.'

'You can see it in their eyes.'

'The pain.'

'They know that you know. Every day out there, they are getting these looks of pity. And you never do business with a man that you pity.'

'Freddie Dowd isn't one of us,' says LJ. 'This is his one shot.'

Paddy pushes away his plate of corned beef and cabbage. He scratches his chest hair furiously. 'I don't know anything about money,' he says. 'All I know is I like it in big fucking heaps.'

'You love it.'

Paddy lifts a sliver of corned beef. He throws his head back and laughs like a schoolboy.

'I love you,' he says.

The waiter arrives. Paddy Lamb scribbles a note on a paper napkin. He asks the waiter to bring it over to Bricks Melvin.

The note says, 'I love what you do.'

Bricks shows it to Nadine, sitting underneath a signed photo of Cyril Cusack.

'The way this works,' he says. 'He wants me to do it now.'

'OK,' she says.

'He wants the good stuff,' he says.

Bricks takes his case from under the table. He assembles his saxophone, giving a signal to the piano player that he will be joining him. The last time they did this, Fellaz had gone straight to number one in the UK charts, and Paddy tipped them a grand.

The waiter brings another bottle of Wolf Blass.

'If you'd like a main course, Mr Melvin . . .' he says.

'We're fine,' says Bricks. 'Just the wine.'

This was the deal, no big eating-out scene, just a glass of wine for minding Bricks on the DART, and for suffering an afternoon of studio hell, listening to Bricks laying down the phantom horn of Johnny Shine.

'Any requests?' Bricks says.

The waiter laughs. 'Anything to stop the piano man,' he says.

'That's Ray Blacoe Senior,' Bricks says. 'A first-rate musician.'

'I'm sure he is,' the waiter says.

'He only plays like that in here,' Bricks says.

Ray Blacoe Senior starts to play something different, something much louder than the slush he has been squeezing from the keys.

Bricks straps on his saxophone. He drains his glass of red wine.

'Excuse me,' he says to Nadine.

These jazzers, she thinks, they're all taking the piss. And when Bricks tears into a solo straight away, like he and the piano player were building up to this all night, she longs for the simple stuff of the afternoon, for 'Yesterday', for something with a tune.

But she doesn't hate this jazz as much as when she was walking the pier. She still can't figure out what Bricks is playing, or what the point of it might be, but she's sort of glad that he's doing it. And maybe if she spent the day with Charlie Parker or Miles Davis, she might feel the same way. Not exactly thrilled they're doing it, but sort of glad that someone is doing it.

It's different when you know the guy. It's different when you're drinking wine with him, and he just gets up calmly and blasts the head off everyone with this wild burst. It's different when you can actually see everyone in the restaurant wondering how anyone can play so fast without blowing himself up. It's not her thing, but it's some racket when you're in the same room as the guy, and you feel the madness, and you see all he's putting into it, and how brilliant he is at it.

The playing stops suddenly. Bricks bows to Ray Blacoe Senior. He bows to the applause of the clientele, but he pays no heed to their shouts for more.

Bricks is back underneath the photo of Cyril Cusack, acknowledging the whistles of Paddy Lamb with a salute.

'They hated it,' he says.

He fills another glass of wine, and one for Nadine.

'More?' she says.

'They don't really want more,' he says. 'They're only trying to be cool.'

'You think?'

'They're clapping with relief that we're gone.'

Nadine offers him a Rothmans. 'I liked it,' she says.

He laughs, breaking into a fit of coughing as he drags on the cigarette. 'I know,' he says.

Ray Blacoe Senior returns to his post, with a hotel lobby version of 'Moon River'.

'You're good,' she says.

'Thank you.'

The waiter brings a couple of glasses of flaming sambuca.

'No way,' she says.

'Ray likes this sambuca shit,' Bricks says. 'Maybe that's why they threw him out of the army.'

Bricks slopes back to the piano with the glass of sambuca for Ray. They chat while Ray plays 'Moon River', on and on.

Nadine finishes her third glass of wine. Three is perfect for her. She looks at Bricks leaning against the stand-up piano in his snazzy black suit, this dude who has nowhere to live.

All day they talked very little, and it was fine. It was like that thing he said last night about privacy. She was with him, and he was with her, and they started to feel right with each other, and she felt right in the head for maybe the first time since last summer, and Bricks blew his head off playing the saxophone for her, and still she had her privacy, without him poking and prodding her with stupid fucking questions about life, about Dorothy.

Freddie told her about the touching thing, that Bricks doesn't touch people or even shake hands if he can help it, and she figures it's actually a pretty brilliant idea, keeping yourself to yourself.

Bricks comes back to the table, smiling. It feels right to be with someone cool for a change, instead of Freddie with his fuzz.

'Ray had a good Christmas,' he says. 'He visited his family on Christmas Day. And he had his Christmas dinner on a tray on his own, because he couldn't take part in a Christian festival. Then he went home to his flat and put on *Songs For Swingin' Lovers* and had a good cry.'

Bricks offers Nadine another glass of wine, but she refuses. If nothing else, Freddie taught her how to drink.

Chapter 7

Freddie wakes up wanting a cigarette. Paddy Lamb's champagne is still giving him the buzz. It reminds him that LJ Carew is interviewing him today. Against all he stands for, he is up for it.

The showbizzy high of the previous day is coming back to him, but then there's no great sellout in getting plastered now and then with Paddy Lamb, and feeling a sense of oneness with LJ Carew. Was he feeling a sense of oneness with that lady? Is it allowed? He knows enough about certain ladies to know they have a soft spot for men who bring up a child on their own. But he also knows that this is a generalization that doesn't apply to him. She kept touching him, for sure, and the ladies never touch Freddie Dowd.

Ah, it hurts his head to think of how LJ might react, as they lie there hot and naked on Paddy's leather couch, smoking after an afternoon of wild poontang, and Freddie drawls in an ironic way to LJ, 'Incidentally, we don't need to broadcast this on the World Service, babe.' Ah, it hurts when he gets to that part. So he'd have to somehow swear her to secrecy and keep the whole thing from everyone else.

Everyone with half a brain in this town thinks that LJ is the complete airhead. And anyone that Freddie knows would completely condemn him if the word got out, which it would.

Still, he could maybe do with an occasional airhead in his life. After Dorothy, he decided that brains were not important in his lady as long as he felt safe with her. He just couldn't stand any more of those vicious mood swings, the smell of danger when things were getting out of control and he was in that place where he could hear the strange music. But there was no lady after Dorothy. And, weird though it might seem to anyone looking at the two of them with normal eyes, maybe Freddie Dowd has too much to lose by hooking up with LJ Carew. Not because she'd be after his mazooma, but because his hardline attitude to the industry of human happiness was all that sustained him through his bad years, his bad life, and to ditch it all after becoming a one-hit wonder would be a complete fucking outrage.

People like her are always flirting anyway, touching everyone everywhere. There's a sort of innocence about it. Anyone with such naked ambition seems somehow innocent to Freddie, this strange innocence that protects them from what people are saying about them at dinner parties.

Compared to most men she touched in the last twenty-four hours alone, Freddie reckons he just barely qualifies as a valid human being in the eyes of LJ Carew. He has money. If he didn't have a dime, it would never become an issue, and he could continue to bask on the high ground with this sense of otherness.

He looks over at Bricks Melvin, asleep on the couch. Bricks looks calm.

Freddie remembers that he has a packet of cigarettes, but he tries to fight it. He has this sensation again, with the buzz of the hangover, and Bricks there snoozing, that he has travelled back in time to the wild years.

The thrill of feeling young again, is quickly replaced by the thought of all that destruction.

Bricks is stirring. Bricks and his kind will be the theme of the interview with LJ Carew. Whether she likes it or not, Freddie Dowd will tell her that the music business sucks, that there is no place for grown-up musicians any more, that the industry just wants a blank space on which it can weave its sick designs. It wants kids, it wants poor dumb boys, because men and women of genuine talent and distinction are just too much trouble.

He is riffing in this vein, thinking that this is exactly the type of thing that he ought to be doing with his windfall, using these opportunities to tell people the truth while he still has the chance. And if LJ says he's just biting the hand that feeds, he can say, Fair enough, lady, but it's feeding Bricks Melvin too and many more like him.

This morning, he figures, he will tell Bricks about his plans. They might even go down today to The Crowbar, and see about booking the room for a weekly session. Bricks seems settled enough now to hear the good news, to get himself ready to blow some jazz.

Nadine comes in to make coffee. She is dressed for her walk, he thinks, wearing this brilliant jumper he bought her, some sort of South American peasant thing. She checks that Bricks is still asleep. She makes two mugs of coffee. Usually she would come in wearing a long T-shirt and take her coffee straight back to the bedroom.

She brings the coffee to Freddie. She smiles.

Whatever she wants, she can have it just for that smile.

'Great,' he says, taking a sip.

He squeezes in on the couch to make room for her, Nadine who can silence them all with her unapproachable beauty, her darkness, like she owns all the air around her, and going in there is just not worth your trouble, man.

He is so proud of her, astonished to think that he could have given her life. Nadine, his Nadine, could crush the hearts of men who have seen her once, and only once, walking the pier like some lovely saturnine ghost.

He is proud that there is some small physical similarity between then, this serene vibe that he has and that Nadine has sometimes, when they're together. It doesn't really mean anything, it's just a natural thing that makes the straight world think you're tripping, when you're actually just in neutral. But he's proud that she has it sometimes, anyway. He is proud that she is so sussed on the lipstick-and-powder front, though that is mainly down to Dorothy who wrote once advising Nadine about make-up, and the ethics of it, urging her to hold fast to Mother Nature, at which point Nadine decided there was something inherently wrong with Mother Nature, that she was taking the piss.

He is proud that she is much cooler than him, that she doesn't feel the need of all that talk, all that explaining, all that rabbit. He is proud that men would throw themselves off the seven spires of Dún Laoghaire for her. But he is afraid of it too. About three minutes after she was born, he began to dread the day when some dude would call to the door for her, and take her away. In the blackest version, the dude would be wearing a leather jacket with Motorhead studded on the back, and he would roar away with her on the back of his Kawasaki to Brittas for the bank holiday weekend, and then, in all likelihood after seven flagons of cider, he would fuck her right there in the sand dunes. His sweet little child, fucked by a tramp. He has been dreading such a thing for seventeen years, running through many variations on the theme, and he's sure it's going to happen pretty soon, and he just won't be able to deal with it.

Ah these fears can crucify him round midnight, terrible fears, much worse than this, lacerating fears that his baby will encounter some catastrophe. Like that Kawasaki could crash doing ninety, like she could get burned like she nearly got burned in the back of the car, like she could wander in for a swim with that dude in Brittas and never come out again, Jesus H. Christ how is a man supposed to live with such a thing, all those men who have seen the gendarmes arriving to the door and who know in an instant . . . *Awwww, Mama . . . awwww Mama*. Nadine is talking. She is here. She is totally one hundred per cent here and alive and well and rocking in the free world. She speaks softly, like him, with a Bob Geldof accent turned down from ten to one, like him.

'Mad last night,' she says, as if a morning smile needs some explanation. 'Guy that Bricks knows . . . mad piano player,' she says.

'Nice one,' he says.

'He stays?' she says.

'Bricks?'

'I mean, when we move, he . . .?' she says.

Freddie has a fierce urge for a cigarette but he fights it again. He is quietly delighted that Nadine has raised the matter, not him. He had no idea how long was long enough for Bricks to be crashing here.

'I thought you hated jazz,' he says.

'Actually . . .' she says.

'You're hanging in there?' he says.

'Mad,' she says.

'So you actually like it?' he says.

'Actually last night . . .'

Bricks is waking up. He looks confused for moment, like he is trying to make sense of a dream. He focuses on Freddie and Nadine.

'Howdy,' he says.

Bricks searches his pockets for tobacco.

Nadine goes to make coffee. The room smells stale. She feels like she has wandered into some student flat.

'Howdy,' Freddie says.

Nadine looks at the two men surfacing. Freddie has the big sofa, but Bricks somehow looks more settled in the sleeping bag on the couch, perhaps because he is still wearing his good suit.

He produces a two-thirds empty bottle of Wolf Blass from beside the couch. Nadine takes down a wine glass.

'It was a delightful evening,' Bricks says.

He takes a slug of wine straight from the bottle.

'We had this thought, man,' says Freddie. 'Maybe you'd like to stay here?'

Nadine brings the glass to Bricks. He pours a little wine into it, and swirls it around.

Freddie sits up on the sofa.

'Silly money,' he says. 'Paddy Lamb's boys have done us a favour. Well, the Duke really . . .'

And he tells it again, how Duke Ellington did him a big favour.

Through the morning mist of alcohol, Bricks Melvin sees the head of Freddie in an oddly exotic light, his serene expression like that of a Native American chief. But he is not hearing much of Freddie's wisdom after the bit about silly money and Paddy Lamb's boys. He is battered and dazed by these words, because instead of poor unfortunate Freddie Dowd he is looking at a rich guy, another Irish success story founded on shite music. And in his condition it sets off the sparks of resentment, the old familiar beginnings of some atrocity. But as the Native American chief's head comes into focus, suddenly the words reveal their full meaning to Bricks.

This money, this silly money is setting Bricks Melvin free, free to live in the moment, and to enjoy it. Sure, he got a big lift from being around Nadine, to steady the nerves. But this is sounding like a second message from the gods, like they're serious, like the fucks finally took pity on Bricks Melvin down there at the crossroads, sending him to the door of poor Freddie Dowd who turns into rich Freddie Dowd, leaving Bricks Melvin on this first morning of the year zero with nothing to feel bad about.

'So how would you feel then, about setting up a regular gig?' Freddie says. 'Like, jazz?'

Bricks composes himself. 'You mean . . . me?' he says.

'You, Bill Dewar, Tommy Hale, Ray Blacoe, whoever . . . say, down at The Crowbar?'

Bricks downs his wine and fills the glass again with

what's left of last night's booze. Down it goes, along with last night's guilt.

'This tastes sweeter,' he says. 'Coz of where it came from.'

'If you based yourself here,' says Freddie, 'you wouldn't even need to get a cab.'

Bricks sips and ponders. 'It's responsibility,' he says.

'You can do it man,' says Freddie.

'What I do now, pretending to be Johnny Shine, there's no responsibility in that.'

'You're world class, Bricks.'

'No one will come.'

'They'll come.'

'Everyone hates jazz. They hated it last night.'

'Actually . . .' says Nadine.

'They hated it,' says Bricks. 'People only like jazz if it's Dixieland.'

'Nadine, did you like it?' says Freddie.

'Mad,' she says.

'Sunday morning pissed at the yacht club, that's why the lady is a tramp,' says Bricks. 'That's the way they like it.'

'Fuck them,' says Freddie.

'Right,' says Bricks with a big grin. 'Fuck them . . . the fucks.'

'I don't care about the size of the crowd,' says Freddie. 'This is not about making money.'

Bricks laughs. 'So what is it about, my man?'

Freddie reckons it's about making a stand for quality, putting his money where his mouth is, maybe steering Nadine towards the good shit before it's too late. But it doesn't quite come out of his mouth like that.

'I love what you do,' he says.

Bricks Melvin has a son somewhere. He'd be sixteen now. Or seventeen.

The walk down to Dún Laoghaire is clearing his head. Coming out of Waterloo Terrace, he was startled by the blast of a car horn. He has a feeling it was Paddy Lamb but it could be anyone in a big car, maybe some punter who saw him playing last night. They all love what he does. One of the things you discover as a full-time drinker, is that you are always meeting people you don't know, but who know you.

'We met before,' they say, when they see the lack of recognition in your eyes. Usually they're pretty cool about it.

Bricks stopped feeling remorseful about this a long time ago. He fancies getting them all together in one place some night, moving through the crowd, maybe even shaking hands with one or two of them if he's really up for it, and them all saying we met before, we met before, we met before, we met before, we met before, enough to fix all these faces in his head again, and no hard feelings.

He has a son somewhere who would be seventeen now. Aaron. Aaron Finnegan.

Aaron's mother volunteered him to come up to Stepaside to confront Bricks. She warned that Aaron was about two feet taller than the last time they met, briefly and by accident when the boy was fourteen, leaving Bricks once more with the prospect of someone he met before, but couldn't place. Maybe this, added to the Stepaside trifle, was bugging him when he lost it back there.

78

He would make his peace with Aaron Finnegan some day, with this good karma that has come over him, this fresh start. But today is for giving thanks that he is not locked away with all the other loopers in Stepaside, but marching down to Dún Laoghaire with a grand in his pocket to blow away the January blues, and to help him reach a decision about Freddie's offer, sipping hot ones on a high stool in the Ferryman. The trick now, is not to get carried away by the breaking ball.

It is time for the simple pleasure of drink, freely taken. Time to live by the logic of the drink. Because it's a thing that the therapy gang and the AA gang really don't understand, this logic that there is in drink, which is totally different to their logic, but which makes a barrel of sense if you come to it right.

There's actually not much that can go wrong for you when you are on the drink. You go from one pub to the next pub, and if you fall off your bar stool you just get right back up again. It's only when you try to give it up that you start getting these fucking urges.

One hot brandy will be perfect, one after the other. Then he will consider his options one after the other – to keep playing for brandy the way he likes it, or to play for love the way Freddie Dowd likes it.

Freddie is too kind. That's the problem with guys like him. With a prick like Paddy Lamb, you get a grand for pretending to be Johnny Shine, and you'll take ten grand without blushing if you can get it. From the kind ones, you have to take whatever they give you. You have to take their kindness, and if you're not careful, you're feeling one of those little spasms of hope.

79

Like last night, blowing with Ray, when Bricks Melvin spoke to Nadine with his jazz, with that thing that he has, and she said she liked it, and he believes she did. Such a spasm of hope went through him at that moment, it was like he was back in Paris twenty years ago, when a look, a vibration, would tell him for sure he had clicked with a woman, that it was all there for him after the show.

It was there for him again last night, he is sure. It is still there for him, and he can still take it all the way. Or he can drink. It was the saddest thing he ever learned, that in this world of fucks and even in Paris you just can't do both.

Chapter 8

Paddy Lamb parks his Bentley on the footpath, tight against the railings. Freddie Dowd's three flash cars are taking up all the space at the side of the house. Paddy finds it an amusing scene, the Merc, the Range Rover and the Ferrari belonging to the guy in the basement round the back, and an old lady's bike at the top of the front steps for whoever owns the other three storeys.

Paddy knows this muso who lives in a flat down the road, one of the first guys he managed back in college, a folkie with a lot of promise who lost his looks when he gave up the drugs. He used to look a bit like James Taylor, now he looks like whatever James Taylor would look like if he sat on his arse all day drinking pints.

To call on him would be just too distressing. For both of them.

Paddy Lamb allows himself another minute in the car to compose his thoughts, but on the main point he will not fuck about. The main point is, the money is on its way, guaranteed. He will spin some old bollocks about the bean-counters sitting on it, because you can spin almost any old bollocks about money to a chap like Freddie, who only knows about art, and who has no idea what a lucky, lucky man he is to have LJ Carew batting for him, taking pity on him.

On the whole, Paddy Lamb would prefer if LJ had no feelings for any other man. He feels very close to clinching it with LJ, and he fears that the slightest distraction could wreck it, even if it's just this bout of pity on her part for old Freddie. But it's an opportunity too, to show her a side of Paddy Lamb other than the big player that she loves to gossip with, the two of them talking telephone numbers, two gypsies so turned on by this crazy business. It is tremendous, dirty fun. But Paddy thinks he deserves more from this relationship than fun. He wants her to love him because he is a nice man, not just for his power and for the devil in him.

He has worked it out, done the math. There must be something decent inside him that she brings alive, some innate goodness. Sometimes he feels like he is making history here, a man of his background besotted with LJ from the council houses at the far end of Dún Laoghaire, LJ who barely went to school at all, let alone to the right school. He is hip to this moment in Ireland when a new aristocracy is emerging, the aristocracy of talent. And he keeps trying to explain to that old gang of drunks in the Arts Club that talent means LJ Carew as well as George Bernard Shaw. Talent is whatever the market says it is.

Men of his background will never understand why he is hanging on in there. Most of them couldn't even handle the concept of going the distance with some totty off the telly, only to discover that she's the one who sees it as a one-night stand, that she has no interest in his background and all the cachet it can bring her, just in gossiping about money and mischief.

She is one of the real people. Where she is at now, in her life and her career, she is looking for a nice man. She says this to Paddy, as if he could never be such a man himself, for all his charm. So to show her what a nice man he can be, as well as a charming man, he will be gentle with Freddie Dowd. He always had a soft spot for old Freddie, still the maverick, buying these cars with money he has not seen. Paddy Lamb will go the extra mile here, even though he has personally made Freddie a millionaire, on paper, and will shortly make him a millionaire in actual fact.

It is not a privilege extended to many in this business, because most of them don't want it enough. Not really. They want other things, like fame, and attention, and sex. They want a few toys, for reassurance. And Paddy Lamb can make all this happen for them, because he has this perfect eye for raw Irish talent, for tailoring it to the taste of an international audience and for enjoying all the success that it brings until the inevitable day when the artistes start showing signs of temperament, such as body-piercing and writing their own material.

They don't realize that they can't do it without him. They lose their humility, and along with it, much of their charm. They don't realize that they don't have careers like Bob Dylan or James Taylor, that they are instead given a couple of great years with little girls screaming at them and nice things to wear and nice places to visit, and all the toys. It comes so easily to them, they assume they can do it by themselves, and so they embark on ghastly solo projects and are bewildered to learn that their moment has passed. They just don't get it. And when the fun stops, they come back to Paddy Lamb, whingeing about money. If they wanted the money enough, the serious money, they would damn well take the trouble to know something about it in the first place, or to know somebody who knows about it, instead of raising bloody hell about unscrupulous managers when their solo album dies, and dies horribly.

For Freddie Dowd, who must be twice as old as the oldest member of Fellaz, there is no excuse at all. Still, whatever it takes to please the fair LJ, must be done. He will bring Freddie the good news, and then take him to be interviewed by LJ and love-bomb the fuck out of him, if that's what it takes to land this little cracker, who has his heart in her handbag. If Freddie can't stick the pace after all the booze of yesterday, Paddy Lamb will teach him how. He will show him how to drink champagne all day, and wake up the next morning like Paddy Lamb, to a full fried breakfast in The Shelbourne, blaming no one except himself, and then forgiving himself with a couple of lines of The Lad.

Already this morning he has had an idea, passing Bricks Melvin up the road. The paper said it will be a creative day for Gemini, and so it is coming to pass. It's a brilliant idea, actually, and that's not just The Lad talking.

He gets out of the Bentley and stretches. He always liked Dún Laoghaire, the Victoriana, the sea air, the old dears walking their poodles, a few hippies and the real people all side by side, the ships coming in, the Britishness of it.

He checks the top pocket of his denim shirt. There's enough in the little bag to send an army into battle laughing.

Nadine opens the door to him. They mumble-mumble a few pleasantries about the restaurant last night, and Bricks. She leads the way into the main room, where Freddie still lies on the sofa.

Paddy sees Freddie on the sofa and it just breaks him up, the curly-haired countryman who can't stop laughing at the good of it all.

'Rock'n'roll!' he says.

Paddy falls into the old brown couch where Bricks slept last night.

'No rock'n'roll,' Freddie says. 'This is the way we live.'

Paddy straightens himself up.

'On the first of March,' he says, 'you can live any way you want.'

Freddie signals to Nadine that she should stay for this. He asks for a cigarette. She throws him a Rothmans. He lights it and sucks on it hard. It seems to send his insides spinning down to his bowels.

'What's that?' Freddie says. 'Four, five weeks?'

'It's going to happen,' Paddy says. 'I am assured by the bean-counters that there's a large cheque with your name on it.'

'In the post?'

'You can always go to their offices to collect it, like a Lotto winner.'

'First of March?'

'It would be first of February, but the guy is in New York.'

'Cheque in the post, Nadine?' Freddie laughs good-naturedly. 'Do you believe this guy?'

'No,' she says.

Paddy snuffles a stray grain of cocaine, shaking his head from side to side in wonderment.

'I always said that if I ever amounted to anything in this business I would do two things,' he says. 'I would return people's calls – it's always some scumbag that never returns your call; the top guys always return your call – and the second thing is, *The cheque is in the post* means *The cheque is in the post*.'

Freddie takes a long drag on his cigarette. He knew there was no irony in the way that Nadine said no, she didn't believe Paddy. There was just hostility.

'I always said . . .' Freddie says, his mind wandering. 'What did I always say? Until yesterday, I always said I'd never be interviewed by LJ Carew.'

Paddy takes the bag out of his top pocket. 'The Lad,' he says.

'Not for me,' says Freddie.

'It's good stuff first thing,' says Paddy.

Nadine is staring at Freddie now.

'LJ Carew?' she says. 'Vampire fuck?'

'I'm using her,' Freddie says. 'I'm using the interview to say some things. Subversive, you know?'

'The fucks,' Nadine says quietly.

Paddy puts the bag away. 'I forgot the lady was present,' he says.

He picks up the empty bottle of Wolf Blass that Bricks left beside the couch. He remembers that brilliant idea he had when he saw Bricks up the road. He hesitates about sharing it. He is being so nice to this guy it is starting to hurt. But then he reckons he needs Freddie on board.

'I saw Bricks Melvin on my way over here. And last

night in the restaurant with Nadine. I take it he's a house-guest?'

'He's a mate,' says Freddie.

Paddy looks sincere. 'You see, I pay Bricks a few grand to play on those Johnny Shine albums, right?' he says.

'Right,' Freddie says.

'You mightn't think it, but those albums sell. We're talking heap big numbers here,' Paddy says.

'Fuck,' says Nadine.

Paddy scratches his chest hair. 'As it happens,' he says, 'Johnny Shine tells me he has his money made and where he is in his life now, he'd like to play some golf. And I'm thinking we've had a good run, and Johnny is great but, you know . . . And then I see Bricks and I'm thinking, maybe if we can keep Bricks off the sauce . . .'

'Good night,' Freddie says.

'We might even sell a few records to the more discerning listener,' Paddy says.

Freddie takes a fit of coughing from the cigarette smoke and the thought of Bricks as the new darling of the Mogadon Set, the man with the magic horn bringing evergreen classics to the Irish across the foam.

'You have got to be fucking kidding,' he says.

'I would consider it a personal favour,' Paddy says, slowly, clearly, like a lawyer is examining each syllable.

'No can do,' Freddie says.

'I'll leave it with you, my friend,' Paddy says.

Nadine is still staring at Freddie.

'Going on that crap show?' she says.

'With Paddy's best friend,' says Freddie. 'Yes.'

Paddy laughs like a man incapable of taking offence.

Nadine picks up the rest of Bricks's empty bottles and a full ashtray and takes them over to the bin.

'Down the pier,' she says.

Freddie starts panicking in the bathroom and, by the time the TV people are wiring him for sound, waiting for LJ Carew to appear, he is so pale they are offering him the full make-up job that LJ gets. Which he refuses, partly on the principle of warts-and-all, partly because he is stuck to the seat with stage fright.

A quick comb of the hair perhaps?

No thanks.

Is Mr Dowd happy with his hair?

Yes, he is.

'Leave the man alone,' says Paddy Lamb, sitting across from him in LJ's executive swivel seat. 'He is trying to compose his thoughts.'

'Say something,' says Freddie, his voice a petrified squeak.

'Blah-di-blah,' says Paddy. 'LJ Carew takes longer in make-up than it takes Freddie Dowd to get up and dressed and a line of The Lad up his hooter and all the way in from Dún Laoghaire.'

'Say something . . . you know . . . that I disagree with,' Freddie says.

'All right. U2 was a one-off,' Paddy drawls. 'It's just not on any more to be waiting and hoping for some guy to put a sign up on the school notice board and, lo and behold, it just happens to be seen by three of the smartest and most talented young men of their generation. The industry in Ireland has moved on now, it's actually an industry, and we must recognize that and try to be creative around it.'

Freddie takes out a new packet of Rothmans.

'No smoking,' a voice says from behind the camera.

'Go on,' Freddie says.

'All right,' Paddy says. 'We Irish have lost our inferiority complex. We don't leave it to chance any more that some genius will emerge from our midst to astonish the world. We hear all this pop music coming at us, and instead of thinking that it's all too slick for us we think, Why can't we do that? Why can't we do it in our own way? Why can't we do it better, and do it again and again and again? Why not?'

Freddie is struggling to find his voice.

'But Paddy,' he says, 'it is all shite.'

Paddy laughs, swivelling in a full circle. 'Louder, Freddie,' he says. 'Let it rip. The people can't hear that little bourgeois voice of yours.'

Freddie speaks again, softly.

'It is all shite,' he says.

Paddy is on automatic.

'My friend,' he says, 'if it is shite, then, as we say in rural Ireland, it is powerful shite. There is an industry growing out of it that allows Paddy Lamb to delegate down the line, leaving me free to drive out in my Bentley to pick up my friend Freddie Dowd and take him in here to the great LJ Carew, who is giving him a platform to say these terrible things about the people who made him a wealthy man. Tell me, Freddie, can you deal with this?'

Freddie is still hung over, and the lights, the TV people, all this rabbit is making it worse. Maybe Paddy's coke is disagreeing with him.

LJ Carew is suddenly beside him, squeezing his clenched fist.

'Just be yourself,' she says.

Paddy stands up to touch and to be touched, virtually a massage.

'Here in one piece,' he says. 'The excellent Freddie Dowd.'

'The millionaire Freddie Dowd?' she says.

Paddy leaves them to it with a quip. 'And what do you see in the millionaire Freddie Dowd?' he says.

Freddie feels like his brain is seizing up. He feels that Paddy Lamb and his champagne and his coke and his money and his bullshit and everything and everyone in this TV studio is sucking his soul out of his body. He has a desperate need to be with Nadine, to have words of wisdom with her. He hates the way she left like that, down the pier, no goodbyes.

It's all eating away at him, and he tries to draw a deep breath but it seems there's not enough air in here. In panic, he goes for another gulp but it's just not happening for him. He is aware of someone ripping off his mike, and then nothing.

Chapter 9

It was the fact that Freddie didn't make the call himself.
That he couldn't be arsed. That LJ Carew in person got on
to Bricks in the Ferryman, saying not to worry about
Freddie, she was just kidnapping him for a few hours and
she was keeping him until they paid the ransom, ha-ha.

It was that and the waiting all afternoon to see Freddie
making a dipstick of himself on the telly, and then the relief
when he never showed. It was the pub atmosphere in the
afternoon, like they were shut off from the outside world,
like they were in some cave under the sea and they could
stay there as long as they liked.

It was the music in the restaurant last night, it was
walking down the pier and straight into the pub and up to
the bar where Bricks was sitting with a brandy, like he was
waiting for her.

It was these things and a few other things that got
Nadine on to the third and the fourth and the fifth glass of
wine, and on and on into the unknown.

With a sweep of his ankle-length black overcoat Bricks
leads the way from the bar to the corner of the lounge, like

91

they are settling in for a long night, a session. He sits with his back to the window, she takes the stool opposite him. She wants whatever he's having. Freddie taught her how to drink. But he also taught her that people like LJ Carew were the pits of the world. He kept feeding her this shit about jazz, and then the first chance he gets, he's hanging out with these fucks. Giving it large. Sending messages to the pub. The big sap.

When she switches to the brandies like Bricks, after six or seven glasses of wine, she can see clearly all the things that are bugging her about Freddie, the things that they never talk about. She starts to wonder how she can get through the average day with all the things that Freddie does to bug her, and none of this brandy to flush it all out of her system.

She names them to Bricks. There's the way he's an expert on everything until he runs into these fucks in real life, LJ Carew and Paddy Lamb, who can run rings round him. There's the way he fucked up her life completely by sending her to this posh school, meaning she had no friends because she was ashamed to ask any of them over to the flat, so they stopped asking her to their mansions. And even if she had asked them, there was no TV because Freddie wouldn't have it in the house until he had filled her head full of shit about records and books and films, like he's got it all sussed with his fuzz, and some guy adored by millions like Billy Joel is just some sad bastard. This one only occurred to her the other day, when something else started bugging her, Freddie telling Dorothy he didn't need her stupid money any more, shortly before she went out the window.

Bricks reckons this is the drink talking.

'Dorothy had issues,' he says.

'She didn't do a fucking crap TV show,' she says.

'I'm kinda disappointed now, that he wasn't on it.'

'Crowd of fucks,' she spits in a venomous whisper.

'We are all whores. Well, I am.'

'Fucks are ripping him off. Sure of it,' she says, liking the to-and-fro, the drink-driven rhythm of the conversation.

'If he's relying on Paddy . . .'

'We're fucked?'

'It won't be simple. It won't be like, here's this money I owe you, thanks very much for your song. There will be . . . talks.'

'He could phone the fucks,' she says. 'Send faxes. The Royal Marine Hotel lets him send faxes.'

'Is it worth it for the Ferrari?'

'Fucks are laughing at him.'

'I want you to know something,' he says. 'I want you to know that Freddie Dowd is one of the few guys in this town who is worth a shit.'

She grunts.

'So?' he says.

'That's about it,' she says. 'And later for the garbage, later for the garbage, later for the garbage,' she says, mimicking his schmoozy little voice.

'And the other thing is, he doesn't really do anything, does he?' she says with a high-pitched note of triumph, like she has nailed it at last.

Bricks shrugs. Nadine gets stuck into this, like it never occurred to her before.

'I mean, if someone asked what my father does, what do I say?' she says.

'I dunno,' Bricks says. 'The arts? Show business? Something like that?'

'But what does he *do* in the arts, in show business?' Nadine says, swirling her brandy around the way Bricks does it. 'I mean, you play the saxophone. That's what you do. That is your talent. What is Freddie's talent?'

'Maybe he's got a talent for working with talent,' Bricks says.

'Like who?' Nadine says. 'All these arty-farty Dorothy types? All these . . . losers?'

'So he's not driven by commercial success,' Bricks says.

'Like, he has a choice?' she says.

'He's after having this big hit, give him his due. Maybe by accident, but it's one more big hit than a lot of us.'

'Yeah, but you're good,' she says. 'You can do something.'

The lounge is filling up. They debate going to this new pub in Dún Laoghaire facing the sea, full of light and air. Bricks is called to the phone again. The barman gives him the phone, and a dirty look. Nadine takes another sip of brandy. She doesn't fancy the new pub after all. It is two storeys high, with spectacular views. This place is better, it's got sentimental value. It will be the first place she got really drunk in.

She knows she's drunk, but she doesn't know how drunk. Maybe there's no way of knowing it. You just keep bobbing along like this, cut loose at last, saying all the things you can hardly even think when you're not drunk. She thought she might be worse by now, after something like twelve drinks. But instead there's a lightness coming over her, like the hard part is finished.

Bricks is back, the same super-cool Bricks as when she sat down beside him this afternoon, so long ago.

'Freddie mightn't make it home tonight,' he says. 'LJ Carew says she'll take good care of him.'

'Fuck,' she says.

'Funny lady. Says the ransom is going up all the time. Says he's a lovely man.'

'Fuck him,' says Nadine. But there is no venom in it this time. The brandy is taking her somewhere else. 'Just fuck him.'

'I want you to hear me,' Bricks says. 'Freddie Dowd is one of the few guys in this town who is worth a shit.'

Nadine starts another brandy. She is overcome with this lightness. She smiles to herself, feeling totally light inside, totally right. The thing about Bricks is, she wants him to like her. She wants him to think that she is not like the others. Maybe she picked it up off Freddie, this wanting to be liked. Just being on the drink with Bricks, getting all these looks from the locals, is a buzz.

'The fucking barman is staring at you,' she says.

'People look at me,' he says.

'The fucks,' she says.

'I'm going to shave off this moustache. Maybe then they won't look at me.'

'I like it,' she says. 'I like it when they look at you.'

Bricks bows his head, like he has remembered some old sorrow.

'Freddie said you didn't talk much,' he says, his head still bowed.

'I don't.'

'You say *fuck* a lot.' He looks up and smiles.

She holds up her glass of brandy to explain that it's the drink that's making her say *fuck* a lot. The drink and some notion that jazzers everywhere like it when you say *fuck* a lot.

She sees at this moment how free he is, how together, how he's so good at what he does, you would forgive him anything. She slides in beside him. Her mouth is suddenly on his. She grips the hair on the back of his head. Bricks knocks a glass of brandy onto the floor, thinking, sick old bastard, taking advantage of a lovely young woman.

The barman comes over with a cloth to clean up the spillage. He gets another stoned smile from Nadine. He tells them they are barred.

Bricks buys two bottles of wine and a bottle of gin and a bottle of brandy in the downstairs bar.

They laugh about it all the way home.

The only cure for passing out in a TV studio is steak, according to LJ Carew. So Freddie is coming to, looking at a huge steak on a plate. No onions, or sauce, or potatoes, just a big, thick fried steak, on its own.

'I thought you were having a fit,' she says. 'Hate that.'

Her accent to Freddie seems slightly different. She seems less mad-for-it, less blonde. She is not touching him. Everything about this seems off-centre, out-of-left-field. He sits on a stool at a marble table in a white-towelling robe, with a vague sense that he has woken up in the time of Julius Caesar.

He takes a long drink from a large glass of mineral water. LJ sits opposite him in a towelling robe. She seems to like this Roman Emperor vibe, the matching togas, all the marbling and the plants and this strange water-feature running down the wall, like they have woken up in some bathhouse in Pompeii.

Freddie is waking up, but he can't remember going to bed.

'You were out for the count,' she says. 'Eighteen hours.'

'Oh, shit,' he says. The water is reviving him, he is awake enough now to put the pieces together, the flakeout in the studio, the fact that he appears to have spent the night in LJ's celebrated pad in Ringsend, sparko.

'Oh, shit,' he says, 'oh, shit.'

'You kept mumbling about Bricks in some pub in Dún Laoghaire,' she says. 'I rang them all.'

'Did you get him?' he says.

'Keep your hair on,' she says. 'I got him.'

Freddie rubs his eyes.

'It's just . . . I never actually spent a night away from Nadine . . . under a different roof.'

'You want to call her?' she says.

'I must call her,' he says.

'It's only ten o'clock,' she says. 'Have your steak.'

Freddie cuts a forkful of the steak. It is well done but tender.

'I'll call her later,' he says.

'I just popped down the road for it,' she says. 'My brother is a butcher.'

Freddie vaguely recalls some article he read in a doctor's waiting room about LJ coming from a family of butchers. Or victuallers, as they put it. It makes his head hurt.

'I'm just anxious about Nadine getting the message,' he says.

LJ hands him a cordless phone. She is smiling at him like an air-hostess negotiating with some drunk guy.

'So call her,' she says.

He dials his home number and then cuts it off before it rings. It has suddenly occurred to him that he is not fit for words of wisdom with Nadine about spending the night with LJ Carew, sitting at LJ's marble table, wearing her toga, watching her floating around in this Roman fantasy, eating her brother's steak.

'She doesn't surface till twelve usually,' he says.

'Teenagers,' LJ says.

'You're very sweet,' he says.

'You like this place?' she says.

'It's . . . it's cool.'

'You want to buy it?' she says.

'Do I what?'

'Maybe Nadine would like it. A place of her own.'

'Eh . . . I've been looking at some other property.'

LJ lets out a big laugh. Freddie judges it to be a laugh with him as well as a laugh at him. He can tell.

'This place is a disgrace,' she says. 'I was ashamed bringing you here.'

'No, no, no. It's me who's ashamed. Conking out like that.'

'So then, we're both ashamed.'

'There's a lot of stuff been happening to me recently,' he says.

'Welcome to the business,' she says.

'The other day, I was rapping with Nadine about the jazz albums she never listens to. She's got this Billy Joel CD that I took out and bent in front of her. This is after I spend my whole life telling her how good this stuff is, and how bad Billy Joel is. My whole life. How many times do you have to keep saying these things?'

'You're very brave,' she says.

'There's all this money to worry about,' he says. 'And maybe a funeral coming up.'

'I can get you the best meat in Dublin,' she says.

'I'm sure you can,' he says.

'It's the only thing in a crisis,' she says. 'Meat.'

'It's not all bad,' he says. 'Bricks Melvin has moved in with us.'

'Oh, that's great,' she says. 'Super.'

'The money is coming in,' he says. 'It'll put Bricks back where he belongs, up on a stage, man.'

'Finish your steak,' she says.

'Apologies about the interview,' he says.

'We would have chopped it up anyway,' she says. And she brings her hand down like a butcher wielding a cleaver.

'You're very easy to talk to,' he says. 'It might have been a blast.'

'I just wanted to meet you again,' she says. 'Fuck the show.'

She sits on the stool next to Freddie. She touches his hand.

'It's like what Paddy Lamb said,' he says. 'We're all gypsies, right?'

'That's just Paddy Lamb talking shite,' she says. 'The way I see it, you're a gypsy, and LJ Carew is . . . LJ Carew lives here . . . disgraceful.'

She is massaging his hand, like she is practising some technique of reflexology.

'It's sort of . . . Ancient Rome vibe,' he says. 'There's the sound of running water. It's different.'

'It's just vulgar,' she says. 'I've got gold taps.'

'You looked happy in it, in the colour supplements.'

'I was happy for a while. And then . . . people change.'

'Maybe the place could use a few books,' he says.

She finishes the massage.

'I can't read,' she says.

Freddie laughs.

LJ is still looking at him with the calm eyes of the concerned air-hostess. Then she lets out a huge laugh.

Freddie shivers with pleasure and pain. It's a laugh that goes right through him. It's like she heard that dirty joke that Dorothy heard the first time they met, only with an improved punchline.

'Would you like me to maybe bring you a few books?' he says. 'Maybe a few albums? To take, like, the bare look off it?'

'I'd love that,' she says.

'You might really connect with some of this material,' he says.

'Just tell me about it,' she says.

'Just give it a shot,' he says. 'Just . . . hang in there.'

'I told you, I can't read,' she says.

'You're . . . eh . . . you don't mean that,' he says.

And she lets out another huge laugh.

'You take everything so seriously,' she says. 'But I like that.'

She takes his hand again.

He feels safe.

*

Bricks Melvin knows where he is and how he got here. He is waking up in an armchair in Freddie Dowd's flat, the morning after the day's drinking with Nadine. He knew it straight away, without opening his eyes. He's accustomed to it, drifting out of sleep like he is emerging from a coma, discovering that he is still alive, and that most of his organs seem to be working.

There's no doctor to give him the lowdown, he has to figure it all out himself, and quickly. He's got a dressing gown on, somehow, a man's dressing gown that seems to add a touch of permanence to his position here.

Then the brain starts releasing its recollections of last night, raw, uncut. Last night was all Dorothy. Her face fills his consciousness, images from way back, her eyes burning with bitter disappointment, her spirit capsizing and still something inside her gallant. Yes, all the time he knew her, she looked like a woman jailed for a crime of passion, for breaking some taboo. In the early morning cold, Bricks Melvin thinks of women waking up in a freezing cell, vilified but unbroken.

This is what he told Nadine, what kept them talking most of the night, this arty intellectual part of Dorothy, the unbroken part, this thing that she had that seemed to stay working after the rest of her had closed down.

They were back at the flat and Nadine couldn't find the corkscrew. They could have gone back out again for a corkscrew, but they decided instead to smash the bottles open at the neck against the wash-hand basin in the bathroom. The first bottle went down hilariously, Bricks pouring it through a tea-strainer to catch the splinters.

He went at it again, and knocked a chunk out the basin.

Nadine was intrigued by this, examining the jagged piece of green porcelain like it was an art object. But they got the thing with the tea-strainer going again, swirling the wine around in their mouths to be extra careful about the splinters.

With all the complications she stopped kissing him. Instead, they got stuck into the booze again until they found themselves talking about the early years of the Phoenix Arts Centre. Which seemed important at the time. A couple of times Bricks and Dorothy shared the bill at the Phoenix, Dorothy giving a reading, Bricks squalling on the horn, maybe Neil Crumb doing a piece of performance art, jumping around in a vat of piss or something.

'It had to be his own piss,' Bricks said. Which made Nadine get a bit hung up wondering how it could be anyone else's piss.

The council were always looking for a reason to shut the Phoenix down. They had Crumb bang to rights on a hygiene rap. But they backed off, saying it would only give Crumb the notoriety he craved.

Amazing to think that art was still so despised just fifteen, twenty years ago, whereas now the council is ferrying tourists round Temple Bar, showing them the spot where Crumb did the famous piss show, watched by members of U2 and The Virgin Prunes. Bricks reckons so many of the Phoenix crowd became bad drunks because there was nowhere for them to go afterwards, no Bohemian all-night café of the type he used to long for, as he sat there slugging wine in Leeson Street clubs with every asshole in the city.

Getting barred from the Ferryman like that made Nadine

seem less like Freddie Dowd's little girl, more a soul mate from the Phoenix, an outcast. It made her seem more like Dorothy's girl, wanting to know all about Dorothy.

Fifteen, twenty years on, and these outcasts are pouring wine out of broken bottles into a tea-strainer, still with no all-night café to their liking, no place out there that will treat them kindly at four in the morning, when they are destroyed.

But they kept going last night until they were finished with most of the wine, and some gin and some brandy, at which point Bricks reckons he must have fallen asleep. He doesn't remember them parting for the night, or him putting on the dressing gown, he just wakes up with this image in his head, from way back, of Dorothy at her most severe, sitting up very straight in that boiler suit which looked increasingly like a prison uniform, talking very seriously, her eyes streaming at times, disappointed, so disappointed.

He pours a brandy. He takes it into the bedroom. It is dark in here with heavy curtains, darker than the main room. He finds the bedside lamp and switches it on. It is her eyes he sees first, looking straight at him with that expression of the woman who knows she has done terrible things, but who was left with no decent alternative. It is a picture of Dorothy on Nadine's bedside locker, with Freddie and Nadine when she was a child.

Nadine is sitting up against the headboard, perfectly still. Something about her doesn't look right to Bricks. It's like she put on too much make-up the way women do at weddings, like she started and absentmindedly forgot to stop, here in this dark room.

She has her cigarettes and the cordless phone beside her. She lights a cigarette. Her shoulders are bare above the duvet.

'Is he back?' she says, looking at Bricks for the first time since he came in.

'Nope,' Bricks says.

'Time?' she says. She sounds a bit hoarse, but calm.

'Don't know,' he says. 'Morning time.'

On the wall facing Nadine there is a full-length poster of Chuck Berry playing the guitar, doing his duck walk.

'Chuck up there. Song called Nadine,' she says.

'Sure,' he says.

'Up there all my life,' she says.

Nadine reaches for the glass of brandy in Bricks's hand. She takes a sip, then another. She puts the glass on the bedside locker, beside the picture of herself with Freddie and Dorothy. She douses her cigarette in the dregs of the brandy. It is a new sound to her, the hiss of a cigarette doused in brandy.

'It's cold,' she says. 'Come on.'

She switches off the cordless phone and puts it back on the bedside locker. She slides under the duvet.

Bricks looks at the picture again, at those eyes and all the sorrow behind them. He looks at the half-smoked cigarette in the glass, damp at the end.

'I'd love to,' he says. 'But . . .'

She switches off the bedside lamp.

'But what?' she says.

She is there for him, like all those visions of the fabulous woman he played for, the woman who did not exist.

The right thing to do is to get out of there, and make

them both a pot of coffee, and forget about it. But the right thing has its terrors too, one more vision to crucify him, to give him bad dreams about the things he did and the things he didn't do.

He gets in there with her. Still wasted, only half-sober, face to face on the pillow he suspects she's been crying.

In his head, he's already over that line, they're already rolling all the way up until they come together like they're hearing the crack of the same drum, he can think it all the way through, and for Bricks Melvin thinking is next to doing. But he can't do it.

He can't cross that line.

'When the time comes . . .' he says.

He turns his back to her. He reaches for her hand but she turns the other way.

Then they sleep.

Chapter 10

Around noon, the taxi stops outside the People's Park. Freddie pays a tenner and tips the driver a twenty. He wants to walk the rest of the way up to the flat, to get the sea air, and to get his story straight for Nadine.

He stops to buy a ninety-nine. This is what he bought the last time he abandoned her, when he took her to the pier and bought the paper announcing the killing of Marvin Gaye, and walked home in a trance, leaving Nadine in her buggy being comforted by the ice-cream man.

Yes, they have spent every night of their lives under the same roof.

The average single parent would have ways around it, a support system as they call it. But Freddie isn't even sure what a support system is. Nadine talked a couple of times about a sleepover but it never happened, probably because those nice straight parents didn't want getting any closer to the local weirdo.

It is a potent symbol, this ninety-nine. And it's another small sign that he still has a soul, that money isn't the answer to everything. When you've given your daughter the keys to an apartment, and a brilliant South American peasant type jumper thing, and there's a Ferrari with her name on it, what do you buy her to see that smile? There's only so much that money can do when you've been getting it together with a TV personality, when you are on the record identifying that TV personality as a public menace.

Were they getting it together? Yes, by any gossip-column standard, that little scene over the breakfast steak would rank as getting it together. But in the world where Freddie has been living most of his life, there's no name for it. So this is another little hassle ahead of him, finding the words to explain to Nadine that LJ Carew . . . well, she has her moments. Like, she is a child of the universe, no less than the trees and the stars she has a right to be here.

And she patches you up pretty good if you faint, and finish up in her place. And she sees the amusing side of living in a Roman bath-house in Ringsend. And if you were to meet her yourself . . . Ah, that would be pushing it. That would need more than a ninety-nine, on one of the coldest days of the year. For that, Nadine would need Ferrari lessons from Mr Ferrari himself. Which can be arranged, perhaps.

He skips past the three flash cars with his ninety-nine. He opens the back door and picks up some junk mail. He hears the bathroom door slamming and then the sound of someone vomiting.

He goes straight to Nadine's room. He switches on the bedside lamp. She is waking up. He picks up the brandy glass with the sodden cigarette. He offers Nadine the ninety-nine. From across the hall, Bricks can be heard retching.

Nadine sits up, gathering the duvet around her shoulders. She takes the ninety-nine.

'Everything all right?' Freddie says.

'Fine,' she says.

'I'm sorry,' he says. 'I left messages . . .'

'Got them,' she says. 'From LJ Carew.'

'I took some kind of a turn,' he says. He nods towards the bathroom. 'Sounds like it's going round.'

Nadine is getting through the ninety-nine.

'Hangover,' she says.

Freddie sits on the bed beside her. Whatever happened last night, whatever it was, it looks like she escaped unhurt. He tries to look her straight in the eye but she is focusing on Chuck Berry.

'What's happening here?' he says.

'Too much last night,' she says. 'OK?'

'And . . . Bricks?'

'Guess,' she says.

'Good time?' he says.

'You?' she says.

'No,' he says. 'I conked out in the studio. Sparko.'

'Oh,' she says.

'Ended up in the famous house of LJ Carew,' he says.

'Fuck,' she says.

'Actually . . .' he says.

'Actually what?' she says.

'Actually nothing,' he says.

'Are you actually . . .?' she says.

'It's just,' he says, 'I don't actually . . .'

'But you're not going to . . .'

'Oh, no.'

'I mean, you're not actually . . .'

'Oh, no. Nothing like that.'

Nadine finishes the ninety-nine. Bricks emerges from the bathroom.

'Bricks, man,' Freddie chirps. 'I hear she drank you under the table.'

Bricks gives a weak little salute and shambles into the kitchen.

'Finished,' Bricks says.

Nadine slides back under the duvet.

'Are we . . . are we all right then?' Freddie says.

There is no answer.

It lashes rain all afternoon. Freddie makes a stew. Bricks is sitting at the table perusing the letter officially releasing Dorothy's body. They will cremate her tomorrow at Glasnevin.

'I was thinking we might go to town tonight? To The Bailey? Tonight?' Freddie says, stirring the stew.

'I'm off it,' Bricks says, his voice full of shame. 'As of now, I'm off it.'

'Nice one,' Freddie says. He keeps stirring, stirring, like the motion will somehow restore his serenity.

'Maybe play something at the funeral?' Bricks says.

'Fantastic,' Freddie says. He turns away from the stew and he gives Bricks the thumbs up, for the good times.

'I owe you,' Bricks says. 'I owe you big.'

'Just eat this stew,' Freddie says.

'Taking me in . . . getting me sorted . . . and what do I do? I take your daughter on the piss,' Bricks says.

'The trick is. . .' Freddie says. 'What did you say? The trick is not minding it.'

'But you do mind,' Bricks says. 'You seem nervous. Sort of excited.'

'There was no trouble or anything?' Freddie says. 'Nothing . . . dangerous?'

'Naw,' Bricks says.

'Nothing else?' Freddie says. 'You think it was, like, a one-off?'

'I think she was miffed,' Bricks says, 'about you and . . . that TV lady.'

'Actually . . .' Freddie says.

'But it's not you, it's me,' Bricks says.

Nadine comes in drying her hair with a towel after a marathon stretch in the bathroom.

'Great,' she says. 'Trayton's gone.'

Freddie turns away from the stew. She gives him that smile.

'American guy?' he says.

'Got rid of it. This . . . perfume or something.'

'I was saying to Bricks,' Freddie says, 'tonight, the three of us might go to The Bailey?'

'The pub?' she says.

'I thought with Dorothy's funeral tomorrow . . .,' Freddie says. 'It was a place we used to hang out.'

'Whatever,' she says.

'Bricks will play at the . . .' Freddie says. 'You know he's off it? Off the booze? Isn't that fantastic?' But there is no joy in his voice, like he has trouble believing it, or anything else, on this day.

Bricks gets up and goes to the other end of the room. He

takes out his saxophone. He gives it a few lazy swipes with a duster.

'Beer,' Nadine says.

She takes a can of lager from the fridge. She sits where Bricks sat, glancing at Dorothy's death papers.

'Hair of the dog?' Freddie says.

'Can't believe it,' she says. 'Trayton's gone . . . magic.'

'Magic,' he says.

She takes a long swig of lager. She throws her head back. Her long wet hair nearly touches the ground. She seems to be talking to the ceiling.

'It was so, so embarrassing,' she says. 'We went up to Kilbrittan beach . . . had a little beer . . . couple of cigarettes . . . babbling on about this and that . . . and he said all these corny things you know? Then we watched the sun go down. I'm not making this up. He must have . . . sprayed me or something with this . . . this . . . you know?'

Freddie turns back to the stew.

'No,' he says quietly. 'I don't.'

They sit on high stools at the bar of The Bailey. Freddie drinks red wine. Nadine, who skipped the stew to drink cans of lager all afternoon, drinks a pint of lager. Bricks tries a fizzy water.

Freddie raises a glass to Dorothy.

'To a free spirit,' he says.

They clink their glasses.

'A legend,' Bricks says.

Freddie is trying to create the right mood, to lighten some darkness that has fallen on them.

'We're going to do this gig in The Crowbar, the full works,' he says. 'On one condition.'

'Right,' Bricks says.

'The condition is, you tell us that story about Dorothy and you and the rubber plant,' Freddie says.

Bricks sips his fizzy water. He looks around the bar, all new to him with punters out on the pavement by day, trying to imagine it the way it was before they renovated it, when Phil Lynott used to drink here, when U2 were just getting their shit together, and there were no boybands and no Riverdance and no nothing, just a few peroxided posers ordering Harvey Wallbangers.

'The rubber plant?' he says.

'Like . . . in the nightclub? The Pink?' Freddie says. 'You remember The Pink Elephant?'

'I remember they had a rubber plant in here,' Bricks says. 'And a few ceiling fans? Casablanca vibe?'

'This was in The Pink . . . you know, you and Dorothy?' Freddie says.

'Maybe it's just the shakes,' Bricks says. 'But I don't remember.'

'The time you were barred?'

'I was barred from every place.'

'You really don't recall being barred from The Pink for dancing with a rubber plant?' Freddie says.

Bricks laughs. He scans The Bailey again, seeing himself here on afternoons twenty years ago, drinking all day with guys who looked like rock stars and talked like rock stars but who couldn't really do anything apart from selling each other speed on the way to The Pink for more. He can remember all that but nothing about dancing with a rubber plant.

'Fucking hell,' Bricks says.

'Maybe it's the fizzy water,' Freddie says.

'I've done stuff in blackout. I've played sessions in blackout. I pissed in the lobby of The Shelbourne in blackout. I've gone to foreign countries in blackout . . .' Bricks says, scouring his memory.

'You're in shock,' Freddie says. 'We're all in shock. So much happening.' He's half-dreading where the complete list of Bricks's blackouts might lead.

'I'm turning yellow,' Bricks says.

Nadine is getting through a lot of pints, hardly part of the company at all. Then she moves her stool between them.

'Why cremated?' she says.

'Why?' says Freddie.

'Yes, why? I mean, did she ever say?'

'I just assumed . . .' Freddie says.

'Yeah?' Nadine says.

'I'm sure she would have wanted it that way. I'm positive. What do you think Bricks?' Freddie says.

'Bricks is turning yellow,' Nadine says. 'Whaddaya think?'

Freddie's heart sinks. She is trying to pick a fight with him. Her eyes are all over the place. It's the beer, it's all the fucking beer. He has no idea how to deal with this. He has never seen her drunk before.

'I think what I think,' Freddie says. 'She was just that type of person.'

'You can tell?' Nadine says.

'You can get a kind of a feel for these things,' Freddie says.

'Can you?' Nadine says.

113

'Ah, come on . . .' Freddie says.

'She told me she wanted to be fucking buried,' Nadine says.

'Come on . . .' Freddie says.

'She wrote to me once and she said she wanted to be fucking buried,' Nadine says.

'She told you that?' Freddie says.

'In the fucking ground,' Nadine says.

'The ground?' Freddie says.

'Some fucking shit about the earth,' Nadine says.

'But you sent all the letters back,' Freddie says. 'And the money.'

'I used to read the fuckers and then send them back,' she says.

'You didn't tell me this,' Freddie says.

'Thought you'd know,' Nadine says.

'Didn't think she had strong views on it,' Freddie says.

'Fuck it,' Nadine says. 'She had strong views on everything. She was a fucking loony, right?'

'At times . . .' Freddie says.

'You said she was a free spirit,' Nadine says. 'That means fucking loony, right?'

'Please, Nadine . . .' Freddie says.

'If she was fucking mad,' Nadine says, 'then you should say she was fucking mad.'

'Please . . .' Freddie says. 'What do you say, Bricks?'

Bricks can hardly hear what they're saying. He is in the horrors, and he has never heard two people fighting so quietly.

'What do you want, Bricks?' Nadine says. 'Buried or cremated?'

114

'I just want to die,' Bricks says.

'OK, I hold my hands up,' Freddie says. 'I have fucked it up.'

Nadine finishes her pint of lager.

'And me,' she says. 'You have fucked me up.'

She is out the door of The Bailey before Freddie can stop her.

Bricks takes off after her. He can't help himself. This is what hope does to you, he thinks, has you running.

Freddie gets to the door to see her disappearing up Dawson Street in her long leather coat, Bricks in pursuit. The worst of the rain is over now but it's still a dirty night. So many nights he went after Dorothy when she caused a ruckus. Many times in this bar. He lets them go.

Bricks catches up with Nadine around the corner. She seems happier now, maybe just drunk.

'I'm going to tell him about you and me,' he says. 'He'll be cool about it.'

Nadine starts laughing at Bricks in this solemn mode.

'And what if he's not?' she says, lighting a cigarette.

'Then I guess we're out of there,' he says.

'We?' she says.

'I'm . . . eh . . . I'm really going to give it a shot . . . giving up the sauce,' he says.

Nadine looks past him towards the Mansion House.

'Why?' she says.

'Because it's time,' he says.

'You're mad, Bricks,' she says.

'I know you're not worth it,' he says, stroking her face.

Nadine pushes him away, gently bringing him down, softly extinguishing his hope.

'Don't tell him anything,' she says. 'I mean . . . there's not much to tell, is there?'

'He'll take it from me,' he says.

'Listen Bricks, the way he saw it, you'd crash, you'd hang out, maybe you'd give me a few sax lessons. He never saw us in the same bed,' she says.

'So we just mooch around like this until . . .'

'Until what? Maybe it was nothing,' she says.

He strokes her face again. 'It was nothing?' he says.

As she walks away towards the Green she calls back to Bricks.

'Anyway it's doing his head in,' she says with a note of triumph. 'Him and that LJ fuck.'

'Bitch,' Bricks says quietly.

Back in The Bailey, Bricks is looking jaundiced with his fizzy water. The melancholy in his eyes makes him resemble young Einstein all the more. Freddie sits on the stool beside him. They both look defeated.

'I let her go,' Freddie says.

'She's over it already,' Bricks says. 'That's what she said.'

'She never went for me like that before,' Freddie says.

'It's hard. It's her mother.'

'I'll tell you something, Bricks, between the two of us, about how I felt when they told me Dorothy was dead.'

'Relieved?' Bricks says.

'Fucking right,' Freddie says.

'Human nature,' Bricks says.

'She knows that. Nadine knows that. She was right,' Freddie says.

Bricks looks at him wearily.

'Make it up to her,' Bricks says. 'Scatter the ashes somewhere nice.'

'Like a girl saying yes,' says Freddie. 'That's what Eddie Condon said about the first time he heard Bix Beiderbecke playing the cornet. Like a girl saying yes.'

He lights a rolled-up cigarette. He pushes the pouch of Old Holborn across the kitchen table to Bricks.

'That's nice,' Bricks says.

Bricks sips his fizzy water. He feels like he has been hit on the back of the head with a plank. He is drinking fizzy water all day, but he is still parched.

He watches Freddie opening another bottle of The Bailey's carryout lager. He craves one, he is delirious for one. He'd like to collapse into a coma on the couch, but Freddie is still up for it, throwing jazz quotes at him, all agitated.

Nadine is still out there somewhere, but Freddie is stuck on jazz. If he stops talking about jazz he will have to talk about Nadine, and how she is out there somewhere. And he has no words for the fear that brings to him, so he keeps talking about jazz.

'Dizzy said of Bird, it was like putting a bomb in your mouth, and lighting it,' Freddie says.

'Right,' Bricks says.

'I saw this documentary about Miles,' Freddie says. 'And Miles says you fall in love with the first woman you can feel. Right?'

'Right.'

'He said that love songs are nice to listen to, but they aren't true.'

'Sure.'

'He was very fucked up for a few years, Miles. He was a bum and maybe a pimp. The needle you know?'

'Yeah.'

'He left nothing to his first wife. The great ones have this thing about them, this cruelty. They've all got it. Maybe you've got it.'

'Maybe.'

'You just have to live with it, this cruel streak they've all got. Like Bob Dylan taking the piss out of Donovan. Cruel, so cruel.'

'Huh.'

'And still, the thing that Miles had, that people liked, was this vulnerable sound. Am I right?'

'You think Nadine is all right?' Bricks says.

'She's . . . vulnerable.'

Bricks is drowsy, wiped out, with no drink to keep him going into the night.

'I've had it,' he says. He finishes his fizzy water and lets out a long sigh of fake satisfaction.

'Buried or cremated?' Freddie says.

'Whatever.'

'You'll get through tomorrow on the water?' Freddie says.

Bricks shrugs. 'Yeah,' he says.

'It's the thought of never drinking again, like never, that would be the hard part for me,' Freddie says.

Bricks stands up. He winces from the effort. 'Can I play the horn sober?' he says. 'Don't know.' He puts his glass back on the draining board.

'Leave that,' Freddie says. 'I'll do it tomorrow.'

'Relax,' Bricks says. 'Nadine . . . the kid is very together.'

'She's cool,' Freddie says. He pushes the pouch of Old Holborn across the table.

'One more,' says Bricks.

'One more,' says Freddie.

Slowly, Bricks sits back down. He takes a brown envelope from his inside pocket and slides it across the table with a nod.

Freddie opens it. It is some sort of legal document.

'It's the rights to everything I do,' Bricks says. 'Just sign it and it's yours.'

Freddie scans the page. 'All recordings . . .?' he says.

Bricks butts in. 'Worldwide,' he chuckles.

'All territories . . .' Freddie adds.

'It's not worth a shit really. But it's a token,' Bricks says.

Freddie is moved by the gesture. 'I'm so honoured,' he says.

'I don't do much around here to pay my way,' Bricks says. 'Maybe I'll be worth a few quid when I'm gone.'

Freddie reaches over to shake hands.

'I'll frame it,' he says.

He finds a biro and signs the contract. Contract seems too heavy a word, it's more of a souvenir.

'Would you do me the honour of having a last drink with me?' Bricks says.

Freddie hesitates. He opens a bottle of lager.

'On the night that's in it . . .' he says.

Freddie hands over the bottle, opened. Bricks drinks half of it in one go.

'Like a girl saying yes,' he says.

Freddie stubs out his cigarette. Nadine is still out there

somewhere. He pushes the ashtray to the edge of the table, inch by inch, until it falls to the floor.

'Steady,' Bricks says.

'In seventeen years never a bad word between us,' Freddie says.

'Never?'

'Nothing like tonight.'

'It's a one-off.'

'I was watching her today. She was in another world,' Freddie says.

'Nah.'

'She was in another world, without me in it.'

'She's seventeen.'

'Never a bad word.'

'It's natural.'

'It's me. She hates me. She's suddenly discovered I'm a fucking fool.'

They both hear it, Nadine's footsteps crunching on the gravel as she walks past the window. They hear her coming in and going straight to her room. Freddie closes his eyes, ecstatic with relief.

'Another world, man,' he says.

Chapter 11

'We can do both,' Freddie says. 'How's about that?'

The bedroom is smoky. Nadine puts out her morning cigarette. She grunts. She squints at Freddie, at his afro poking around the door.

'We can cremate her, and we can bury her,' he says.

She grunts again.

'It was actually Bricks's idea,' he says.

'Two funerals?' she says, like it is too much for her to comprehend.

'Bricks had a dream,' he says. 'In this dream, he heard Dorothy talking about it.'

'Oh?' she says.

'She said, you've hired the hall so burn me. Just go with it, maybe it's a sign.'

Nadine goes back under the covers.

'She wanted to be buried,' she says.

'I got the gravedigger on the phone and for an extra few lids he'll open the old family plot in Dean's Grange. So we can bring the ashes there, and . . . whatever . . .'

He is trying to sound chipper, making it seem like a day out.

'What time is it?' she says.

'It's nine. We need to be . . . you know . . . I'll run out for cornflakes and shit.'

Nadine's head appears above the duvet. To Freddie, she looks all right after the freak-out in The Bailey. He wants her out of bed now without her thinking he's hassling her. He wants no more scenes like last night. It hurts too much.

She grunts again, in a more affirmative tone.

'You know you can tell me anything,' he says. 'Like, fuck off Freddie,' he adds, getting out of there.

He looks in on Bricks again before he leaves for the cornflakes. Bricks is sitting at the table fingering his sax and making the odd scribble on the back of Dorothy's death papers.

'Ten minutes,' Freddie says with a big smile of approval.

Bricks waves him away and scribbles some more.

Freddie resists the urge to drive the few hundred yards down to Dún Laoghaire. He decides he must rise above it, this horrible suspicion that he can't leave Bricks with Nadine. He didn't sleep much last night with this terrible shit running around his head.

He was so relieved when Nadine came back he thought he would conk out for eight hours of perfect peace. But he couldn't stop the shit racing all over the place, taking him back to yesterday morning when he sat on the bed with a ninety-nine, knowing in his heart that nothing would be the same again.

And could it be just the drink that made Bricks so remorseful? Could he really have been feeling so guilty about going on the piss with her, if he hadn't done a lot more besides?

Bricks signed his life's work away last night. Freddie would love to think that it was what it seemed, a gesture, a mark of big respect. But in the depths of the night, it seemed for a long while that there was a lot more to it, that it was just the type of desperate move you'd make if . . .

Ah, there could be a lot less to it as well, it might have been no more than Bricks crazy for beer. A big price to pay maybe for a bottle of lager, but then Bricks is an alcoholic and that's the deal.

The trick is, not minding it.

It's a very cold, bright day as Freddie walks down to the People's Park and then left into the main street. He is wide awake with the cold and still he feels the lack of sleep, this bad shit running around his head, eating away at him.

In the mini-market he buys a box of cornflakes and four packets of Rothmans. He imagines they will smoke most of them today, saying goodbye to Dorothy, goodbye and safe home.

He tries to walk at a normal speed on the way home but his pace quickens anyway, driven on by this nervous energy.

If . . . if, say, they were having actual sex, like if there was wild poontang involved, Freddie feels there's a very great danger that he just won't be able to handle it. That, after a lifetime fighting the good fight against the forces of medieval darkness, after supporting the campaigns for contraception and abortion and after designing an award-winning poster for the local pro-divorce group, he is about to turn into a family-values freak at the notion of his

123

daughter getting it on with Bricks Melvin under his own roof.

Under his own roof. Christ, he even heard himself saying that last night round about four-thirty. Under his own roof.

He is sounding more like a mad mullah than a free rockin' spirit of the Borough of Dún Laoghaire, where they always vote more liberal than the rest of Ireland, because they just know better, man.

But it goes deeper than that, he tells himself, it's not some morality shit, it's these lowdown blues that he never saw coming, blues for Nadine, that yesterday she was maybe three-quarters grown up and today she's maybe, like, seven-eighths grown up and maybe more, maybe much more, and fuck it, she's only seventeen and, like, what else is out there for her?

All right, when Freddie himself was seventeen he'd have sold his soul for anything even vaguely resembling the beast-with-two-backs, but it still seems such a sad old situation, to have all that sussed and sorted at seventeen. Like, it's the one advantage the unwanted people have, they're still out there living the dream, wanting it, chasing the beast when the pretty people have all had it.

He is nervous now going into his own house, under his own roof. With a major effort of will, he composes himself. With the rational part of his brain, he figures that Nadine is a teenager and, as a teenager, she is obliged to be doing his head in. She is only doing what she's supposed to do, he thinks. He leans against the railings outside, trying to let a few sensible thoughts trickle through his addled brain. He opens a packet of Rothmans. She is finding out that her father is not a thousand per cent perfect, he thinks. She is freaked out at the company he is keeping. She has lost her mother and it may be bringing her down in ways she does not understand. She is drinking a bit too much. She is drinking a bit too much with Bricks.

Bricks, who was brought into the house by Mr Freddie Dowd. So then who's to say what's too much and too little? The same Mr Freddie Dowd who once hitch-hiked to a club in Montreux, to see Bricks Melvin playing with Gerry Mulligan, and arrived just as they were stacking up the tables? The same stonewall genius who is burying his wife today on the northside and later on the southside?

Nadine is only doing what she's supposed to do, he decides, which is to find her own level, to make her own mistakes. And what he's supposed to do, is to love her without question.

He inhales deeply. He blows a lungful of cigarette smoke into the cold air.

'He knows,' Nadine says, and walks past Bricks to the fridge.

She is wearing just a long T-shirt. She takes a can of beer from the fridge. She thinks about opening it. Then she puts it back in the fridge again.

Bricks is still sitting at the table, concentrating on the instrument, putting a shape on the music in his head. He doesn't acknowledge her presence in any way. He plays a flurry of notes on the sax. He pauses. Finally, he looks at her.

'Knows what?' he says.

'About yesterday morning,' she says, filling two mugs of instant coffee.

'Knows what?' he says.

'Knows that we. . .' she says.

'We what?' he says.

'You know . . . in there,' she says, looking towards the bedroom.

Bricks shakes his head in bewilderment.

'Fuck,' she says.

'I'd remember something like that,' he says.

Then he smiles.

'Winding me up,' she says. She puts a mug of coffee down in front of him.

'Sorry,' he says.

'Watching me all day yesterday. Watching you. He knows,' she says.

'He knows about the booze.'

'He knows,' she says.

'He's just worried about you right? Running out of The Bailey . . . the booze . . . rapping with him at this table last night . . . we rapped about all this . . .'

'You wouldn't . . . by accident or something?' she says.

'I wouldn't tell my own mother,' he says.

She laughs. 'Mad,' she says.

'Fucking brandy,' he says.

'Wine, gin . . .' she says.

'Stick to the pints, that's what they say. Just stick to the pints and stay away from the shorts.'

She sips her coffee.

'Maybe I'll go off it too,' she says.

'Hangover?'

'It's like . . . still a bit . . . pissed.'

'Sort of woozy?'

'Sort of . . . buzzing.'

'You need a beer,' he says.

He takes two cans from the fridge. He opens one for her and one for himself.

'Back on it?' she says.

'Just the beer. Stick to the beer and stay away from the shorts.'

Freddie can be heard on the gravel outside.

Bricks lowers his voice. He points to his can of beer.

'He knows,' he says.

Bricks plays like a god at the cremation. For an audience of two. And some undertaker's son who brought the coffin.

Freddie reckons it's a shame that more folks can't hear this, or that it wasn't recorded, but then it mightn't have happened at all with the folks in on it. Maybe it's the intimacy that inspires Bricks, just the three of them. 'She Loved You Madly', he calls it.

A couple of scribbles on a sheet of paper at the kitchen table, a tin of beer for breakfast, and by noon, Bricks is producing world-class improvisatory art. It makes Freddie want to cry.

After the music, Dorothy's coffin goes into the flames. They spend about ten minutes in silence, Bricks standing with his head bowed, the odd little smile passing from Freddie to Nadine as they remember Dorothy, all that infectious madness that has them here today and down in Dean's Grange cemetery later on. Madness is infectious, you can actually catch it from other people like catching the flu, she said so herself.

But some magic in Bricks's playing brought the best

part of Dorothy alive for them, all that funny New York stuff.

They come out into the cold. Freddie is holding the black urn containing Dorothy's ashes, just a few token ashes for the occasion, because the full Dorothy would still be too hot to handle. He puts the urn into the front passenger seat. He opens the back door for Bricks and Nadine.

'I feel like a taxi man,' Freddie says.

Bricks and Nadine get into the back of the Merc, a dozen cans of Tennents on the seat between them.

Freddie revs up the car, turning the heater up full blast. They are on their way to the southside, to Dean's Grange cemetery.

'May I?' Bricks says, rolling a cigarette.

Freddie throws back a packet of Rothmans.

'Have one of these,' he says. 'That was sensational.'

'Mad,' Nadine says.

'I kinda expected . . . the rich guy . . . Richard Madigan? I half-expected him to show up,' Bricks says.

'Yeah?' Freddie says, looking at Bricks in the mirror.

'I have a funny feeling he's still out there somewhere,' Bricks says.

'You don't believe he killed himself?' Freddie says.

'Just . . . just a hunch,' Bricks says.

'I kinda expected . . . what's her name . . . LJ?' Nadine says.

'Ha-ha-ha,' Freddie says.

'Beer?' she says.

'Maybe,' Bricks says, taking a can.

'Maybe I'll call LJ later, get her to come to the house for a few drinks?' Freddie says, returning the taunt.

Nadine opens a beer. She drinks it with a childish sucking noise.

'Vampire fuck,' she says.

'Maybe another time,' Freddie whispers.

Bricks takes a long slug of beer.

'For the graveyard,' Bricks says.

'Same again?' Freddie says.

'In a minute,' Bricks says. He takes another long slug.

'I mean, will you play that number again?' Freddie says.

'Depends. . . depends on how cold it is,' Bricks says.

Freddie is looking at Bricks in the mirror. Their eyes meet.

'It struck me, you were maybe the last person to see her alive,' Freddie says.

'Right,' Bricks says.

'I know it's a downer and all, but do you reckon her . . . her spirit, by any chance, got into the music . . . like she was speaking through you?'

'You reckon?' Bricks says.

Nadine throws her eyes to heaven. 'Fucking hell,' she says.

'Cosmic shit, I know,' Freddie says.

He puts the boot down whenever he gets the chance in the traffic. Crossing the river, he has this vision of being stopped for speeding and having to explain the urn in the front seat to some cop. He slows down just in case. The Merc is eating up the ground anyway, heading south along the coast road and out through the suburbs.

'Where is this fucking graveyard?' Nadine says.

'We're nearly there,' Freddie says.

He looks back at Bricks again. Bricks seems agitated.

'I wish I coulda done something,' Bricks says.

'If you ever want to talk about it. . .' Freddie says.

Bricks clicks his fingers, like he has suddenly remembered something.

'You know what we were rapping about, me and Dorothy? The Gestapo,' he says, clicking his fingers again. 'The counsellors and the AA and all that crowd? The Gestapo? That's what we were rapping about.'

'The psychobabble?' Freddie says.

'All that shit,' Bricks says. 'Invading your privacy?'

'Sure,' Freddie says.

'Except . . . well, she was for it and I was against it,' Bricks says.

Freddie laughs. 'No shit!' he says.

Bricks is scouring his memory. It seems to be causing him physical pain.

'She said . . . she told me, at the top of the stairs, she told me I could have a life beyond my wildest dreams,' he says.

'You know something? That might be the last thing she said. Her last words,' Freddie says.

'Hold on. The nurse saw her after me,' Bricks says.

'Actually, the nurse saw her after she . . .' Freddie says.

'Oh, right,' Bricks says. 'Listen, don't go by me, OK?'

'I don't get it,' Freddie says. 'I don't get it the way people do the hari-kiri thing. I knew this guy, top advertising guy, went out drinking with a bunch of friends, great night in the pub, off to a nightclub, riffing and rabbiting, then he goes home and hangs himself in the shower. No one has a fucking clue why he did it. Something about a woman? I don't buy it. No one knows shit about this stuff.'

Bricks is wilting.

'I wish I could remember more,' he says softly.

'It'll come to you,' Freddie says.

'If I can't remember dancing with a rubber plant in The Pink . . . ,' he says.

Nadine interrupts with an angry grunt.

'Stop it. Stop this fucking shit,' she says in a furious whisper.

'Sorry,' Freddie says. 'Dark shit.'

'Where's this fucking bastard graveyard anyway?' she says.

'We're nearly there,' Freddie says.

Freddie swings the Merc through the gates of Dean's Grange cemetery. He spots the gravedigger waiting beside a mound of earth. He parks as near as he can get to the grave.

He gets out of the car with the urn.

'I have to talk to this guy,' he says.

Bricks and Nadine stay in the car, watching Freddie paying the gravedigger a lot of cash. Then the gravedigger places the urn at the bottom of the headstone marked *Dowd*.

It is cold. It is too cold to be standing around. It is too cold for jazz.

Freddie gives them a signal and they get out of the car.

Bricks takes his case with him. He opens it at the graveside.

He straps on his saxophone. He blows on his hands.

Freddie introduces the gravedigger, a former muso with very long, very clean hair and a strong smell of aftershave.

'This is Trevor. I knew him in a previous life,' he says.

Trevor finds no humour in this. He is watching Bricks

nervously. Bricks is looking at him like he is waiting for the go-ahead from the master of ceremonies.

Trevor nods at him. 'Howya, Bricks,' he says, with a slight shake in his voice, like there is some history between them.

'Howdy,' Bricks says.

'We met before,' Trevor says.

Bricks hasn't the faintest idea who he is. His mind starts wandering to that night when all the people he met before and can't remember will gather in the one place and make their peace with him and tell him what he's been up to for the last twenty years.

'You must come to this thing . . .' Bricks says.

Freddie intervenes. 'Bricks is going to play something,' he says.

Bricks blows on his hands again. He is about to play and then he hesitates, like he hears some signal on the wind.

'For an American artist,' he says.

And he plays 'The Star-Spangled Banner'.

No improvization, no Jimi Hendrix version, just the plain American anthem as it is heard when they give out the medals at the Olympic Games.

Nadine shoots a look to Freddie, a look that says, here is a man taking the piss. But as 'The Star-Spangled Banner' soars over Dean's Grange, each note sent out with absolute conviction from the land of the living to the land of the dead, they see that something is happening to Bricks. They see that his eyes are full of tears.

'It was trite,' Bricks says. 'That's what it was.'

He is lying on the floor of the flat, smoking cigarettes and drinking beer and trying to rationalize what came over him in the cemetery.

'It worked,' Freddie says. 'It worked for me.'

He turns for assistance to Nadine beside him on the couch. She grunts in a supportive tone.

Bricks seems severely rattled by the experience, like he was gripped by some malign force beyond his control. He has literally to lie down to take it all in. No matter how much he is told that it worked, that it was very simple and moving, he feels the need to explain himself.

'I wasn't playing it for her. I was playing it for me,' he says.

Freddie and Nadine make empathetic noises, engrossed by Bricks talking about himself.

'You find that at funerals,' Freddie says. 'People are sad for things in their own lives . . .'

Bricks interrupts.

'I played that tune in the orphanage,' he says. 'OK, I call it an orphanage, but it was Devil's Island, you know? The gulag. And this brother gave us a few tin whistles, the old black ones, to see if anyone could knock a tune out of them. So, I had an ear for music, as it happened, and I picked out "The Star-Spangled Banner" first thing. Knew it from some old movie. And I played it and the brother came round and beat the living shit out of me.'

Bricks does the voice of the brother, a culchie accent riddled with sarcasm. 'You want to go to America do you, Mr Melvin? Is that what you want to do? Is it America? Is it?'

Freddie laughs. Bricks keeps going, in his own voice again.

'I hate this fucking country,' he says. 'All I ever wanted was to go to America. Hear a bit of decent music. You know, the fucking morons up in Leitrim once had a march against jazz? They went out on to the streets and they marched against jazz? The stupid fucking cunts.

Freddie wants to crack up at this but he stops himself. Nadine is just quiet, downing her beer. Bricks keeps going.

'I got so good at the music they had to stop abusing me. They needed me. There's some old film of me playing some poxy Irish music to show the people what happy little boys we were. The stupid fucking cunts.'

'I come out of there at the age of seventeen dying to get to America and meet Louis Armstrong, and the first thing I do is get a criminal conviction, so then America is off.'

'We can work on that,' Freddie says.

'I went to Paris, had a wonderful time. They like a bit of decent music over there. And then all these dudes would come over from New York and we'd play and they'd want to take me back with them but . . . then other shit happened to me . . . life . . .'

Freddie breaks in. 'Your day is coming, Bricks. I'm getting loads of feedback.'

Bricks waves his words away. 'You're a sincere man, Freddie. But you're pissing into the wind.'

'Nadine likes your stuff. Young people . . .'

'You're a sincere man,' Bricks says. 'But there's only one of you and there's millions of them, and they don't like me.'

Freddie holds the line. 'Your day is coming,' he says.

Chapter 12

They come up here every Sunday. They'll be up here this afternoon. At first, Paddy Lamb thought it was just traffic congestion, all those Sunday drivers choking up the narrow little roads from the bottom to the top. And then he sussed it. He had some people from Sony over for drinks and they were up on the battlements of his little castle, when one of them remarked that the folks were gawking in at them.

You can't see much through the trees. Like every property on Kilbrittan Hill, it is heavily walled and gated and guarded by mature trees. But there is this opening for a couple of seconds that gives the folks their buzz.

Paddy and his Sony party got raucous watching the cars crawling by all afternoon. They started waving and hollering at the folks, who started waving and honking back, guessing that this must be some celebrity booze-up, another golden happening in the homes of the stars. Maybe the folks were guessing that they wouldn't be able to do this much longer, that soon the Hill would be the private domain of Ireland's new elite, and it would get all regimented like Hollywood, with bus tours. Till then,

Paddy would savour the pageant. He has people up for drinks on the last Sunday of the month, and they watch the parade go by.

In a few minutes, today's guests will be here. Richie Earls will be up if he's in the country, and maybe after a few libations, he'll sing a bit of blues. If not, Johnny Oregon, his house sitter, will be along, for the vibe. These days the rockers get along fine with the pop acts, probably because they keep bumping into one another at airports, dashing from territory to territory in their private planes.

So there'll be half-a-dozen guys from Paddy's various boybands knocking back the champers with Richie Earls or Johnny Oregon or Bones Morrissey, the great traditional fiddler.

The boys will come armed with a cracking bunch of models which should settle any musical differences. There'll be a crowd of absolute lunatics along from the Spielberg shoot in Wicklow, and the great Esther Pilkington, who is shameless about using these occasions to drum up big-name support for all her good causes, to make a difference.

They don't know it yet, but most of those models will leave here today tied in by Esther to some massive fashion show against slavery.

All these mad, wonderful, talented people will get down and dirty with the bean-counters and the legal eagles who know what everyone up here is worth down to the last Swiss franc, and who keep Paddy Lamb abreast because, when it comes to pushing the next Fellaz their way, he can make a difference.

And LJ Carew will be there, and Freddie Dowd, who has

gone one better than Paddy Lamb by staying the night in LJ's love palace and who is, therefore, shall we say, on probation.

Paddy stands on the battlements looking at his staff scurrying around the roof making the preparations, a terrific bunch of kids with a great attitude. Watching them laying out the food and the drink and beavering away at every detail in their black T-shirts and their excellent haircuts, he feels proud to be Irish.

It's all about detail now. Like having a canopy prepared on this fine spring day just in case it rains on Bricks Melvin playing the saxophone. Like bunging all the leftover bottles of Bollinger down to the eco-warriors in the Glen o' the Downs.

Right now he's getting flak from the neighbours for partying in this public fashion, and he respects the neighbours for that, for their obsession with security. But maybe the neighbours, even the heaviest hitters among them, are still learning, still a tad naive about protecting their ass.

Paddy Lamb's people have been out there for a few generations, and if Paddy could impart just one nugget of wisdom to the neighbours, it would be this: if they are up for it, the natives will get you, and there's nothing you can do about it, pal. The neighbours will discover this in time, like any emerging aristocracy. They will learn that it's not about having money, it's about having fun.

The folks out there, they want to have fun. They want to dream. They want money, but they don't want to do what you have to do. The ugly stuff. They wouldn't really like it up here, and deep down they know it. They wouldn't have

137

the stomach or the stamina for it, for the lifestyle, for hanging on to what you've got and keeping up all these fucking standards. There are duties associated with living in a little castle on Kilbrittan Hill, an understanding of which doesn't come to you overnight, like Freddie Dowd's money. Because it's not about money, it's about having fun.

Watching the folks watching you every Sunday is fun. It's nice to know where everyone is, in the old pecking order. And they're a sophisticated, demanding crowd. They're Irish, for God's sake.

So you can't have your Jack Nicholsons every Sunday. You don't want overdoing it with just a load of famous faces. That would be crass. The folks like to glimpse the dudes behind the scenes, the ten per centers, the guys who fire their imagination with visions of sweet deals and heavy manners. So you mix and match them, right, the famous and the mysterious, and on both sides of the wall the arousal can be intense.

The day after they buried Dorothy, it seemed clear to Freddie that Nadine was getting into some dark shit. She withdrew into herself and took to watching the three *Godfather* movies one after the other, day after day, night after night.

It was Bricks who started it, bringing home the videos and a few cans of beer to begin his new regime of beer and beer only, of couch and takeaway pizza and remote control.

Nadine pulled up the beanbag and opened another can and soon the two of them were locked into this beery-eyed routine, the curtains drawn all day, smoking like beagles.

She was watching *The Godfather* and Freddie was

watching her, as discreetly as he could manage it, for what amounted to twenty-four-hour surveillance.

He has finally decided that he was completely off the wall with his suspicions of sex under his own roof. If anything, she is grunting even less at Bricks than at him. So he has decided this is not a sex problem. He is maybe ninety-nine per cent sure, if the truth be told, but he just can't bring himself to think of that other one per cent, of a truth so pure and so final.

He has decided that this is basically a drink problem. Which is some consolation, as he has vast experience in the field.

He keeps repeating to himself that this is pretty typical teenage behaviour, these wordless days stretching to more than two weeks of grunting and groaning and wincing and rolling of the eyes to heaven. But he knows that this teenager is the daughter of Dorothy McIlroy, who started hearing the strange music at this point in her life, and who never stopped.

Today she watches the movie on her own. Bricks is engaged to play at Paddy Lamb's bash, a taster for the gig proper in The Crowbar tomorrow night. A chance to put the good word around, and a grand for Bricks. A chance to remind Paddy that the first of March is getting closer.

Maybe they'll stop laughing at him then. Down at The Crowbar they couldn't believe he was hiring the venue for six weeks. They asked him for two weeks up front and a deposit in case Bricks caused any damage. When he produced his wad of crisp notes fresh from the machine, it was like they couldn't wait to see this shit. Like, could he start tonight?

As Freddie left the bar, he heard them laughing.

Freddie peeps through the curtains at the three flash cars belonging to the Bank of Ireland that will be his, bought with his own money on the first of March. This madness is just days, minutes away from becoming real. Nadine seems to have gone off the cars too, given up the struggle along with talking and walking.

There they stand, the fuckers, representing maybe half-a-million in borrowed money, to get it out of his system. Bought because of something that Dwight Yorke said, but Dwight never said what you should drive when you're on your way to Kilbrittan Hill and a near-certain meeting with a TV personality who treated you kindly, and who will want to know why the fuck you never called her as promised. Dwight said nothing about that. Dwight never spent the night in the love palace of LJ Carew.

Freddie goes for the flaming Ferrari. They are going to a party, after all, and technically that's fun. And probably a hell of a lot more fun than watching your daughter curled up in the foetal position watching *The Godfather*, and watching you in case you call that terrible woman.

Though it was never spoken in actual words, Nadine would not be going to this bash. She snorts a goodbye, which to Freddie seems full of scorn for his weakness, his inability to just stay away from these fucking people like he always said he would.

He tries on an old blue beret. It looks kind of shit, but he keeps it on anyway to remind himself that with the fuck-off money on the way, he is beyond ridicule. Except under his own roof. After a fortnight of stalemate, it seems that he is the one who has cracked, while Nadine digs in, giving nothing away.

You can't be silly about it, they say. You have to let them go. But it doesn't happen with some joyous parting of the ways, or a touching ceremony climaxing with the release of doves.

'It happens like this,' Freddie says.

'What?' Bricks says.

Freddie starts the Ferrari. For a few moments the two men sit contemplating its phenomenal elegance and power.

'You get sucked in,' Freddie says.

'Yeah,' Bricks says.

'The cars, the parties, the bullshit,' Freddie says. 'Before you know it you're one of them.'

Bricks straightens his tie. His good black suit is crumpled but he still fills it with a shambolic grace.

'The trick is . . .' he says.

'We could walk,' Freddie says. 'It's only up the road.'

'Miles . . . Miles had a Ferrari,' Bricks says.

Freddie laughs. 'That's OK then,' he says.

'OK then,' Bricks says.

'I'm sorry,' Freddie says. 'Of course we'll drive.'

'Right,' Bricks says.

Freddie reverses out the gate and points it towards Kilbrittan Hill. He joins the traffic down by the People's Park, the flash car just one of many inching along in the Sunday jam.

'Forgive me,' Freddie says. 'You've got to play for these people. I forgot you don't take public transport. Man needs his space, his privacy, right?'

'Right,' Bricks says.

141

'Just tell me if I'm giving you a pain in the ass, OK?' Freddie says. 'I'm a fucking nervous wreck.'

'You're too kind,' Bricks says.

'Nadine too,' Freddie says. 'Goofing off like that.'

'Seventeen,' Bricks says.

'She likes you,' Freddie says. 'It's hard to tell, but she likes you.'

'I know,' Bricks says.

'Really,' Freddie says. 'I can tell.'

'Seventeen.'

'Is everything all right, Bricks? Anything you want to say to me? I mean, are we crowding you? How are you doing on the beer?'

They are bumper to bumper at the bottom of Kilbrittan Hill. The queue is forming for a glimpse of Paddy and his people.

'Just stay in the moment,' Bricks says.

The cars crawl up the hill. A ten-minute journey from Dún Laoghaire is taking an hour.

'If you don't fancy this gig I can just give you the grand,' Freddie says. 'Just ask. I always say that if the artist asks you for money you just give it to him. Because he wouldn't ask for it unless he needed it.'

Bricks looks away. 'We're nearly there,' he says.

At the gates of Paddy's place, they are stopped by a smiling pony-tailed security man wearing a black T-shirt.

'Freddie Dowd and Bricks Melvin,' Freddie says.

'Sir,' the security man says.

The gates open and they park at the front of Paddy's castle alongside a few other motors straight from the showroom.

'You need to know something about Nadine,' Bricks says.

Freddie reacts like a loud noise has gone off beside him. 'Oh,' he says.

Bricks drums his fingers on the saxophone case.

'That beret,' he says. 'She hates that fucking thing.'

Freddie laughs. He takes off the beret and leaves it in the car.

Paddy Lamb comes trotting towards them with an outstretched hand.

'Special friends,' he says. 'How the hell have you been?'

'Been better,' Freddie says.

'There's a lady up here called LJ Carew who says you never phone, you never write,' Paddy says.

'Know that one,' Freddie says.

Paddy escorts them into the castle and leads them scurrying up several flights of stairs to the roof.

Most of the guests seem to be here already, about forty of them in little groups, drinking glasses of wine and beer from the bottle and nibbling on finger food while the cortège passes by the front gate.

Paddy takes the two new guests to the battlements on the other side, to show them Dublin Bay. He seems elated, like he has put this spectacular view together with his own hands, and this is the unveiling ceremony.

He directs Bricks to a small bandstand in the far corner, where Ray Blacoe is setting up an electric piano.

'In your own time, sir,' Paddy says.

Bricks salutes Ray Blacoe. 'My main man,' he says.

Paddy steers Freddie towards another entrance to the roof, down a flight of steps into a small room with a few leather armchairs and a huge TV screen. The walls are covered with gold and silver and platinum discs for Fellaz, The Cisco Kidz, Johnny Shine.

Freddie is nervous. He has seen several familiar figures who have disturbed his spirit, faces he knows from the gossip columns, notorious people he can't quite place.

'Football today,' Paddy says. 'United and Villa if you fancy it.'

'Do you still go over?' Freddie says.

'We'll go again, my friend,' Paddy says. 'Maybe we'll buy the fucking club.'

Freddie produces a freshly printed set of business cards announcing the start of a weekly residency by Bricks Melvin and friends at The Crowbar. Paddy sits at the low table and produces a little bag of The Lad.

'I wouldn't go doling the cards out to this lot,' he says.

'Maybe I'll just leave them on the table here,' Freddie says.

'The way I see it,' Paddy says, 'the future for an artist like Bricks Melvin is at events like this. Private parties.'

He straightens the white powder into lines with one of the business cards. He takes a huge blast of the powder through a twenty-pound note. He hands the note to Freddie. In this alien place, Freddie feels the need of it. He takes one snort and then another. It's so long since he had any, he can't recall what's supposed to happen next.

Paddy lays two more lines, deep and crisp and even.

'You've got the beak for it my friend,' he says.

Freddie goes for the three-in-a-row.

A gust of raw energy blows through the door and down the steps.

'Hiding,' says LJ Carew.

Paddy gets up and wraps himself around her.

'Guy stuff,' he says.

LJ extricates herself from Paddy's embrace.

She kisses Freddie on the cheek. She touches him all over, like she is frisking him for more of the drugs. This to him is the original LJ Carew, everything cranked up to ten. The thing is, he is starting to like this one too.

'The thing is . . .' he whispers.

'Forget it,' she says. 'Are you better?'

'I feel fine,' he says.

'I'm trying to tell this fellow that jazz is over,' Paddy says.

Bricks and Ray Blacoe can be heard from the roof, softly swinging.

'That's nice,' LJ says.

She sits on Freddie's knee.

'It's not nice, it's wonderful,' Paddy says, trying to find the football with the remote control. 'I love what these guys do. I'm just trying to tell this lunatic that the folks won't pay to see it any more.'

Freddie moves LJ off his knee so she is sitting between his legs. He puts his arm around her middle, and squeezes. He kisses her neck and nibbles her ear. He feels a moment of pure joy, as if it can all come right for him, the music, the money, the women, everything.

'So guys like us, we put out this boyband stuff, and keep the good shit all to ourselves?' Freddie says.

Paddy is still smiling, but he sounds a little colder. He picks at his chest hair, as if to demonstrate that there's nothing artificial about it.

'Jazz is over,' he says. 'The folks won't go there.'

LJ slips out of Freddie's hands.

'The football starts, I'm outta here,' she says.

'Later?' Paddy says.

Paddy and Freddie sit looking at one another for a few moments, disorientated, like LJ has taken all the oxygen with her.

'There's an etiquette . . .' Paddy says quietly. He brushes a few grains back into the bag.

'You mean, the coke?' Freddie says.

Paddy shouts. 'Not the coke, not the coke, for fuck's sake.'

Freddie wants to laugh but he stops himself. 'An etiquette?' he says.

'An etiquette, that when you're partying with Paddy Lamb, you don't make a play for Paddy Lamb's woman,' Paddy says.

'A play?' Freddie says.

'It disappoints me, what you did there my friend,' Paddy says.

'I don't . . .'

'Not officer material,' Paddy says.

Freddie sees a large tin of cigarettes on top of the screen. He takes one. Paddy throws him a lighter.

'If she's your woman . . .' Freddie says.

'We're all a bunch of fucking gypsies, all right?' Paddy says.

'All right,' Freddie says. His temples are pounding. He suspects that his heart is about to explode.

'But that woman . . .' Paddy says. 'She's mine.'

The football keeps drawing Freddie's attention. United are all over Villa. Paddy zaps it off. He looks wounded.

'If she's your woman . . .' Freddie says.

Paddy gets up and embraces him.

'You're a sophisticated man,' Paddy says. 'Paddy Lamb is not very sophisticated.'

He takes a cigarette from the tin. He looks for a light from Freddie, holding his hand steady.

'If I fucked up . . .' Freddie says.

'Today, I have given her a diamond,' Paddy says.

It sounds a bit creepy to Freddie, a bit Edgar Allan Poe.

'And . . .?' Freddie says.

Paddy guides him up the steps. 'One of these days . . .' he says.

All afternoon, Freddie keeps feeling these rushes of joy, dashing from the roof to the football and another hit of Paddy's coke. He tells about twenty people the story of how he copped that title from the Duke. Twenty people he wouldn't normally be talking to, on general principles.

He finds himself telling the story to Bones Morrissey for a second time as the floodlights came on in the early evening.

'Relax,' says Bones. 'It's the way of all successful men . . . how I did it.'

And he is relaxed about it. He feels like going easy on himself for a change, and on all these creatures who are only trying to make a living. He can't even fault Paddy for warning him off LJ. In fact, with all the drugs inside him, he reckons Paddy took that scene pretty well.

'I am not very sophisticated,' Paddy said. And this afternoon he could listen to Paddy's shit and laugh with him, not at him.

He is even thinking that a lot of these people, a lot of them are actually down to earth, even though they say so themselves.

He took a lot of phone numbers, including those of three models.

He heard the two members of Fellaz who can sing crooning *a capella* as the sun went down. He told them about a few decent records from which they might learn something. He put all their names on the list for Bricks at The Crowbar, because they say they are mad for it.

The road up the hill is empty now.

LJ is long gone, to think about her diamond.

He has a terrible urge to be with her now, to explain things to her, to apologize for taking liberties, whatever, so that everyone knows where everyone stands.

A vision of Nadine comes to him, curled up in the foetal position, smoking and sulking. He will call in to her on the way to LJ and tell her exactly the way it is, that LJ is Paddy's woman, and she's a human being who just needs to read a few good books.

Catch-22 is the one. He is saying his goodbyes to everyone when it becomes blindingly obvious to him that *Catch-22* is the perfect book to bring to LJ tonight. He'll pick up a copy at the flat, but he could nearly recite it by heart. Three times, cover to cover, he read it to Nadine at bedtime.

Bricks is finished for the day. He stands in the darkness looking out over the bay. He is back on the brandy.

Chapter 13

'I'm losing it,' Bricks says.

They are back from the Hill. Freddie is reversing the Ferrari on to the gravel. He keeps the engine running, as if Nadine inside might hear him whispering in the car. Bricks's melancholy seems immense.

'Take it easy,' Freddie says.

'This thing that I have . . .' Bricks says, cradling his saxophone case. 'I'm losing it.'

'You sounded good today,' Freddie says.

'They hated it,' Bricks says.

'They were mad for it,' Freddie says. 'They're all coming to see you tomorrow night.'

Bricks sniggers.

Freddie takes a hold of Bricks's arm.

'Listen, is there any shit you want to tell me? Are we crowding you? Maybe you're picking up the wrong vibes from Nadine?' Freddie says.

Bricks shakes his head.

'Fucking brandy,' Bricks says. 'That's all I need.'

Freddie turns off the engine.

'You know what I think?' he says. 'I think you should try this shit I'm on.'

'Doesn't work,' Bricks says.

'I guess I've got a grudge against the booze. Even to see Nadine drinking beer . . . and this movie thing?' Freddie says.

'This what?' Bricks says.

'Watching movies all day. Drinking with the big boys?' Bricks rolls a cigarette.

'I've . . . ehh . . . I've got a son somewhere,' Bricks says.

Freddie lets out a loud laugh.

'You have a son?' Freddie says.

'I know what it's like for you,' Bricks says. 'He's about seventeen.'

Freddie laughs again. 'No way, baby,' he says.

Bricks looks bewildered. 'Aaron . . . he's called Aaron,' he says.

'So you're trying to get him hitched to my lovely daughter?' Freddie says.

'Fuck,' Bricks says.

'The two of you, plotting and scheming over a few cool beers?' Freddie says.

'I'm losing it,' Bricks says.

'He doesn't by any chance ride a motorbike and like Motorhead?' Freddie says.

'To be honest . . .' Bricks says.

Freddie squeezes Bricks's arm. 'Joke,' he says.

They get out and walk down the narrow steps to the basement door. It is pitch dark inside. Freddie turns the key and walks quickly through the flat, switching on all the lights.

'No note,' Freddie says.

He goes into Nadine's room and comes back with *Catch-22*. He grabs a handful of classic jazz CDs from the huge pile in the corner. He takes a bottle of brandy from the kitchen cupboard.

'Hennessy OK?' he says.

Bricks slumps into his couch.

'I want you to know that you're one of the few guys in this town worth a shit,' he says.

Freddie is already on his way out.

'Tell her I'll be back but it might be late,' he says. 'Tell her it's all good shit . . . tell her I'm on a roll.'

Nadine walks the pier on Sundays when the darkness has driven away the crowds. Even out here, she feels that Freddie is watching her, perched like a fuzzy vulture, accusing her of things that he is too much of a wuss to say out loud.

She wouldn't mind seeing Dorothy again at the end of the pier, just to ask her if she was born mad or if two-faced Freddie drove her mad.

Nadine gets up on the bandstand for the last time. She's finished with the walking. It just seems like the right time in her life to stop marching up and down here like a fucking loony, talking to herself.

She roots deep in her pocket. She puts the Billy Joel CD into her Discman and turns it up high. She leans on the railing of the bandstand looking across at Howth, with Billy giving it loads.

She feels that somewhere out there Freddie can sense this. She can imagine his suffering. And it makes her feel better.

No shit, he can really pick up on stuff like this, the way these mafia guys know deep down that some member of the family is betraying them. He can hear what she's thinking from miles away. So he knows, he knows, he knows that she was in bed with Bricks, he just can't face it.

And Bricks . . . Bricks is putting it all behind him, and getting on with the drinking, and that's cool.

That's how she's feeling about it herself, stepping off the bandstand for the last time. It's funny the way things slip away, just because of the mood you're in for about ten minutes. A few beers go down, and you're stuck with something for the rest of your life. Like, when she ran out of The Bailey and Bricks ran after her, and she turned him down, she wanted to give it another shot almost as soon as she walked off to the Green that night. But the moment passed.

Fuck it, Bricks is not some sad old fucker pawing you in a nightclub, who will never take no for an answer. You turn Bricks down once, he walks away.

So it's like this. She was pissed, she wanted it, but it's cool now. She wanted it just to get it out of her system, yes that's it.

Freddie would understand that. And it killed the smell of Trayton, at last. And replaced with the faintest taste of Bricks. Her drinking buddy.

Freddie knew that LJ would be at home. He never doubted it, all the way into town along the coast road from Dún Laoghaire to the red-brick cottages of Ringsend. He knew that when she opened the door she would not be angry with him for feeling her up at Paddy's place. He felt safe. He knew that Paddy would be angry if he could see him now, calling again at the house of LJ, but it was Paddy's fine drugs that had brought him to this place, and they're still working, so he's not in touch with Paddy's anger right now.

He doffs his beret and bows.

'Peace,' he says.

He gives her *Catch-22* and then the jazz CDs.

She opens her mouth wide with surprise, like this had been foretold and had finally come true.

'Brilliant,' she says.

She leads him by the hand into the marble interior. Huge candles are flickering, there is a smell of incense. This is the first time he has seen Ancient Rome by night.

'You'll love these,' he says.

He sits on a stool at the marble table and riffles the well-thumbed pages. LJ sits opposite him, watching him.

'Tell me about it,' she says.

'*Catch-22* is just the greatest,' he says.

He shuts the book firmly, a last goodbye. He slides it across the table to her.

'It'll stun them at the dinner parties,' she says.

'They said to Joseph Heller, "You've never written another book as good." And he said, "Who has?"' Freddie says.

LJ laughs. 'Have you any more of them?' she says.

'I've got all his stuff,' he says.

'I mean, any more stories like that?'

'You just want to show off at dinner parties?' he says.

'I don't get asked to dinner parties,' she says. 'You know that.'

She goes to the tiny kitchen. She comes back with a half-

153

drunk bottle of red wine and two glasses. She fills the glasses.

'I know that,' he says.

'So we have something in common,' she says.

'You want to come tomorrow night?' he says. 'A real classy event?'

'Bricks?' she shudders. 'Mad bastard.'

Freddie holds up a Charlie Parker album. 'Later for the garbage,' he says.

She takes the CD to a little machine in the corner. Charlie Parker can be heard coming through the walls and the ceiling.

'I feel like I'm on a journey,' she says.

Freddie laughs. 'Most people I know,' he says, 'they'd say that all ironic.'

'Come on Freddie,' she says. 'Life is too fucking short for that.'

Freddie is hearing the music anew, imagining how amazing it must sound to LJ, remembering how it was for him.

'Wouldn't it be great if it was like this all the time?' he says.

She sips her wine. This is LJ again without the manic edge, not the one she sends out to work. Freddie gets the impression she is actually listening, LJ Carew listening to Charlie Parker.

'Welcome to the business,' she says. And she taps the side of her nose.

'The coke,' he says. 'I can take it or leave it.'

'Enjoy it,' she says. 'Everyone does it once . . . or twice.'

'You?' he says.

'It was Paddy got me into all that, pleasing him,' she says.

'And diamonds?' he says.

She fills his glass. 'Paddy is a total crook,' she says. 'You know that?'

She is looking at him calmly, the concerned air-hostess.

'You think?' he says.

'How . . . would you . . . like it . . . if he never paid you?' she says.

'How?' Freddie mumbles.

'He rips people off for fun,' she says. 'People he likes.'

'I kinda suspected . . .' he says.

'Do you think I should marry this guy?' she says.

'Not really,' he says.

'Think about it,' she says. 'If I refuse him, who will he blame?'

'Who?' he says.

'Well, you can bet your ass he won't blame it on himself,' she says.

Freddie takes a long drink of wine.

'It's crazy,' he says. 'But I'm almost flattered.'

LJ looks at him intensely. For an odd moment, he thinks she is going to slap him in the face, to bring him to his senses.

'Do you hear what I'm saying to you?' she says.

Freddie hears her, but there is still something abstract about it, like Charlie Parker is what's really happening, and this money shit is a vague proposition that he will look at in due course.

He holds his hand up to stop LJ pursuing the matter.

'I hear this,' he says. 'I hear Charlie Parker, the Bird himself, trying to find that thing that he lost. You know?'

155

LJ nods, like he has become unwell, and he is telling her his symptoms.

'The Bird?' she says.

'The bird of paradise,' he says. 'That day when everything happens for you. That one time when your heart and your head are totally together. And you keep going back there trying to find it but you can never get it back. It almost drives you crazy because you know what it feels like, it's just you can't feel it, not really, never exactly the way it was. And you can get drunk or drugged up and you're nearly there again but you're only dreaming, you're wasting your time and fucking with your head. And then you hear the Bird and you know that he's looking for it too. That's what he's doing, he's looking for it, he's going crazy looking for it, he's saying, I'll find it if it kills me, you hear? I know I left it here somewhere, and I'm going to keep on looking for it until I find it, you hear?'

Freddie slides off the stool and starts crawling on his hands and knees in a parody of Bird looking for what he lost. He looks under LJ's cushions and throws them around the room in mock frustration.

LJ gets it. She gets down on her hands and knees, looking for it.

'I know I left it here,' she says, while the Bird soars and swoops.

He tackles her from behind and pins her to the floor.

'Found it,' he says.

They make love on the cushions. It happens so sweetly and it feels so right, Freddie feels he has been possessed by the spirit of the Bird. Or if not the Bird himself, at least some extremely talented black man. Freddie gets a bit mystical with the intensity of it, the sheer strangeness to him of a woman's skin, sensing that it was planned, or it was meant to be from the day that LJ Carew first saw him pushing Nadine along the pier, and knew even then there was a connection, that he didn't fit and she didn't fit into anyone's idea of cool.

It keeps him from coming several times, savouring this feeling of destiny. It makes it sweeter, to be doing it and to be removed from it just a little bit, just enough to realize that he has found that thing that the Bird never found, when your heart and your head are totally together, and you know it.

LJ turns her back to him and he puts it in there one more time. He takes it all the way to the top, and the Bird plays on.

They lie there for minutes just looking at one another. LJ gets the notion to snip a few strands of his hair, just shaping it, she says, nothing that would change his aura.

As she snips, there is just one vaguely blue note for Freddie, as he wonders if she wanted it from behind because she couldn't handle the sight of his face contorted in ecstasy. But it's such a sweet little white ass anyway he lets it go this time. In fact he is kind of longing for it again as she steers him to the exit, all sanctified.

'Fantastic,' he says to LJ at the door. He gives her a quick salute as he gets into the Ferrari. He feels like Steve McQueen.

Like a black Steve McQueen.

He cruises into the petrol station on the coast road. He buys the early edition of *The Irish Times*. There's an ad for Bricks at The Crowbar, a little box stuck away in the bottom corner of a page full of big promotions, Robbie Williams, Bob Dylan, Destiny's Child.

He can't feel Paddy's drugs any more. He can only think about Paddy screwing him. He suddenly feels down. He suddenly feels so down.

It is four in the morning as he pays the kid at the hatch.

'Nice car, pal,' the kid says.

Freddie suspects he is taking the piss.

'You should see where I live,' he says.

Chapter 14

Jazz is for the middle of the night. *Kind of Blue* is never going to sound wrong, but Freddie feels it sounds most stately at this time. If you hear it any hour before midnight, you're always missing something that reveals itself only in the dead of night, to one solitary, sleepless man.

Freddie is sitting at the kitchen table listening to *Kind of Blue* on the Discman, making a list of the things he owns. It's five o'clock in the morning and he can't rest. He's still coming down, all the way down from the summit.

He got it straight from Paddy in the most exquisite and precise public-school tones, like there was a lawyer measuring each beat, that LJ Carew was Paddy's woman. And now Freddie has just gone and stolen Paddy's woman, high on Paddy's hospitality.

It's starting to sink in that he is going to stay poor.

He's got three bars of the Super Ser on, and he's just remembered that he doesn't own that thing. He doesn't own the cup that he's drinking coffee from, in fact he's probably down on that deal because all the Delft came with the flat and Dorothy destroyed most of it.

159

He doesn't own any of the furniture. Not the kitchen table or the chairs, or the sofa he sleeps on or the couch that Bricks sleeps on. It all looked fine when they moved in, the furniture matched the carpet and the carpet matched the curtains, all in shades of brown which used to depress Dorothy, and make her threaten to redecorate.

It's all still there, looking better than the tenant at this hour, but sadly the property of Mrs Williams, who owns the rest of the house, who is still spry and who personally collects the rent every month, which means she would probably notice her big brown sofa going out the gate.

So he's got the cars and the apartments to sell. He's got a sound system and about seven hundred albums in vinyl and CD and hundreds of videos and books, which he won't sell. He has to leave something to Nadine, and it's all good shit. He's got the worldwide rights to everything Bricks Melvin does for the rest of his life, which at this point on the open market is worth about twenty pence, and anyway he's not selling. In other words, he has fuck all. On the luxury goods, with the amount of cash flying around this town, he might get lucky and break even.

When he was in the players' lounge at Old Trafford as a guest of Paddy Lamb, shooting the breeze with Dwight Yorke, he figured his days of renting flats and furniture and breaking even were behind him. It's a long way down.

His grandfather became a successful barrister and built a villa just up the road. Freddie's father, in turn, became a hugely unsuccessful barrister, but a lovely man to talk to in the pub. When Jack Dowd died of cirrhosis, the solicitor, who allowed Freddie and his mother to live in the villa after he bought it, said he was doing it mainly for Jack, because he was a lovely man.

So if it keeps going like this, Nadine will be living in a cardboard box with a superb album and video collection. Because her father couldn't hack it, with all his hippy-dippy, rama-lama bullshit and his father before him couldn't hack it. Growing up comfortable, Freddie Dowd just didn't have the stuff you need to take the money when it was going, and to hang on to it. He didn't have the appetite, the sense of vast entitlement of an operator like Paddy Lamb, who could give you champagne and take you in a private plane to watch United and make you feel like you can play with the big guys, and then screw you and your rented couch. You and the boys in the band, back to zero.

But the boys will have another hit in summer because they're hungry. And maybe Paddy will diddle them out of that too, but they won't lose heart the way that Freddie Dowd is losing heart, because they're hard little fuckers behind all the grinning. Smart enough, too, to be getting hitched to hard-headed little models who want to have babies, and not some head-case like Dorothy.

But there's no use in blaming this on her. He doesn't deserve any better with his effete little voice giving out all that cosmic bollocksology. He doesn't deserve to be listening to *Kind of Blue*, to Miles Davis and John Coltrane and Cannonball Adderley, great artists, hard, hard men. Hard like Van, like the Man himself. You have to be hard to be an artist in this world, to go at it like a bull the way that Miles and Cannonball and Coltrane did it, playing these sessions back in 1959, and no one knowing what the fuck they were on about.

Freddie Dowd has been around for nearly forty years, and no art has come out of him, unless you rate an award-winning poster for the local pro-divorce campaign. No art, no money, no furniture.

He can do a few things now, for dignity's sake. He can sit down with Nadine and tell her there will be no cheque in the post. Then, he can tell her about LJ, and about finding the thing that he lost. Then he can retrieve that copy of *Catch-22* before Nadine notices it's gone. And then he can take the keys of the Mercedes and drive himself off the end of the pier. It feels like the right thing now, at five o'clock in the morning listening to *Kind of Blue*. Except he'd be sure to fuck it up.

But Freddie is going to do one hard thing for sure. One thing that is hard enough to justify his belonging to the same species as Miles Davis. He is going to go ahead with these six weeks at The Crowbar, give it a shot, defy the bastards who say that jazz will never pay its way.

Miles is whispering to him from beyond the grave. All these guys are dead now. John Coltrane died young, but he left this music behind him, and it's all that is keeping Freddie Dowd together on this long night, nearly forty years on. It is keeping him together because he knows, he just knows that these guys understand exactly what it's like to lose everything, to have your furniture taken away, to be mocked, to be alone at the darkest hour – and then what? To fuck it all out of the way like so much garbage, and play.

Chapter 15

First thing in the morning LJ Carew has a CD of *Catch-22*, the talking book, biked over to her. She listens to it in her Porsche on the way out to Kilbrittan Hill. It sounds like a howl.

She calls Freddie on her mobile. He sounds wrecked.

'Unnnh?' he says.

'Love it,' she says.

'Unnnh?' he whispers. 'Hiiiii.'

'Love the book. Love the start of it anyway.'

'Awwww . . . listen . . .' he says

'I'm off to see Paddy . . .'

'Listen . . .' he says.

'Give him back the rock . . .' she says.

'Listen, I'm really, really sorry about this,' Freddie says.

'Uh-oh.'

'The book,' he says. 'I need it. I'll get you another copy. I'll get you a new one.'

'This one'll do.'

'No, no. I'm just a little bit . . . it's just . . . just in case . . . sentimental value . . .'

'Ah, Freddie, you give this to all the chicks?'

'No, no, no,' he groans.

'It's all the same to me. Really.'

'Nadine . . . it's got a bit of history.'

'All the same to me, baby.'

'Great. Great. You're off to Paddy right now?'

'Shoulda done it long ago.'

'Lunch? Maybe the Bandillero? Give me the bad news?'

'Bandillero at two?'

'Maybe . . . we can celebrate.'

'You sound wrecked, Freddie.'

'Last night,' he says. 'Fantastic.' And his voice softens almost to nothing.

Freddie rolls off the couch and slumps to the floor like a dead man. He's going to stay poor. While he was rabbiting on the phone about getting *Catch-22* back, he had a desperate urge to ask LJ to turn back down the road, to tell Paddy nothing and to keep the ring, at least until Paddy parts with the big bucks. But it would be so against the spirit of what happened last night, so uncool after all the things he said and all that crazy love, he couldn't get the words out.

Now maybe it's the last of the white powder finally leaving his system, maybe it's the sight of Bricks conked out there in the sleeping bag, yes maybe it's the sight of that old sleeping bag that makes him want to try one last time. But he can't actually do it. He finds LJ's mobile number scrawled on a piece of paper in his back pocket. He dials three digits but then he stops. What is he to say to her?

He pulls on his jeans. He goes to the kitchen and finds an ancient tin of Andrews Liver Salts. The powder is gone hard. He digs out a spoonful of it and it fizzes a little in the water and he swallows it in one go, thinking it might clean out whatever mad shit is left in his head. It just makes him hate himself a little bit more.

He'll have to call LJ, for Nadine. Yes, if he can't do it for himself, he must do it for Nadine, so that she will not stay poor. And he must do it now, before LJ gets to Paddy's place.

With the fear rising in his gut, he dials the number. It is engaged. He dials it again. It is engaged. He makes a cup of instant coffee and tries again. It is engaged. He is going to stay poor.

When she stops talking to Freddie, LJ makes another call to the station to run through the line-up for today, a new Corrs video, Justin Timberlake in town, Naomi on about the supermodel bash against slavery in The Point. She reckons that nine out of ten drivers in the next lane going into town are gawking and grinning at her, the blonde in the silver Porsche, the blonde in the Porsche who is none other than LJ Carew, driving and talking on the mobile because she can't be arsed obeying the law.

She used to wave at a few, even the horn-blowers. Now she keeps looking straight ahead. She didn't like what she saw in those faces, the envy and the sneering. Blokes she knew all her life would look at her like that, when she became a somebody. And they'll jeer her even more if she gets it together with Freddie. Because that's wanting it every way. That's having the fuck-off money and the bit of culture besides. It's not you, LJ, they'll say, you're breaking out of your box, LJ, it's like Ronan Keating getting it together with Björk or Yoko Ono or some other artsy-fartsy nutter.

Only with the fuck-off money can you tell them all . . . to fuck off.

She is getting a good run out the southside, not many hold-ups in this direction. She'll have to warn Freddie off the coke, in case he gets too fond of it. She had a fuck of a job getting off it herself. It was Paddy who got her into all that, pleasing him.

Still, she owes Paddy this trip, she owes him a bit of face-time as they say in the business. Maybe they're too alike, maybe that's the problem. Having the *craic* the way they do, laughing all night about the business they call show, Paddy forgets that she doesn't fancy him, doesn't think about him that way, at least not while he's a total crook and a degenerate. You might party with those guys, but you wouldn't want them inside you.

By the leather jacket and trousers she is wearing, Paddy will know straight away that she is going in hard. It's a tip he gave her himself. When you want to get something done, you don't fuck about. After that, you can fuck about all you like.

She is listening to *Catch-22*, thinking about Freddie. He is a nice man, no badness in him after all the abuse. But an aura, this quiet thing. And good on the job too, straight into orbit at the first attempt.

A good guy, is what her instinct is telling her, good guy, good guy, good guy.

At Dún Laoghaire she has an impulse to call on him. A surprise, a quickie, whatever. Then she thinks no, just in case. She is nervous of making a wrong move. It's a sure sign she's got the fever.

It will come down to the same old thing in the end, she reckons. It's one thing saying you're on a journey. A freaky-deaky guy like Freddie will give you that one, at least he won't laugh in your face. But she slipped it in at the start, she told him she can't read and he took it as a joke, which is how every other tosser takes it. They find out soon it's not a joke, and that's it. They can't get past it. Strange how even the stupidest man in the world will look down his nose at you if you can't read.

She remembers every little jibe and put-down, from every little tosser. She remembers everything.

She phones ahead to Paddy's place. She leaves a message on the machine, that she's coming, and she's not bringing good news. You don't fuck about, the man said. He'll be ready for her, even if he has to kick some model out of the scratcher still pissed from yesterday.

Paddy, in fairness to him, never gave a shit about the reading thing. It probably gave him an erection, like, it proved she was the real McCoy, a total scrubber from the council estate. Paddy said, make the most of it, confess it on the *Late Late*, tell everyone the truth, you were a bad girl and they kicked you out of school and they wouldn't let you back because that's what they do to poor people, still.

He likes the bad girl bit, it gives him a stiffy.

Go for the charity angle, he said, and straight away Esther Pilkington will whistle up the supermodels for a bash at The Point and a long weekend of non-stop partying against illiteracy. He said it's a really cool one, that, as cool as slavery was last year. The folks can get a handle on illiteracy, not like Friederich's ataxia or some of these syndromes. Illiteracy could be as big as landmines, he said.

167

You need to have a feel for these things, he said. He always overdoes that charity gag.

The gates of Paddy's castle are open. For the first time, she starts to feel nervous about this caper. She thinks about Freddie back there in Dún Laoghaire, willing to give up a few million for her. She stops the car outside the gates. It doesn't feel right now, to be letting Freddie do this. Sure, she's got enough money for both of them, but there's the daughter who mightn't be too chuffed when she finds out what Freddie did for love.

Look, he's made the gesture, and that's all that counts. That's the bit that makes him different from anyone she's ever met. She wonders now if she is rushing this, though deep down she suspects that it makes no difference anyway. When it comes to getting money out of Paddy, all she has is her instinct, a gut feeling that you're better off standing up to him, that in some animal way he'll respect you for that. When it comes to Paddy paying people there's no guidebook, no map. There's not a lot of people who've been there.

She phones Freddie.

'I'm outside Paddy's place, bottling it,' she says. 'Having second thoughts.'

Freddie, from the depths of resignation, feels a crazy surge of joy. He tries to show restraint.

'How's that?' he says.

'Not about you, Freddie, not about you. Just about the way we're doing this. The rush of blood. . .'

Freddie feels such relief it's like another hit of the devil's dandruff.

'You reckon there's some other way?' he says.

'Maybe there's another way.'

'Like, keep a lid on it, somehow, until Paddy delivers the bread?' Freddie says, in his softest tones.

'Like, that could be for ever,' she says. 'Still . . .'

Freddie wants with all his being to tell LJ to turn back, to stall it, to postpone the evil day in the hope that the baleful gods will smile on them some other way. But as he wrestles with it, he finds himself looking at a picture of Miles Davis blowing hard on the cover of *Birth of the Cool*. He can't escape Miles, his clothes and his attitude. He can feel all of Miles's scorn for his weakness now, Miles dissing him, Miles cackling at the smallness of his soul.

Yes, it would be a bummer for Nadine if he blew the big bucks by making the wrong call in this situation, but you get no guarantees anyway in this business, as Miles well knows. And Miles seems to be telling him that what Nadine needs most of all is a father who can say what he is going to say now, at the count of three . . .

'Go in there, baby,' he says to LJ.

'Nice one,' she says.

'Do your stuff,' he says.

'I'll see you later,' she says.

LJ drives into Paddy's place and parks outside the front door, no security for her. She loves it up here, she could spend all day just looking across the bay, glorious. But right now, she doesn't need it.

The front door is ajar. She hears Paddy calling her from the basement. She expected he'd be down in his lair after the message she left. He comes here when he's depressed.

The basement looks like a gentleman's club, all oak and

leather and Axminster and a huge fireplace. No big TV screens or gold discs down here. No sign that Fellaz and The Cisco Kidz and even Johnny Shine are paying for this.

Paddy is standing with his back to the fire. He looks like he is still in the Caribbean, the white trousers, the flowery shirt. He is smiling, but it is the smile of the brave loser, not the lover of life. He is beginning a huge cigar.

'Leather trousers,' he says.

LJ gives him a little wave. She puts the diamond ring on a small table with magazines on it. Paddy keeps talking about leather trousers.

'It's so bloody sad. They come to me all the time wearing leather trousers, these old pop stars from five, ten years ago with a new album, a solo project, terrible stuff,' he says.

'You have to run them?' she says.

'It's a whole new category of music,' he says, 'the leather trousers album.'

'I'll take these off if you like,' she says.

Paddy sucks on his cigar. 'That won't be necessary. Will it?'

She sits on the arm of a leather couch. 'Me and you, we're too alike,' she says.

'If you don't mind me asking . . . from the message you left . . . you were in the colours last night?'

Go in hard, she thinks. Don't fuck about. 'With Freddie. Yes.'

'Officer material,' he says.

'Freddie?'

'He's a very nice man. And a very talented man.'

170

'You love what he does?'

'No. But he's a better man than I am, isn't he?'

Paddy sounds gracious, every word exquisitely spoken.

'I'm sorry,' she says.

He goes to the oak dining table. He pours two cups of coffee from a big silver pot. She won't partake.

'You have my heart,' he says.

It sounds like his voice is breaking. She needs to get out of there.

'You're taking it well, Paddy. I'll remember that.'

'I just hope it's the right thing for you.'

'Who the fuck knows?'

'That's how it is in our business, LJ. Who the fuck knows?'

Paddy goes to the drinks cabinet beside the fireplace. He takes out a crystal decanter of whiskey. With an absent-minded air, like this was part of some ancient routine that he could perform without thinking, he pours the whiskey into his morning coffee.

'Nobody knows,' she says.

Paddy takes a sip of the coffee laced with whiskey. It is not quite to his satisfaction. He adds another dash of whiskey.

'Nobody knows except you and me and Liza Minelli,' he says.

'Early in the day, Paddy,' she says. 'Early for whiskey.'

'We were in there drinking with Liza Minelli, remember that?' he says.

He starts to scratch his chest hair, but he stops quickly, like it involves some secret technique that doesn't work for him any more.

171

'Whiskey for breakfast, they'd have you in rehab for that,' she says.

Paddy brings his cup and saucer back to the fireplace. The saucer adds an odd delicacy to the scene. He seems to perk up somewhat with each sip. He starts to hold forth.

'My friend Frank Mahaffy told me that in all his years of managing rock groups there was one addiction worse than all the others put together. You're probably thinking heroin, cocaine?'

'Tell me,' she says.

'Golf,' he says. 'You see, you can throw a guy who's on heroin into a limo and kick his arse on to a plane. You can function. You can never even find the bastards on the golf course. The real killer, they say, is golf.'

LJ swings an imaginary club. 'I hope it never gets to that, Paddy,' she says.

Paddy takes another decorous sip. 'That would be the last straw,' he says.

LJ takes a step backwards, the hard part done, the open door beckoning. But she is not quite finished yet.

'You'll . . . you'll see him right?' she says. 'Freddie?'

'I can do business with a man like that.'

'He's not in the business, Paddy. Just give him his dosh like a good man.'

'You think . . . you think I can be a good man?' he says, like the notion just occurred to him, and he's warming to it already.

'You could try,' she says, matter-of-factly.

'I am trying,' he says.

She taps her wrist. 'Lunch. I'm doing lunch.'

'Now you're breaking my heart,' he says.

'We've done a few,' she says, echoing his note of sadness.

He drains his cup. He takes LJ's hand and he kisses it where the ring would have been, a last exaggerated show of gallantry. He ushers her up the stairs.

'I really, desperately wanted to give you lunch to talk about *Big Brother*. The Irish version?'

'Don't know about that,' she says.

'It's got your name on it. One of those pop moments . . .'

'Kids . . .' she says.

'They love you . . .'

'I'm on . . . I'm on a . . . a journey, Paddy.'

'Oh dear,' he says.

'You ever hear the Bird? I mean Charlie Parker?'

They reach the front door. Paddy studies his shoes, like there's something he can't bring himself to say.

'Oh dear,' he says again.

'Don't worry, Paddy,' she says. 'I know my place.'

He smiles, again the smile of the good loser.

'It's just this old saying I have,' he says. 'Top-of-the-range music, bottom-of-the-range life.'

'I'll remember that,' she says. And she kisses him quickly on the lips.

He sees her into the Porsche. He puts his head in the window.

'I was in the colours m'self last night,' he says. 'As it happens.'

'Good for you,' she says.

'Terrific mount. Quick out of the stalls. Ran a bit green in the closing stages.'

'Did you give her a few reminders?'

'Up in front of the stewards. Over-use of the whip.'

173

'Again?'

She starts the Porsche and drives away to the sound of their laughter.

Chapter 16

The music wakes her up. Nadine lies there listening to Bricks playing in the next room. It's the tune he played at Dorothy's funeral, the one he wrote, or made up on the spot, or whatever jazzers do.

Nadine sits up and lights a cigarette. She looks at the family photograph beside the bed. Bricks's tune seems to suit Dorothy in some way, it makes her look sort of normal.

She reckons it will be pretty cool at The Crowbar tonight, to sit there drinking and listening to Bricks, and then to get pissed with him. Maybe he'll blow her away again with his playing. If it was some guy her own age, he'd be doing her head in looking for a bonk. With Bricks it's like, can we just shut the fuck up about it and have a few beers?

She heard Freddie leaving just as she was waking up. He looked in on her and then thought better of it. He must be off again with his showbiz friends, the big sap.

She tries on a psychedelic T-shirt and torn jeans. Maybe she'll wear this tonight, like some hippie-chick groupie.

The music stops. She goes inside for coffee. Bricks is at

the table filling a glass of brandy. He jumps when she comes in the door, like he has been found out. Then he sighs, and pours another drop.

'Nerves are shot,' he says.

'Dorothy's song?' she says.

'Can't play it,' he says.

'Sounded fine,' she says.

'Brutal,' he says.

She makes coffee. He takes a hit of the brandy and goes back to his couch.

'Freddie out?' she says.

Bricks is preoccupied with his own problem.

'I can play the notes,' he says. 'But the tone is brutal.'

'Sounded fine,' she says.

'Fine?' he snaps. 'What the fuck is "fine"?'

'Freddie be back?' she says.

'Left about an hour ago,' he says. 'Probably out all day. Shopping, I think.'

'Shopping and fucking, right?' she says.

Bricks laughs. He rolls a cigarette. 'More like a book at bedtime,' he says.

Nadine sips her coffee.

'Fine,' she says, not really getting it.

'*Catch-22*,' Bricks says. 'Pretty heavy for that lady.'

Nadine stirs her coffee.

'What?' she says.

'Big book,' he says. 'Big for LJ Carew.'

Nadine puts down her cup. She walks quickly into the bedroom. *Catch-22* is gone. She's got about ten books that she keeps between bookends on the floor and it's nearly the first thing she sees every day. *Catch-22* is gone.

She wanders back in a daze. She sits on the edge of the sofa, looking into space.

'He gave that book to her?' she says.

'I think he meant to tell you, but you weren't here,' he says.

'Right,' she says, like she is still in a trance.

'Are you . . . are you here now?' he says.

'He used to read that shit to me every night,' she says. 'We didn't have TV.'

'I know,' Bricks says.

'Couldn't have any friends over here . . .' she says.

'I know,' he says.

'So he read this book to me, like, every night,' she says.

'He said it's all good shit,' Bricks says. 'He was on a roll.'

Nadine lies back on the sofa. She stares straight ahead for several minutes while Bricks cradles his brandy, head bowed.

'You lost it, Bricks, man?' she says, dead calm.

'I tried to tell him . . .' he says.

'You can't play any more man?' she says.

'Not the good stuff,' he says. 'My tone . . .'

'If you can't play, you can't play, right, man?' she says.

Bricks swallows his brandy.

'Freddie Dowd . . . is one of the few guys in this town . . .' he says.

'Would you get us more brandy?' she says.

Slowly, Bricks puts his saxophone into the case and shuts it.

'They hated it up at the party,' he says. 'Paddy's people.'

'Fuck them,' she says. 'The fucks.'

'The punters hate me . . . and I hate them,' he says.

177

'Maybe get a bottle of port as well?' she says.

'One of them told me he loved Billie Holiday,' he says. 'Said she was a tragic lady. I hate that shit.'

'Fuck that shit,' she says.

'If these guys knew Billie Holiday,' he says, 'they wouldn't say she was tragic, they'd say she was a drunken bitch.'

'Never mind,' she says.

'Billie was just a great musician,' he says. 'And the punters really, really hate music. It tells them things they don't want to hear.'

'Enough of that shit, man,' she says. 'You're sounding like fuck-face Freddie.'

Bricks stands up and buttons his crumpled jacket. He picks up his ankle-length overcoat. He takes a fistful of money out of his pocket and checks it, and sweeps out the door.

Freddie had his eye on this coat for ages, a chequered overcoat in Copeland's window that looked exactly like what Barney Bigard was wearing in a Milt Hinton photograph taken at Beefsteak Charlie's in New York circa 1955.

It's a gift for Bricks, to mark his official comeback. Freddie tries it on in the shop. It's way too big for him and he looks ridiculous in it, like a small boy trying on his father's clothes. But they figure it would be perfect for Bricks.

It costs nearly a grand, maybe Freddie's last extravagance. But then jazz is more than music. Like Lenny Bruce said, it's about the clothes and the attitudes.

He's having this late lunch vibe with LJ at the Bandillero but until then he'll be incommunicado, doing what he must. He walks across Capel Street Bridge and up the quay to O'Connell Street. He buys a new copy of *Catch-22* in Eason's. The lack of sleep is starting to waste him. He goes into Bewley's on Westmoreland Street for coffee.

He likes to keep moving on the day of a gig, just buzzing around town and leaving the artist alone to get his shit together. But he needs to sit down with LJ, because LJ has been sitting down with Paddy.

It's the first time Freddie has been in Bewley's with major negotiations in progress elsewhere, as a result of which he will maybe drop a few million.

Usually it would be one mug of coffee to last all day, a read of a borrowed paper, and enough left for his bus fare. And in those simpler times, in spite of how he dissed the music business, Freddie sort of assumed that if someone wrote a freak hit, they would simply get paid, and then go home. This now seems like more softness on his part, considering that the writer of a freak hit is of no further use to a big hitter like Paddy Lamb, so there is no need to keep him sweet, no percentage in paying him his due.

A lot of things Freddie sort of assumed were soft and simple. He sort of assumed that anyone connected with LJ Carew was some bastard with forty off-shore bank accounts. The sort of bastard he sees in Bewley's these days making phone calls to some other bastard in Budapest, telling him to get over here quick while it's hot, before it all goes wallop.

Now they will have to stand in line twanging their braces because Freddie's black ass is in the way.

Freddie's system feels all out of whack in Bewley's, because he is wilting from fatigue, but speedy with the coffee and the prospect of the gig.

He wanders out of Bewley's and up in the direction of Trinity College to the Bandillero. It bugs him that he recognizes no one on the street, to stop and rap and to get the good word out about tonight. There is no love of jazz in any of the faces he sees. He can tell.

He gets his strength back in the Bandillero when LJ comes through the door in full spate. They order corned beef and cabbage. And then there's the laying on of hands.

Dorothy had this huge energy too, but it sucked all Freddie's energy out of him. The stuff that LJ is giving out is lifting him up again, like he could cancel lunch and march her off to the car park right now and make the beast in the Range Rover and then go on the razzle for the day down to Wicklow.

He lights a Rothmans from a new packet. He figures he can use them all today. On the wall there is a framed picture of Peter O'Toole, looking wry.

LJ passes her copy of *Catch-22* across the table and takes the new one in exchange. She is very blonde and dressed for her show, all in black leather which reminds Freddie of Suzi Quatro, though he doesn't mention it on the assumption that LJ has never heard of Suzi Quatro. Yet.

'Regrets?' she says.

Freddie takes it that she's talking about the sex, but she's kinda left it open-ended.

'Well, I'm maybe down a few million and, eh, I don't know yet but I may have turned my daughter against me for all time, but no . . . no regrets,' he says, wry as O'Toole. But his heart is racing, because of LJ, and what she does to him, and what she is about to tell him.

'You're down nothing yet,' she says.

'You told him?' he says.

'The lot,' she says.

'Well . . .?' he says.

'He's devastated,' she says.

'So . . . the cheque is still in the post?' he says.

'Maybe,' she says. 'You wouldn't get a yes or no out of Paddy if you nailed him to the floor. Regrets?'

'No regrets,' he says. 'Not me.'

'Paddy said you were . . . What is it? . . . "Officer material",' she says. 'He said he can do business with a man like you.'

Freddie lights another cigarette. His head is spinning.

'That's . . . that's big of him,' he says.

'But you just want your money, right? You're not in this business. Right?'

'I'm in the jazz business,' he says. 'I guess that doesn't count.'

'It's not a business any more,' she says. 'But it's a lovely hobby.'

'You'll see tonight . . .'

'Paddy got emotional. Said he wanted to be a better man. Sounded like he meant it. But I know my Paddy and I'd say we're not out of the woods yet.'

'So the cheque is still in the post?' he says.

'He's off to London for a few weeks,' she says.

'So?' he says.

'Everyone in the business goes to London for a few weeks if you're looking for money,' she says.

181

'So it's just bullshit?'

'He might go there,' she says, 'but that's not really the point.'

'So we'll know in two weeks?' he says.

'Maybe in two weeks he'll have to go to New York for three weeks,' she says.

'Like, the St Patrick's Day Parade?' he says.

'Why not?' she says.

'Then we're into Easter.'

'You're getting there.'

'And then . . .'

'Then there's Midem, the big trade fair in the south of France,' she says.

'Another holiday?' he says.

'No, that's what they call work. So when they come back from that, they need a rest. Maybe a few weeks in Los Angeles, or just off to London for another two weeks.'

'Very nice,' he says.

'You're looking at summer then, so a top guy like Paddy would take all his staff to the Caribbean for a couple of weeks. They'll have made all their big decisions by then, like whether it's right for Fellaz to cover a song that was a hit for someone else six months ago, and if they should go up against Bob the Builder for the Christmas number one,' she says.

'So this is, like, a big orgy in the Caribbean?' he says.

'For the staff it is,' she says. 'For Paddy it's just more work.'

'New York?' he says.

'Three weeks at least,' she says. 'And then the shit hits the fan around September. The big push before Christmas.'

'So you've got, like, a couple of weeks in September when you might pin him down?' Freddie says.

'No way,' she says. 'I told you, it's the big push before Christmas. So you'd have no chance of getting him then because everyone else is trying to get him.'

'So?' he says.

'So then it's Christmas,' she says.

'Paddy said . . .' he says. 'Paddy said if he ever amounted to anything in this business, he'd do two things . . .'

'He'd always return people's calls,' she says, 'because it's only the arseholes that don't return your calls. The top guys always return your call.'

'Bullshit?' he says.

'Not exactly,' she says. 'His office will call back to say that he's in London for two weeks. I mean, they don't want you arriving up to the door.'

'And the second thing is,' he says, '*The cheque is in the post* always means *The cheque is in the post.*'

LJ looks confused. 'That's not the second thing,' she says. 'No way.'

'He told me . . .' he says.

'The second thing,' she says, 'is that he would blame no one but himself if he ever got ripped off.'

Freddie is losing his appetite for the corned beef and cabbage.

'What's your gut feeling?' he says.

'My gut feeling,' she says, 'is . . . you gave a lot up for me.'

'Oh well . . .'

'Most of the guys I know, they'd give up nothing for nobody,' she says.

183

'But if the money does come through . . .' he says.

'Who knows? You never know what money will do to you,' she says. 'I mean, you've seen where I live. You could become one of us, only worse.'

'Worse?' he says.

'Most of us didn't know any better,' she says.

'Freddie Dowd is not becoming anything. Freddie Dowd just wants to run little jazz gigs,' he says.

'Listen, Freddie Dowd, I can't go tonight,' she says.

'You can't beat the live sound,' he says.

'It's not the jazz,' she says. 'I just don't like Bricks Melvin. He's a mad bastard and he scares the shit out of me.'

'If you knew him . . .'

'If . . . I don't want to badmouth him, OK?'

'He's an artist. He's got that ruthless streak.'

'I've interviewed thousands of them,' she says, 'and I'd say the really talented ones are the nicest people.'

'William Faulkner said if an artist had to rob his own mother he would not hesitate. "Ode to a Grecian Urn" is worth any number of old ladies,' he says.

'William . . .?' she says.

'Faulkner,' he says.

'I'll remember that,' she says. 'But tonight I'll stay at home and listen to Bird.'

'And catch up on your reading?' he says.

She throws her head back and laughs, like she has heard some classic joke. Freddie orders the wine. A hundred quid the bottle, for old times' sake.

They eat a lot of corned beef and cabbage and then LJ insists on a trip to Damien the Trinity Barber for a few

184

more snips off Freddie's fuzz. Nothing drastic that will destroy his aura, just a bit more off the top to show him how he might look if he gave a shit about such things.

And since he has such good taste in clothes for Bricks Melvin, she reckons he can do better for himself in this department as well without losing his soul, just getting rid of these crap ancient jeans and crap denim jackets that are hardly clothes at all.

She keeps assuring him that she will do nothing to him or his appearance that goes against his beliefs.

She walks with him back to the car park, arm in arm. They get some startled looks. In the lift up to level four, a young suit can't stop himself sniggering.

'I feel like that fat little guy who married Sophia Loren,' Freddie says.

'He had brains,' she says, 'he had charisma.'

'I think the word is money,' he says.

She makes him look unflinchingly into the rear view mirror of the Range Rover.

'Brains,' she says, 'charisma.'

'Looks?' he says.

'The way it is now, I wouldn't change a hair,' she says, helping him into the Range Rover.

'Maybe . . . maybe Paddy will give it all up for you?' he says.

She walks away laughing, like it's a self-evidently hilarious thought. At the door, she blows him a kiss.

He watches her leaving the car park the way she came in, a star.

She does live television several times a week. She can take all this madness and she can go on a journey and then she

185

can tell Paddy Lamb to go and fuck himself, and it works for her. She can go on a journey taking Freddie Dowd with her, because somehow, she is able to get past all the shit and make up her own mind.

The only thing that Freddie is sure of is that he can do none of these things without dread. He can smell the danger, he can sense things getting out of control. He has reached that place where he can hear the strange music. And it's too late to stop now.

He sets off for Dún Laoghaire in the late afternoon. It is a dirty day and it is getting dark. He starts to imagine that he will miss the gig, stuck in the traffic. If it takes him half an hour in these conditions to get from the city centre to Nassau Street, a few hundred yards away, it could take him all night to get to Dún Laoghaire, six miles to the south.

He wants to phone the flat, but he has no mobile. He doesn't want to interfere with Bricks's preparations, he just wants to talk to Nadine to tell her he mightn't make it. And maybe, that the cheque is still in the post. And really, he just wants to talk.

The tape in the machine is *Sketches of Spain*. He'd like to listen to it on principle. The jam intensifies. He reckons Miles would be too pure for this horrible scene. He puts on some drive-time shit instead. For the traffic reports.

They're playing his song. He turns it up. The jock talks about Fellaz and what great guys they are, and Freddie half-expects a namecheck before he remembers that this is not Radio 3 where they give you a little biography of the composer.

He is even starting to get pissed off about this, because

he's no Burt Bacharach but he wouldn't mind the odd mention. He even catches himself looking into the rear-view mirror to check if he is starting to look halfway cool. He scans the faces of other drivers, imagining that they are enjoying his work.

Then he catches himself on and remembers that this is a night for jazz, for genius. The chequered coat is on the passenger seat. For a moment, he can see a full house, see himself arriving at The Crowbar late and not getting in. For a moment he trusts his fellow man to deliver.

He even wonders if they could make a go of it commercially, if the gig suddenly took off and then it wouldn't matter if he never got his blood money out of Paddy Lamb. That's the dream. But after a long, long mile of drive-time, Freddie would trade his dreams for a mobile, for a few words with Nadine, with Bricks, just to talk.

He is smoking non-stop. He hates himself now for not getting a mobile on principle. Nadine has been bugging him for months to get one, but he just kept rabbiting on about all the suits who use them to make themselves look busy. He thinks about jumping out of the Range Rover at Ballsbridge and into a phone box, but he bottles it.

He wants to scream with frustration and he does it, at the traffic lights in Ballsbridge. He turns up the drive-time shit full blast and he screams.

The driver in the next lane looks at him and then looks away, as if he understands.

Freddie thinks it is the loudest noise he has ever made, but it doesn't bring him relief. He gets it into his head that some kid on the door won't let Bricks in and Bricks will just go away. It's getting on for seven now and he's reached

Blackrock so he will probably make it after all, but fuck it, will Bricks be barred from his own gig?

The drive-time jock is cracking up over something that the AA Roadwatch guy said. Something about a Ferrari.

They are rapping about some Ferrari, the jock slagging the AA guys about being able to afford one, about Eddie Irvine living out in Dalkey and pulling the birds and all that Grand Prix fucking shit.

Freddie suddenly feels this terrible sense of calm. He is hearing the worst thing he has ever heard and it makes his whole being go absolutely still. The AA guy is repeating that a Ferrari went out of control and crashed in the People's Park. Two people have been taken to Martinstown Hospital.

Freddie has not the slightest doubt. He knows who the two people are. He figures that when the gods are fucking with you, they have a way of letting you know these things.

He sets off for Martinstown Hospital. The traffic seems to be obliging him at last. He will make it from here in about five minutes. He is not panicked any more, he has no desire to scream.

Maybe the worst thing of all has happened. For the last seventeen years, he has sometimes been crucified with fear, imagining a moment such as this. And now that it is happening, the fear has rushed out of him. The fear of the thing has been replaced by the thing itself. He has never been here before. He feels cold.

At the hospital, he parks the Range Rover next to an ambulance. The ambulance doors are open. He has a strong sense that they took Nadine up here in this.

He takes the chequered coat with him. He has no idea

why, but it seems to comfort him. He needs all the help he can get now, from Barney Bigard and Milt Hinton and all the boys in Beefsteak Charlie's in 1955.

Chapter 17

The nurse brings him a cup of sugary tea.

'She's just like you, Mr Dowd,' she says.

They are in the canteen. The nurse takes him there to let the news settle, that Nadine has a hip injury and they are operating on it at this minute, but she should be all right. Her companion has a lot of bruising but they are mainly treating him for alcohol poisoning.

Freddie is feeling no pain. When the nurse gave him a big Filipino smile and kept saying OK, OK, OK, he felt that the universe was filled with goodness, that he had been blind to it all, but now he could see. The statue of the Blessed Virgin in the hall looked strangely benevolent to him. The hospital smell seemed to promise a happy ending. There was human kindness in this fucked-up old institution, and mercy in this world.

He asks the nurse the same thing he's been asking her since they met in the front hall.

'Nothing permanent?' he says.

'She'll be one hundred per cent perfect,' she says.

'Sorry to keep asking, ' he says, 'but . . .'

'Tea is good,' she says.

'You are from the Philippines, Olivia?' he says.

'Yes,' she says.

'And you really think she looks like me?' he says.

'She sounds just like you, that's it,' she says. 'Voice very soft.'

Maybe the nurse reminds him of some corny old war movie on a Sunday afternoon, but he doesn't think she is taking the piss.

'And her . . . her companion?' he says.

'He'll be OK,' she says. 'But the alcohol? He must stop.'

Olivia goes to get more sweet tea and a Wagon Wheel. Freddie's father used to get him a Wagon Wheel on his way home from the pub. It is always there for him in times of trauma, the Wagon Wheel.

Olivia has to go, to say the right thing to some other basket-case who is having the worst trip of his life. Freddie figures he will buy her a new canteen at the other end of this.

He needs to call The Crowbar with some version of events. The official version is that in the late afternoon, Nadine drove the Ferrari through the front gate of the People's Park with Bricks in the passenger seat. Then she revved it up and did a few circuits of the park, watched by the women and children in the playground at the far end who were mesmerized by this crazy display for several minutes until Nadine overdid it on a corner and the car went skidding into the trees.

The services got there quickly, and all were intrigued to find that the joyriders turned out to be a lovely young woman and this dude with a faint resemblance to Einstein, and not a couple of bullet-headed lads with too much cider in them. As to what the fuck drove them down there in the first place, Freddie is starting to have a few notions which are far too troubling to address at this time.

He gets to see Bricks first. Olivia appears again and takes him in the lift up to the third floor to show him Bricks just inside the door of a public ward, looking battered, like some hobo who is sleeping off the effects of a fight. Freddie throws the chequered overcoat on to the end of the bed.

'He's a musician?' Olivia says.

'Sort of,' Freddie says.

The elation is wearing off. The anger is starting to rise in Freddie's gut. He calls The Crowbar from a payphone in the hall. He asks them to give the people their money back and apologize and say that Bricks Melvin has been in an accident. The kid at the other end says he'll tell them, all four of them.

Freddie can see Bricks from the phone. He can see the chequered overcoat on the bed. He feels like a chump.

The kid is still on the line.

'Is that it?' the kid says.

'Tell the people he won't be there next week either. Tell them Bricks Melvin is finished,' Freddie says.

He takes out a cigarette. He is about to light it when he remembers where he is. He turns to Olivia but she is already down the hall, checking out someone coming this way on a trolley. She smiles at him.

This is it, his first look at Nadine to see if she is OK or if Olivia was just feeding him hospital bullshit.

They stop the trolley for a few seconds, like they are

running a brisk production line and Freddie is in quality control. Nadine looks just like Nadine in a deep sleep. Freddie nods his approval. There is something disturbing about this to Freddie, a sense that he is identifying the remains. He feels that he has a formal purpose here as a relative, but these other people in masks and gowns are the ones who count. He is afraid to touch Nadine for fear of disconnecting something. They wheel her into the ward.

Olivia steers him into the lift and then into the front hall. He doesn't question her. She seems to understand his sense of powerlessness, his fatigue.

'You must look after yourself now,' she says.

'Will Nadine have a room of her own?' he says.

'You want that?' she says.

'I can pay,' he says.

'Then, yes,' she says.

'I'd like to be here when she wakes up,' he says.

'You won't be driving then?' she says.

Freddie laughs. 'I mean, can you contact me?' he says.

'I know what you mean,' Olivia says. 'But you really shouldn't drive after a shock like this.'

'I'll walk,' he says.

He starts off for home, half a mile away.

'She'll be OK,' Olivia says.

'I can pay,' he shouts back.

It feels wrong to Freddie to be thinking about money at this time, but he wants Nadine away from Bricks. It really matters to him now, that the money comes through. The very act of walking home, the slowness of it, reminds him that he can't live without money any more. It makes him wonder how he survived so long with the sort of brain damage that poverty brings, to have no money coming in for month after month, and still to keep the faith.

By the time he reaches the flat, Freddie has decided to cancel Bricks at The Crowbar. He can't afford jazz any more, there's a war going on. If Bricks wants to drink himself to death, that's cool. But he's not taking Nadine with him, and he's not doing it on Freddie's tab.

There's only one flash car in the driveway now, the Merc. It makes Freddie's predicament seem more urgent. It makes him think about the wise words of Paddy Lamb, and that bright idea Paddy had about Bricks as the natural successor to Johnny Shine. And right now, he feels he can deliver Bricks. And claim his reward.

The side door is unlocked. He walks quickly through the flat, turning on all the lights. There's not much damage done at first sight, just a load of empty bottles and cans in the main room, the smell of stale smoke.

Then he sees that a Count Basie album in vinyl has been used as an ashtray. And there's a shattered twelve-inch version of *Bitches Brew* on the floor.

He starts to put the pieces on the table. It seems like a natural impulse to match up all the broken bits, futile though it is.

Then he sees the saxophone case in the corner. He opens it. He takes the saxophone out. He straps it on. He blows into it, nothing but a squawk. He takes it off. Then he smashes it against the wall. It gives him some relief but it does no damage to the instrument. He looks at it from every angle but it is still perfect, still beautiful.

He puts it back in the case. There is a small black-and-white photograph loose in the case, of Bricks with Ella

Fitzgerald. Ella is singing, head thrown back. Bricks is hanging loose, waiting to solo. Freddie remembers something about Bricks getting a gift of a gold-plated sax from Ella Fitzgerald.

'Fuck you, Ella,' he says.

Then he is able to sleep.

Bricks Melvin knows where he is and how he got here. One look around the ward and it all comes back to him in horrible instalments, getting pissed with Nadine, knowing he was going to miss the gig, getting into the Ferrari. He was conscious all the way.

He remembers bracing himself for eternity as Nadine lost control of the car. He remembers talking to her after the almighty wallop they took, a weirdly calm conversation about the seat belts saving them, and wondering how a couple of piss-artists could think of fastening their seat belts. Then he stepped from the car. He passed out in the ambulance.

But he is remembering other things too. He remembers now, dancing with a rubber plant in The Pink Elephant. He remembers dancing with the plant to some shit record, and being barred for it. He remembers, too, pissing in the lobby of The Shelbourne Hotel. He knew already he had done this, because a lot of people told him so, but on this morning, he can remember for the first time the actual deed of pissing there and then on the carpet because it seemed like the right thing to do. He remembers a lot of other things now that he did in blackout.

He is starting to remember in some detail how he went drinking one night in Birr, down in County Offaly, after playing an open-air set at the Vintage Car Rally. And it seems quite clear to him now that he looked out of his hotel window the following day to see a lot of strange-looking cars that didn't quite look right for the Birr Vintage Car Rally. Turned out he was in Boston.

The other thing he can remember is that he pushed Dorothy McIlroy out the window of the Stepaside Centre. Maybe she set it off by lecturing him about the booze, maybe it was an act as random and as careless as the act that threw Bricks Melvin into an institution just for being born.

But he did it. And he is getting away with it. He has beaten the house just one time, and it feels sensational.

When Bricks Melvin was a child, he played so they wouldn't abuse him. Then he played for love. And then he played for brandy. But none of it gave him the hit he is feeling now, the shiver of ecstasy as the ice cuts into his heart. This thing that he has, the jazz, has betrayed him. The bastards hate him for it, and he hates them. He hates them all and that includes Freddie Dowd, the kind of guy who gives you hope and then sets you up for another hammering.

Bricks Melvin has played his jazz, he has tried beauty, and it doesn't work. It has destroyed him. He can feel it dying in him now, he can feel the love leaving him, like it belonged to another man who has finally gone away, letting him roam the darkness, and go wherever the badness takes him. There is nothing left for him now, but badness.

There's a grey-faced old man stirring in the next bed. Bricks gives him a big Jack Nicholson smile. The old man can hardly hide his disgust at this leering new neighbour with the black eyes turning yellow and the livid bruises.

'I'm a bad guy, me,' Bricks says.

The old man turns away.

'I have killed before and I will kill again,' Bricks says.

He tries another Jack Nicholson smile, savouring his secrets. Then he sits up in the bed, arms folded, waiting for breakfast.

Chapter 18

Freddie can't stay angry. He is too grateful that Nadine is still in one piece, still unmarked. Next to some geezer roaring away to Brittas with her on the back of a Kawasaki, Freddie's deepest dread was that Nadine would be in a car smash. He thinks – one down, one to go.

He goes up to the hospital with a bunch of stuff, the grapes and the Discman and the copy of *Catch-22* for old times' sake. And cosmetics, every bottle and jar and spray and lipstick that he can rustle up in the bedroom and bathroom, all stuffed into a sort of red velvet bag that could be anything really.

He can see it working out between them, Nadine waking up and giving him that smile. And he thinks, fair enough, there is wrong on all sides. But he has to let it be known that he is pissed off. This is a step down from angry, from smashing-a-saxophone-against-the-wall angry. But he plans to keep Bricks in a public ward away from Nadine, and to send him a note addressed to Mr Gerry Melvin, saying that the gig has been cancelled. He has to let it be known some way.

— *Do Nothing Till You Hear From Me* —

He gets to the hospital and it doesn't work out like that. Nadine wakes up. She doesn't give him that smile. She is already smiling at Bricks, who is sitting on the edge of the bed, smoking. Bricks is wearing a tartan hospital dressing gown. His face is still a shocking thing, some horrendous Hallowe'en mess of black and blue and yellow. He extinguishes the cigarette in a glass of water on the bedside locker. He throws the water into the sink and then takes the wet cigarette-end to the bin. He holds his hands up in a grand gesture of remorse.

'Never again,' he says.

'Fuck's sake, Bricks,' Freddie says.

'I just had to see for myself that Nadine . . . that she was right,' Bricks says.

'You want to move in here?' Freddie says.

Bricks looks amused, like he is above this, like he knows that Freddie in his right mind wouldn't be on his case.

'I've got an AA meeting,' Bricks says.

'A what?' Freddie says.

'I'm giving it a shot. Back to the rooms. There's a meeting on across the yard.'

'You want to take Nadine with you?' Freddie snipes.

'You're right to be angry,' Bricks says gently.

'No he's not,' Nadine says.

Bricks holds his hands up again and shuffles out.

Freddie takes his place on the edge of the bed. He seems stunned for a moment by the confrontation, the fan having a go at his idol.

Nadine is already into the make-up routine, applying lipstick and studying her face in a small mirror with fierce concentration.

199

'I am right to be angry,' he says.

'Me? What about me?' she says.

'Why should you be angry?' he says.

She puts away the mirror and the lipstick. She takes the copy of *Catch-22* from him.

'This?' she says.

'So I'm making you do all these things just by seeing someone you don't like?' he says.

'Who?' she says.

'You know who,' he says.

'Sorry,' she says. 'Didn't catch the name. Who?'

'LJ,' he says. 'LJ Carew.'

'Don't care,' she says.

'So you'd just drink and drive around the People's Park anyway?' he says.

'Fine, thank you,' she says.

'You what?' he says.

'Thank you for asking, I am fine after my accident,' she says.

Freddie is feeling wasted already. He didn't want a row, he has never in his life wanted a row.

'Sorry,' he says.

She gives him half a smile, maybe a quarter.

'My hip,' she says, wincing.

'They say two weeks, you'll be up,' he says.

He kisses her on the forehead.

'Careful,' she says. 'Hurts.'

'Nothing broken. You'll be one hundred per cent perfect,' he says.

'Seat belts,' she says. 'Bricks remembered.'

'I've . . . I've cancelled the gig,' he says.

'Then put it on again,' she says.

'Bricks has to sort himself out,' he says.

Nadine manages to drag herself higher on the pillows.

'So that other thing you said. Is that shit too?'

'What thing?' he says.

'That other thing you said,' she says, 'about people who are really brilliant at what they do?'

'OK, OK,' he says.

'You forgot it?' she says.

'No,' he says.

'So . . .'

Freddie concedes defeat. 'OK, OK. If someone is brilliant at what they do . . .' he says.

'. . . You have to forgive them,' she says.

'Everything,' he says.

'And I mean, everything,' she says.

'And I mean, everything,' he says.

'So?' she says.

Freddie is chuffed that she was listening to his words of wisdom in the first place. It just feels strange to him that Nadine has taken over as Bricks's number one fan.

'Listen, with Bricks, you're not . . .?' he says.

'Bricks?' she says.

'I mean you're not actually . . .?' he says.

'Drinking buddies,' she says.

'Good. I don't mean good, as in . . .' he says.

Nadine riffles the pages of *Catch-22*.

'Does she like it?' she says.

'Hasn't read it yet,' he says.

'You're actually . . .?' she says.

'You'd like her,' he says.

201

'Yeah?' she says.

'Because I like her,' he says.

Freddie feeds the patient a grape.

'Only after your money,' she says.

'If you only knew,' he says.

'No thanks,' she says.

Freddie gets up and rinses the glass that Bricks used for his cigarette.

'Maybe I'll book another residency so, when I see how Bricks is getting on,' he says.

Nadine gives him half a smile, maybe three-quarters.

'He means it,' she says. 'Wants to stop drinking.'

'I thought he was looking well,' he says.

'Bricks?' she laughs.

'Behind it all he looked contented or something,' he says.

'Really up for this AA,' she says.

'So where will you be then, without your drinking buddy?' he says.

'Going off it too,' she says.

'In sympathy?' he says.

'Because I'm worth it,' she says, mimicking the American accent on the L'Oréal ad, and in the process leaving a weird echo of Dorothy in the air.

Freddie gives her the glass of water.

'The apartments will be finished soon,' he says. 'The view will do you good.'

'Cheque in the post?' she says.

'We're very close to it now,' he says.

They go silent for a while. At this point, it feels like bad luck to be even thinking about the money.

'I'll hang out here,' he says.

'They can give you the room next door,' she says.

'Don't think so,' he says.

'Winding you up,' she says.

Freddie takes the sucker-punch with a smile. He has other things he could be doing. He is due to call to the police station, the garage where the wrecked Ferrari ended up, and the bank. Then there's talk of a stroll on the pier with LJ, their first major public appearance. But if he could, he would just stay here all day and all night, watching over his baby.

'I'll book Bricks in again, right?' he says.

Nadine gives him that smile.

'Because there's nothing else out there only shit, right?' she says.

'Right,' he says.

He takes two new mobile phones out of his jacket and hands one to Nadine.

'Hey!' she says, feeling the weight of the little silver phone.

'You're the only one who has my number,' he says.

'You didn't . . . you actually . . .' she says.

'I mean it. No one else can contact me on this except you. Just press this and you're through,' he says.

Nadine tries it out. She presses the green button, top right. Freddie's phone rings and he answers it. She speaks into her phone while Freddie listens on his.

'No one else?' she says.

'No one,' he says.

The first of March comes and goes and there is no cheque in the post. To anyone who wants anything, Paddy Lamb is in London for two weeks. Rumour has it he is cutting up rough, sending for drink and hookers non-stop in a hotel suite in Kensington.

Freddie went to the police who are taking a very dim view of Nadine driving without tax or insurance while completely drunk.

He went to the garage and they showed him the battered Ferrari with the righteous scorn of the serious car freak for some dickhead with fuzzy hair who can't look after his motor, who basically doesn't deserve to be driving this beautiful thing. A terrifying sight, another humiliation, and a bill for twenty grand.

He went to the bank, which is refusing to lend him another penny. In fact they want to start clawing their money back straight away, scared by reports of uninsured cars being crashed in the People's Park. So he didn't bother telling them about Paddy Lamb's allergy to the artist and the artist's royalties.

They eventually get to walk the pier, Freddie and LJ, on a Sunday when the weather isn't too lousy. And then LJ is spotted by a flock of kids and they have to stop for ten minutes, which is a very long time on a bad March day, longer still as they are spotted by more and more kids. Children, no more than eight years old. Freddie is appalled at how young they are, how the boybands and a pop celeb like LJ really are performing for kids as in kids, small children.

LJ works the crowd immaculately, sending them away from the pier with warm thoughts of her and the weirdo standing off to the side, shivering.

She suggests leaving immediately for her place in Marbella.

'You can't be a star in this weather,' she says.

For a moment, Freddie knows she is serious, that she really would take off tonight on some private plane, that she is on a journey, but she is going first class. Instead they go back to his place and fuck.

He has to take charge of something in this life, in this cruel town. Once he might have been ashamed to bring a woman back to the flat, but then he's seen LJ's pad and it will be winning no awards and anyway he has no space in his head any more for life's little embarrassments.

And when LJ squeezes into him on the couch and they go at it frontways and sideways and backways, Freddie Dowd has a home on high. He has another wisp of suspicion that LJ turns her back to him for the last big push because he would be too unsightly at the point of orgasm. But the Bird is on the turntable wailing all their pain, blowing it away.

Later, LJ offers to give him any money he wants, and fuck the bank and fuck Paddy and fuck Bricks Melvin and every other lunatic in this business. She tells him about this other guy who was chasing Paddy for years, a guy who owned a cut of Fellaz from the start.

'Paddy offered him ten grand to fuck off but he wanted two-fifty,' she says. 'And it became his life, chasing Paddy. So Paddy has this power over him, like he has over a lot of people. And he makes the guy an offer of a truck with this portable loo on the back that can be set up at special events, like backstage at a festival for the stars to piss in. So the guy thinks he's doing pretty well out of this, driving this loo around the place. And Paddy cracks up when he tells people that the guy was offered some other job, and the guy says, "What – and leave showbusiness?"'

Freddie laughs.

'Take my money,' she says.

It is an offer Freddie can't refuse in the circumstances, but he refuses it. He couldn't take money from Dorothy and he still can't take it.

'I'm going again with Bricks,' he says. 'I still believe in the old bastard.'

'Bastard,' she says.

'I need to know,' he says.

Chapter 19

There are nine others at the meeting in the little hall in the hospital grounds. It's something that fascinates Bricks Melvin about Alcoholics Anonymous, how these meetings could have gone on without him knowing a thing about it for years, all this sobriety happening just yards away from pubs full of drunk people.

He's not new to the rooms. He did a few months a long time ago, but at every meeting he would run into someone he knew out there. Out there where the pubs were open. And eventually he just went drinking with one of them, a painter who went in and out of AA on a seasonal basis. They both had a desire to stop drinking, which is the only thing you need to attend an AA meeting. They had a desire to stop drinking, but they had a bigger desire to drink.

Two men sit at a table, waiting to open the meeting. There is a card on the table with an AA slogan, 'One Day at a Time'. There is a routine, the same in this room as in every AA room in the world. The secretary reads the Twelve Steps and the Twelve Traditions from the Big Book of AA and then it's over to someone who chairs the meeting, sharing for about fifteen minutes his own experience of the bottle. Then it's open to whoever wants to speak, one by one. It always starts on time and it always lasts for an hour. The unchanging rhythm appeals to Bricks after the turbulence of recent days.

Then there's the rhythm of the DART which runs adjacent to the hospital. In this room they are next to the line, so they can hear the trains going by every fifteen minutes on the button. Another solid back-beat for Bricks.

He closes his eyes and listens to the secretary reading out the Twelve Steps and the Twelve Traditions. It's all just words to him. Then it's over to Jimmy, one of the elder lemons, to chair the meeting.

Jimmy thanks everyone for coming on a such a bad night. He tells his story for about fifteen minutes. Jimmy throws in a lot of AA jargon. He works the room like a real pro, landing all the old lines like they were newly minted, like, *If you keep going to the barber, you're bound to get a haircut*; like, *One drink is too many, and twenty is never enough*. But then, Bricks can see that Jimmy's come a long way, from being by his own account a scum-sucking wife-beater to this dapper little guy talking about getting through today without a drink, about things of the spirit. He has made a long journey to be here in this dank room with bare floorboards, but more warmth in it than all the cosy bars out there.

At least that's how Jimmy puts it. But Bricks isn't buying this shit. He still has this little Jimmy down as a scum-sucking son-of-a-bitch bastard wife-beater, period. It's that hanging judge inside everyone, the same vicious little brute who never let Bricks Melvin get away with anything.

Tonight, Bricks is tired of making allowances for people. They never made any for him. They turned their faces away when he was a child, and bastard children like him were herded into institutions. Behind those walls they buggered him for a few bowls of trifle. They rejected him from the start and then they rejected his music.

But that's all over now. The dapper little pro finishes, and everyone claps. Bricks gets in straight away, to get it over with.

'My name is Bricks, and I'm an alcoholic,' he starts.

The room murmurs back at him: 'Hello, Bricks.'

'I've come a long way in the last few days,' he says. 'I guess we've all come a long way to be here, like our time was up and we finally came in.'

He has an urge to talk about his short stay at the Stepaside Centre, but he guesses that these characters might diss it as country club stuff. And anyway, the killing of Dorothy and the getting away with it is so intoxicating, he wants to keep it all to himself.

'I'll keep it short because I know that other people want to get in,' he says. 'Out there, they've already made up their minds who Bricks is and what Bricks does, and right now it's killing me to think that they will never change their minds. Because in here, I am not that person. I am not what they think I am. And I will show them all. I will show them I am just a man who happens to have this disease. And maybe I will get this woman back too. That is my hope. I have just said to her, today, I am doing this programme for myself, and for no one else. But I want you to be with me . . . I still want that. But she's only seventeen so I better shut up now.'

Everyone laughs. Little Jimmy smiles knowingly. Bricks smiles back at him, feeling he's said enough for now, knowing that these alcoholics in this room are the only people who understand what he's up against now, out there. And even they don't understand a damn thing about him.

'Thank you, Bricks,' says Jimmy. 'You want to get in, Mick?'

Bricks listens to Mick, a man well known to him, a highly regarded sound engineer who used to drink until dawn in the Leeson Street clubs. He's been off it three years now, to Bricks a vast stretch. It seems like everyone, even Mick Mannion, one of the Strip's most dedicated drunks, is further on up the road to goodness than he is.

Mick says you have to accept that people are not going to forgive you. You have to be able to take it, and deal with it somehow, and not drink. You have to realize it doesn't work out sometimes, that your woman or your loved ones don't want you to make amends, they just want you to fuck off and die.

Like, just because Mick has changed, just because Mick is sober today, it doesn't mean everyone is going to turn around and say, thank you very much Mick, that's all right then, just don't do it again. And remember, expectations are just resentments under construction.

Mick says there is more freedom in not drinking than in drinking. When you're not drinking, you always have the option of having a drink or staying the way you are. When you're drinking, you have no option but to have another one.

He welcomes Bricks again to the rooms and talks about

the artist in Bricks responding to this new way of life. It involves, after all, a huge creative challenge for Bricks Melvin to re-imagine himself as someone who is clean and sober.

After the meeting, Bricks has a smoke with Mick Mannion at the back of the hall. Mick says he's living out here now. He doesn't work any more because it would probably drive him to drink. At the age of forty, he lost all ambition. He draws the dole and knocks around Dún Laoghaire. He walks the pier and hangs out at the new plaza down by the car ferry, watching the boatloads coming and going, and the new Pavilion theatre being built. He spends hours in the old Protestant church that houses the Maritime Museum, just sitting there in the quiet like some relic of old Dún Laoghaire, thinking about the sea. There are plaques all along the walls commemorating dead seafarers. He thinks of all these guys who perished in these horrible shipwrecks, and how lucky he is to be alive.

'Just keep it simple, one day at a time,' Mick says. 'You can have a life beyond your wildest dreams.'

Bricks is getting this lovely gentle vibe off Mick. So he feels guilty that he is failing to reach the AA standard of rigorous honesty. Mick shakes Bricks by the hand. He tells him he's come to the right place, and he knew he'd get here eventually.

They can hear the train coming. There's an old wooden fence and then a twenty-foot drop to the railway line below. Bricks remarks that they could jump on top of the train from here, like desperadoes. Bricks figures he could send Mick Mannion through the fence with one shove. He could turn away as the train rumbles by, and slip back into the hospital through a side entrance, and Mick would be dead from the fall before the train hit him.

He could do that to Mick, a nice guy. Really, he could.

Within a week, Bricks is the most popular man in the hospital. It seems that he blossoms from the moment Freddie brings the sax up to him, and tells him he's getting another shot at the title. He moves through the building like a celebrity visiting the sick at Christmas. One of the consultants calls it an institutional swagger, this charisma he has.

His face is healing so that it looks funny instead of grotesque. He is sharing his sense of well being with his new buddies in AA. He keeps remembering other things that happened in blackout, including the one he likes telling best, when he hired a builder's crane to take him to the window of a fourteenth-floor flat to give a bottle of Heineken to the girl who lived there.

It was actually Nadine's idea to bring the kid out of a coma. A kid around the same age as her was brought in after a car crash. He was a passenger, the driver was killed. Everyone was on a downer that day, Bricks was sitting on the edge of her bed tootling, and Nadine made a jokey remark about playing the kid's favourite song to bring him out of it, maybe something by Billy Joel.

The idea got around, and soon the kid's family were desperately trying to settle on one song that might touch him deep down, because he didn't go for sweet melodies as such, but Tupac Shakur cranked up to ten.

There was a sort of ethical debate about whether a

hospital patient could have incredibly loud music blasted at him, with *motherfucker* this and *motherfucker* that, and no way of knowing if it would work.

But Bricks just got on with it. He asked for the curtains to be drawn and he asked from time to time for a smoke, as he sat there in the dark improvizing in the most tender tone, like he was having an intimate conversation with an old friend. He said it's all black music anyway, the kid would get it.

The kid was sitting up for the newspaper snappers the next day, with Bricks refusing to pose for pictures, what with his face all smashed up, just asking for a mention for his forthcoming residency at The Crowbar.

After a week, there are some who are calling him a saint.

Nadine is out of bed and walking with the aid of a crutch, enjoying the buzz. The hospital creates its own reality, an enclosed little world in which Bricks Melvin is boss. And it feels natural for Nadine to go with it, to stake her claim, to let it be known that she has the inside track with the main man. But she gives him no answer yet when he says he still wants her. She's seeing a counsellor soon, maybe then she'll know what she wants.

She tells Freddie she doesn't want him coming up every day, she's given him enough hassle. She'll call him if she needs something.

Freddie is locked into another reality beyond the walls, still chasing Paddy Lamb, while the bank chases him. He wants to sell the cars but he hears that no one will buy them, that the economy is cooling down or some such shit, of which he knows nothing. He's not sleeping, frozen with fear at times when he thinks of all the money he owes, and how he might be relying on jazz to get it back. With the economy cooling down.

Paddy's available only on voicemail now, a vital innovation according to LJ, meaning that in an ideal world, the likes of Paddy will never even have an accidental conversation with some deranged musician.

The big industry buzz at the moment is Eva Cassidy, the perfect artist in that she's dead, and so she is guaranteed never to call some hard-working executive to bitch about her royalties. Paddy is excited about this, and won't be dealing with anything else until he comes back from London.

Freddie reads in the paper about Bricks bringing the kid out of the coma. He waits in vain for Nadine to call him on the hotline.

Chapter 20

Working on his cred as an AA regular and a saint to some, Bricks figures he could get away with nearly anything, indefinitely.

He is lying on his bed after tea. He is alone in the ward. The grey-faced old man in the bed beside him died yesterday on his way to the operating theatre. Just the Reaper keeping his hand in.

At last the urge to drink has left him, replaced by this new obsession, to do bad and get away with it. He'll raise it to an art-form in time. He doesn't want to get greedy, but there were thousands and thousands like him who were thrown at random into the gulag, and to even things up a bit for all the lost boys, he might have to do a lot of bad.

There's a doctor here, a consultant, who is nearly as popular as Bricks Melvin at this time because he is a wizard of a medic and a very nice guy. A prick is just a prick, and shit happens. The nice people are worse. The nice people let it happen.

He has his eye on this consultant, who said he had an institutional swagger. Fine words there, straight out of some south Dublin drawing room. No doubt this guy has a brother who is a judge and another one a top shrink, locking them up, signing them in and out of the funny-farm. No doubt he has been protected by privilege all his life, him and his fine words. But there's a fire escape where he goes for a smoke and there's no protection there, just a very long drop. He's a very long, very bony man so he could be offed almost anywhere with the right attitude.

Here is Nadine now, leaning on a crutch, but still as fine as the first night he saw her, giving out all that stuff, that electricity.

On the one hand, she is really getting on his tits traipsing after him all over the hospital. On the other hand, he would love to fuck her like he should have done the first time. It would be sad, to lose all that stuff.

Maybe he is not completely free yet, free of feeling and conscience and sentimentality. Maybe she is holding him back.

She comes in and, for a moment, he thinks she is pissed, she looks so happy. She tries to calm down, to get the words out. She sits on the old man's bed. She is wearing street clothes for the first time since the accident, a new denim jacket and jeans. For a moment, he thinks she is about to check out of the hospital, which annoys him. The thing that annoys him most is that he knows how her story is going to end about five seconds into the telling, but it takes her a lot longer to spit it out.

'Counsellor, right?' she says. 'I see the counsellor and she's fucking brilliant, right? Like, she reads my mind and now I know what I have to do, OK? She says, there's something between me and you but she doesn't know what.

Like, I said you said you still want me, and you're off the drink and all, but she says it can wait. OK, Bricks? Just give it a while, there's so much shit happening, just . . . I need some space. I need some space, man.' She laughs.

Then she starts up again. 'I just feel terrific now, like I want no big scene with anyone for about ten years, no matter how great they are and it's, like, fantastic . . . but, Bricks, I still think you're doing brilliant here, really, I really mean that.'

Bricks bangs a carafe of water off the locker, like he is calling a meeting to order.

'Congratulations,' he says.

Her legs are pumping up and down in a nervous spasm. 'Mad,' she says.

Bricks rolls off the bed and walks to the old-fashioned sash window. He stands with his back to Nadine, looking at the yellowish glow of the lights beyond the hospital walls.

'Feeling good about going out there again?' he says.

Her legs are still going.

'Just some space of my own,' she says.

'You should be terrified,' he says.

He turns around to face her. He tries to get comfortable sitting on the bars of a radiator.

'Counsellor again tomorrow,' she says.

'Watch it. Watch where they're coming from,' he says, like he is giving masterly advice to another patient about something that isn't really his business.

'Think I've got it sussed now,' she says, getting the words out quickly.

'You think?' he says.

217

'Even thinking of giving up smoking,' she says.

'You might be still in shock,' he says.

She lies back on the bed, sinking into the large pillow. She has that big smile at nothing in particular.

'Feeling sort of . . . happy,' she says.

'Fucks should give you something for when they land this shit on you,' he says.

'I . . . am . . . happy,' she says, with a certain sense of awe.

He attempts a smile. 'Do they . . . does the counsellor want to talk to me?' he says.

She lets out a sudden laugh. 'No way. Couldn't handle that.'

Bricks can't get comfortable on the radiator. He moves to the edge of the bed facing Nadine. He thinks he could reach over and take her crutch and batter her senseless.

'They asked about me?' he says quietly.

'A bit,' she says.

'They're good at that, the bastards,' he says. 'Pumping people.'

'It's cool, OK?' she says.

Bricks looks at her solemnly, like a professional sizing up the situation.

'I'll support you, whatever . . .' he says.

'It's cool,' she says.

'Just take it one day at a time,' he says.

She points the crutch playfully at him, like it's a gun.

'Then I'll kill Freddie,' she says.

'You think?' he says.

'Nah, Freddie'll be sweet.'

'It's your shout.'

'You know it's only really dawning on me now,' she says.

'We're loaded. We're really, actually, rich. Well, nearly.'

Bricks bows his head. He can't look at her any more, lying there. There is so much of her, he thinks, so much sex there for him, so much to lose.

'Funny thing,' he says, 'when you're in something like a car crash, it makes you want to live more. In the moment.'

Nadine thinks he is just shooting the breeze. Then he raises his head and gives her a dirty little grin and she starts picking up his hint. It sets her speeding again. She likes the way he lands it out of nowhere.

'Here?' she laughs.

'Just one time,' he drawls, clicking his fingers. 'Just one time, the counsellor didn't say a girl couldn't have fun, just one time.'

Suddenly Nadine remembers her injury.

'Hip,' she groans. 'Sorry, man.'

'Ah, that's a shame,' he says. 'Tomorrow?'

'Busy,' she says, enjoying the to-and-fro.

'Tomorrow is such a long time,' he says.

'I don't see a time . . .' she says, smiling big.

'When the time comes . . .' he says. 'The time comes.'

'Maybe one time,' she whispers.

'Just one time, baby, just one time,' he croons.

Just one time, he thinks, and probably not two when the Gestapo have filled her with this counsellor shit. And then she will have one more cigarette with him at the old fire escape, and then he can go and fuck himself.

Nadine eases herself very carefully off the bed. She starts to limp up and down the ward without the crutch. Then she rests against the windowsill, looking out at the moon.

'Mad,' she says.

'They should give you something, the fucks, they really should give you something,' he repeats.

'No,' she says firmly.

'Valium,' he says. 'Whatever. Fucking brandy.'

'I'm not sick,' she says. 'I am happy.'

'The fucks,' he mutters.

He eyes her. She must be at least six foot and her legs alone are indescribable to him. Maybe once back in Paris when he was playing like a demon and he could describe anything on earth in a few arpeggios. Not any more. One night in Paris long ago he conjured her up, and now he is sure she's getting away from him. Did he just dream her up? If he got a grip on that long hair would she scream? She seems to be partly talking to the moon and partly to him.

'I am happy,' she goes on, 'this is my life, it is happening to me.'

Bricks clears his throat. He's not entirely sure if she knows he's there any more.

'All my life, Freddie fills me with . . . stuff,' she says. 'Freddie stuff.'

She goes silent for a while, like she is remembering every jazz record, every old movie, every good book that Freddie gave her whether she liked it or not.

Bricks breaks the silence. 'Freddie Dowd is one of the few good guys in this town . . .'

She cuts across his standard tribute to Freddie Dowd. 'I know that, OK?' she says quickly.

Now that the words are out, and they can't be taken back, she seems to relax completely.

Bricks just listens. Him and the moon.

'I know he's not a fuck, like Paddy Lamb. I like it that he

knows about things that these fucks don't know about. All the jazz, the books, all that stuff. I like it, OK?'

It seems to be a challenge as well as a question. Bricks responds.

'OK,' he says.

'He'll be sweet about all this. He'll be cool.'

'OK.'

'I've got this burn. Dorothy lost the head, nearly killed us all in the car once. So this is all nothing, it's baby stuff. Freddie will laugh at this. He'll be sweet.'

Bricks makes affirmative noises. She is making him feel things he doesn't want to feel. He has a son out there somewhere, who would be seventeen. If anything happened to his son, to Aaron, the last light would go out on Bricks Melvin.

Even that nice doctor who hangs out at the fire escape is somebody's son. Then again Bricks Melvin was somebody's son, and they drove away with him one day and dropped him off in hell.

Nadine keeps talking, mostly to herself now it seems.

'All my life, it's been Freddie. I go to bed and I know he's there, with the headphones on. I wake up and I know he's there. I see his afro coming round the door, and I hear the jazz starting up inside. He gets me off to school always with a couple of quid, you know? Don't know where he gets a couple of quid he just gets it, selling albums or selling his body, I never ask. He sold his body, you know? He sold his body for medical experiments. Testing new drugs. I got nightmares, waking up screaming, with the car on fire, and he would sit up all night with me, all night till dawn. And he'd tell me about it, how half the world was walking around because of all the drugs he took, but I was the first, I was the special one. He'd make me laugh. He'd do anything for me, you know? Anything except get his fuzz cut off,' she says.

'Right,' Bricks responds.

'But he can't do my life for me right? This is my life, my own thing, it's happening to me. It's not happening to you, Bricks. OK, it is, but it's still my thing. Not a movie and not a book and not some bunch of jazzers taking the piss.'

'The fucks,' Bricks says supportively.

A couple of nurses breeze into the room. They set about the old man's bed.

'Another customer?' Bricks says.

'Broken leg,' one of the nurses says.

Nadine turns away from the window. She limps back to collect her crutch.

'I don't expect too much,' she says to Bricks. 'Freddie does that, and people let him down.'

'Punters,' Bricks adds.

Bricks watches her hobbling out the door of the ward. He would have given a lot, maybe any talent he ever had, if a child of his had talked about him the way she talked about Freddie.

'Now boys,' the brother would say, 'you will one day have boys of your own and you will know all about it.' He can still hear those voices from the gulag, mocking him. All the bitterness that fills him now, he would burn it up tomorrow in one cold act of destruction. For the boys.

Chapter 21

It was something that Olivia said. Something about conjugal rights.

Freddie bumped into her down at the shopping centre and he suggested coffee, because he owed her one. So she told him again that he sounded exactly like Nadine and, while they were queuing at the cafeteria, she said that Nadine's hip was healing well and that she could still have children and they would all look like him.

They sat down and Olivia said a lot of other things too, but Freddie didn't hear much of it. Just the outline, how Bricks started this campaign that morning to be moved into a room with Nadine, like man and wife. He was bugging the authorities about his conjugal rights.

Freddie is in this weird state again where something that has terrified him all his life is actually happening to him this minute. And this time it has turned him into a zombie, nodding and smiling and stirring his coffee.

It seems perfectly clear to Olivia at least that there is some dark shit between Nadine and Bricks. Dazed, he half-hears Olivia banging on about how their relationship makes sense to her in a strange sort of way, as they are both special people, Bricks with his great talent, Nadine with her great beauty. Olivia says they tend to find one another, these special people. It all seems clear to Olivia, in fact she sounds all for it.

So is Freddie finally going to face the truth that Bricks has fucked his daughter under his own roof, or does he need video footage of them making the beast? The fear of the thing has been replaced by the thing itself. The guy on the Kawasaki has come, and taken her away. Except he was no fan of Motorhead. And he came in a taxi. And he came because Freddie asked him to call. And he stayed because Freddie insisted.

Sure, what Olivia says might just be Bricks going off on one, fucking with the system, demanding his rights just out of habit, like a long-term prisoner with nothing better to do. He wouldn't need Nadine's permission for that, he mightn't even feel the need to tell her about it. But Freddie is weary of reading the signs and coming up with the answer that causes him no pain. It's now for the truth and later for the garbage.

And now an image of Bricks that he has been suppressing for a long time comes into his mind, the scene in the alley off Lesson Street when Bricks kept kicking that bouncer in the head, that night when he was so far gone he was capable of anything. Freddie brought home a jazz genius and a funny, funny man, but he also brought that guy, that mad bastard with no limits. The guy that LJ feared – LJ, who is afraid of nothing.

Through the zombie-haze he hears Olivia talking about Nadine's companion, about Bricks the giver of life, who brought that kid out of a coma.

Maybe Freddie knew it all along. Maybe he just couldn't admit it to himself that morning when he came back with the ninety-nine, like a spare prick.

Olivia is starting to annoy him now, banging on about babies, about spring being a time of rebirth. She's from the Philippines, she must be full of that Catholic shit, Freddie thinks. He keeps nodding and smiling, a puppet with his wires all tangled up, because his soul seems to have frozen over and this is the only physical movement left to him.

'You'll be up today?' Olivia says.

'How is she today?' he says casually.

'She says she's taking it one day at a time,' Olivia says.

Olivia leaves him nodding and smiling and staring like a fairground automaton.

'My soul,' he whispers.

He starts to imagine the two of them up there, a couple, Bricks sitting on the edge of the bed smoking and telling her to play it as it lays. He is able to stop himself before it gets out of control, this imagining. He reckons they would take too much pleasure in seeing him out of control.

He takes the mobile out of the breast pocket of his denim jacket. She didn't call him about anything. Like, what bad shit has to happen before she figures he's worth a phone call?

She answers after one ring.

'Hi!' she says, sounding up.

'I know,' he says, with what he hopes is no expression at all.

'You know?' she says.

'Olivia,' he says.

225

'I'm seeing a counsellor,' she says. 'I'm fine, totally.'

'And . . . eh . . . your buddy Bricks. Will he be seeing a counsellor too? Like a sex counsellor?'

'Listen it was nothing,' she says. 'It'll be cool OK?'

'I knew,' he says.

'I kinda knew . . .'

'Deep down,' he says.

'You knew,' she says.

'I will support you whatever you want to do in your life,' he says.

'That's exactly what Bricks says,' she says.

'And what you want to do,' he says, 'is you want to say goodbye to Bricks, right now.'

He senses immediately that he has lost it. Nadine is silent.

Freddie fills the silence, he can't stop himself.

'I saw him once nearly kick a guy to death,' he says.

Silence.

'You can't wreck your life . . .'

She hangs up on him.

He wants to run up there straight away. He can feel it all getting away from him, seventeen years finishing in the shit, and still he doesn't even know for sure if this thing with Bricks is still going full blast, or if Bricks is just winding everyone up with this conjugal rights shit. But some instinct for survival keeps him from going there, some desperate vision of him making everything worse with everything he says.

He is able to pull back. Against all the craziness in his head, he gives it until tomorrow. And if he's still feeling like this tomorrow, he'll go up there anyway.

He stumbles around the shopping centre for a while, wandering into shops on the top floor, getting odd looks like he is a known shoplifter or just the local weirdo having a very bad hair day.

He starts to remember various presents he bought Nadine in these shops, a book, or a camera, or a watch, seventeen years of birthdays and Christmases. All that time. All that hope.

And in the end, after seventeen hard years, she gets into something that she knows will rip him apart. It's like she's saying, you know that life you never had because of me? Well, fuck you. You know that money you never took from Dorothy? You missed out there, buddy. You know the money you took from her to send me to the posh school? Well, look how I turned out, arsehole. You know all that jazz you made me listen to? I liked it so much, I fucked one of them at the first opportunity.

The more he finds himself riffing like this, the more Freddie feels like a chump. He finds himself getting silly, thinking he would be making a big point by refusing to visit the hospital any more, and then remembering that he's not wanted anyway.

This is the real killer, that she didn't call him, that she didn't rate him enough after all these years to give it to him straight. He's tried to do all the right things, all the hard things, and it has eventually left him wandering around the top floor of Dún Laoghaire shopping centre like an imbecile. A looper. A clown.

He needs a drink. He needs to do something easy for a change, just to sit for a while in a pub with a pint of Guinness in front of him. He never liked going to pubs in

Dún Laoghaire out of some paranoid sense that it would give the straights some ammunition to take Nadine away from him, alerted by shocking reports that he would take the child with him down to the dole office where they would while away the hours with a couple of good books.

Straights. It's a word he hasn't used in years. It was one of their first differences of opinion, when he was banging on about straights one day, and Nadine said it was embarrassing. So he stopped using that word, and started using suits instead.

He strolls with his hands in his pockets into the Ferryman for a pint.

'Give me a pint,' he says quietly to the barman. It even sounds easy to say it.

He gets twenty Rothmans from the machine at the end of the lounge. A lot of people are smoking. It's the first day of the Cheltenham festival and there's a buzz about the place, the punters coming in and out of the bookie's a few doors down, absorbed by the racing, the struggle to pick a winner.

Freddie sits at the bar listening to the punters' bullshit, noticing a face wracked with tension, the pain of a punter who is backing another loser, who reckons that if it wasn't for bad luck, he'd have no luck at all.

'Did you ever notice there's one guy who seems to have all the winners?' he says to the barman.

Nadine once said to him, Did you ever notice that people around here do nothing except notice things? She claimed that she was fourteen before she met anyone who had a proper job.

Yes, it's time for Freddie to leave that life behind. It just gets too hard, keeping the faith. Too hard, trying to interest people in the good stuff, when they insist time after time that they want to hear shite. Too hard, waiting for the magic that makes it all right. Too hard, to be sure of so little. Too hard, too hard for too long.

He drinks his pint of Guinness quickly. He feels this lightness coming over him. He finishes his pint. He walks briskly out into the main street and heads for home. He feels that this is the last time he will do this, walk up the hill to the traffic lights and around the next corner to Waterloo Terrace. But he doesn't feel sentimental at all.

There's a can of Guinness in the fridge. Just what he wants. He opens it and sups at it while he takes the world-wide rights to the works of Bricks Melvin out of an atlas where it was waiting to be framed.

He chuckles at the way he has lived, never owning a briefcase, not even for show. The most useless chancers in the business can rise to the old attaché case, but not Freddie Dowd. Old Freddie could keep it all in his head.

He sits at the table drinking his can and remembering the night that Nadine ran out of The Bailey and Bricks sat across this table turning yellow, signing over his life's work as a friendly gesture. Though it seems clear now he was just so desperate for a beer he would have signed away his own son that night. He has a son somewhere, the fucker, a son the same age as Nadine.

But Freddie has the rights.

He chooses the powder-blue Mercedes. Freddie Dowd, here on business. He drives down through the town to the Royal Marine Hotel. He sits in the car for a few moments looking at all the yachts in the harbour. All the time, it is getting easier for him to see himself out there.

He skips into the old white mansion and up to the reception desk where they know him a bit. They let him send faxes. He scribbles a note at the end of Bricks's contract, saying he can be paged at the Royal Marine for another hour. Then he faxes the page to Paddy Lamb at Kilbrittan Hill.

The lounge is quiet after lunch. He takes a table in the corner. He asks the waitress to bring him afternoon tea and then changes his order to a pint of Guinness. She seems a bit suspicious of him. He's had enough of that shit too.

He is finishing his leisurely pint when Paddy Lamb comes in. Paddy looks around the room and gives a little jump of delight when he sees Freddie in the corner. Freddie remains seated, offering no handshake, just a look of contentment.

It used to come over him as he daydreamed about jazz, this look. Now there's a hint of something else in it, something meaner. Some inner certainty that this is going to work for him, that there's nothing stopping him now. He knew that Paddy Lamb would be down, and here he is. He knows now, there's no telling the good guys from the bad guys.

'Another Guinness?' Paddy says.

'Thanks, Paddy,' Freddie says.

Paddy shouts up for two pints. He looks almost dangerously brown from wherever he's been. He is wearing an off-white linen suit and a Hawaiian shirt and the merry look of a man who has been laughing uncontrollably all through lunch.

'I'm drinking too much,' Paddy says, a bit slurred. 'LJ Carew blows me out for you, you fucking bourgeois bastard and then this fucking polo-player's been staying with me, asking me to go to some fucking bullfight in Spain. Hotel booked and all, five star. He fought me once over a woman, can you believe that? He beat the shit out of me.'

The waitress brings the two pints. Freddie pays for them.

'I got your attention,' he says.

Paddy watches the waitress walking away.

'Long legs and large breasts,' he says. 'Any man would fight for that.'

Freddie lights a cigarette. 'I knew you'd come,' he says.

'You stole my woman,' Paddy says, aiming an invisible duelling pistol at his rival. But Freddie can detect no malice in it. Just a great weariness after a long losing battle.

He knows that feeling.

'I owe you one,' Freddie says.

'I don't hear from you enough,' Paddy says.

Freddie waits for a punchline. There is none.

'Your people hear from me nearly every day,' he says.

'I always said if I ever amounted to anything in this business . . .'

'Right, Paddy,' Freddie says.

'This . . .' Paddy says, taking the fax out of his inside pocket and reading it through like every syllable is precious.

'I want to bring something to the party,' Freddie says.

'This . . . is significant,' Paddy says.

'This idea of yours, to promote Bricks Melvin as the new Johnny Shine. It's so crazy it just might work,' Freddie says, deadpan.

Paddy starts to play with his chest hair.

'You said it, friend,' Paddy says.

231

'Fifty-fifty?' Freddie says.

Paddy looks away, as if caught unawares by a rush of emotion.

'This is not about money, my friend,' he says.

'I know,' Freddie says. 'It's the principle of the thing.'

'It's very sweet of you.'

'It's a big step for me,' Freddie says. 'I used to wonder why a really big player like Paddy Lamb could be arsed with the Johnny Shine albums, could be arsed haggling over every penny with some poor boyband bimbo, and then it came to me – it's the principle of the thing.'

'I couldn't take more than twenty-five per cent of Bricks,' Paddy says. 'It's free money. Hardly any costs. There must be twenty years of material in the can.'

'So, stick a photo of Bricks on the cover looking a bit mysterious . . .' Freddie says.

'Send him out on the road . . .' Paddy says.

'The *Late Late Show* . . .' Freddie says

'Officer material . . .' Paddy says.

'And the Irish in Britain have their new Johnny Shine,' Freddie says. 'Well, the same Johnny Shine, with no Johnny around to fuck it up.'

Paddy orders a bottle of Dom Perignon. He takes a white envelope from his inside pocket. He pushes it across the table to Freddie. The envelope is open. Freddie finds inside it a cheque made out to Mr Freddie Dowd for two point seven million pounds only. Sterling.

Paddy grabs Freddie tightly by the wrist. He looks deep into his eyes.

'Why?' he says.

'You're Paddy Lamb, and you need to know why?'

'As a . . . a partner?'

'OK, partner,' Freddie says. 'Bricks has been knocking a few back with Nadine.'

Paddy squeezes his wrist and then releases it.

'Mother of God,' he says quietly.

'And one thing leads to another,' Freddie says.

Paddy seems knocked back by this. He sits back in his chair like he needs to put some physical distance between himself and such awfulness.

'We've all been down there,' Paddy says. 'Some of the best people.'

Freddie nods. 'No more about it, OK?' he says. 'Not today.'

It occurs to him that he has no inside pocket in his denim jacket. He calmly puts the cheque back into the envelope and folds it in half and slides it into the back pocket of his jeans.

'You need to party, my friend,' Paddy says.

Freddie feels mellow now with the Guinness and the first glass of Dom Perignon, drinking and only half-hearing Paddy obligingly changing the subject to the girl with long legs and big breasts and talking about musicians, how they are a special breed who get used to anything after a while, a bit like the homeless.

He half-hears Paddy telling that story about the guy who drives around with the loo on the back of a truck. He gets Paddy's rap about Andy Williams again. He recalls being so impressed by the first version in Paddy's office, he believed for a while that Paddy genuinely cared about guys like Andy, and was seriously upset about Andy doing it to send some lawyer's daughter through college. He understands, now, that Paddy is passionately in love with this business. He just hates all the people in it.

And he hears something new in Paddy's beautifully pitched voice, a new respect amid all that old bollocks about Freddie Dowd being up there and Paddy Lamb being down here. But mainly he is thinking about the cheque in his back pocket and hearing the strange music like he has never heard it before, taking him to a little spot on Easy Street.

'I want to go to the barber,' Freddie says.

'Shave?' Paddy says.

'Let's say, I'm on a journey,' Freddie says.

'Tommy downstairs is an old friend of mine,' Paddy says. 'He lets me drink in the chair.'

'Let's try Tommy then,' Freddie says.

They gather up their drinks and take them downstairs to the barber shop. It's made to look like an old-style premises with pictures of prize-fighters on the walls. Tommy himself is chatting to a couple of assistants wearing white shirts and black dickey-bows. Tommy seems young to be the boss of a place like this. To Freddie he bears an uncanny resemblance to Engelbert Humperdinck.

'Tommy,' Paddy says, 'special friend.' He's waving the bottle of champagne in Tommy's direction.

'Trouble,' Tommy says, flashing a big Engelbert smile.

'I want to introduce you to Freddie Dowd,' Paddy says. 'A very nice man and a very talented man.'

Tommy sizes up Freddie's fuzz.

'What can I do you for?' he says.

'Take it off,' Freddie says.

'Trim?' Tommy says.

'Like that,' Freddie says, indicating a picture of boxer Steve Collins with a crewcut.

Paddy whistles. One of the assistants ushers Freddie into the chair. He drapes a large white towel across his shoulders. He starts to wash and shampoo. Freddie's afro seems to fill the sink. Paddy and Tommy smile their big smiles.

'The Filth,' Tommy says. 'They're playing Chelsea this evening.'

'This guy calls Man United "the Filth",' Paddy explains.

Freddie grunts.

The assistant is working up a huge lather.

Paddy pours champagne for Tommy.

'Hey, Freddie!' he shouts. 'You want to go and see the Filth?'

Freddie gives a little thumbs up. He would like to do the first thing that comes into his head, like everyone else seems to do.

'I'm a Liverpool man,' Tommy says. 'I wouldn't be seen dead in Manchester.'

'Snip, snip, Freddie, and then off on Paddy's little aeroplane?' Paddy says.

Freddie grunts again with approval.

The assistant washes the shampoo out with a jet of hot water and hands the operation over to Tommy.

'You a fan of the Filth, Freddie?' Tommy says.

Freddie looks at himself in the mirror, his hair much smaller for being soaked and combed out straight, his heart much lighter now in these last few moments before Freddie Dowd's famous afro disappears for ever, extinct, taking with it a world of wishes that never came true.

'I like Dwight Yorke,' Freddie says.

Paddy sits in the next chair, laughing.

'This fucking bourgeois bastard steals everything,' he says. 'Dwight tells him about the cars he likes to drive and next thing you know Freddie steals Dwight's idea. And the minute he gets his bourgeois arse into a Ferrari, he's stealing Paddy Lamb's woman. I shit you not.'

'Fair fucks,' Tommy says. He is cutting large parts of Freddie's hair very quickly. Freddie admires his professionalism, the fact that he passes no remarks on the old hair, like it is a private matter between Freddie and his God.

Paddy is telling the guys about the boyband bloke who goes around with the loo on the back of the truck. He gets a big laugh when he delivers the line about someone offering a better job and the guy saying, '*What – and leave showbusiness?*' The way the line is landed, practised to a point of perfection, Freddie laughs along.

Tommy is finished with the major chopping. Now he is snipping and shaping. In the mirror, Freddie is starting to see a person he could grow to live with. There is still too much eccentricity around the eyes, a softness, but he is starting to see that resemblance to Nadine that Olivia saw, her darkness, an expression that says, I know something that you will never know.

But where is her mystery now? Freddie is visited by a terrible scene of Nadine with a child crawling all over her, or twins for Christ's sake, stuck in some kip with Bricks on the booze, too proud to take any money, no time at all for the millionaire Freddie Dowd.

He was in that place himself a long time ago, and he's fucked if Nadine is going there too. But today he is going to do something for himself for a change, like have another glass of champagne to celebrate his new hair and to look forward to a night of football in the Theatre of Dreams with his partner Paddy Lamb and Paddy's big cheque in his arse pocket.

A tray arrives from above with champagne and Guinness. Compliments of the house. Paddy winks at Freddie in the mirror.

'Now that you're loaded, you get everything for free,' Paddy says.

The assistants are given the Guinness. They all stand around marvelling at Freddie's new look, his new head.

Freddie is feeling giddy on the Dom P. He starts telling a convoluted story about Patrick Kavanagh, and how Kavanagh kept slagging the fuck out of this other poet Padraic Colum, and when he was asked why he kept doing this he said he did it for no reason other than for spite.

'That's what I'll say when they ask about my hair,' Freddie says, enjoying the barber-shop banter, the guy thing.

Paddy pulls him up on this the minute they get into the cab on the way to the airport.

'You're a sophisticated guy,' he says. 'Paddy Lamb is not very sophisticated. And never in a barber shop.'

They pass the hospital on the way. Freddie is still drinking a glass of champagne. Somehow, the baleful gods are letting him know that in the place where it really counts, his money is no good. And tomorrow that world of shit will still be there. But today he is flying. And he figures he is probably pissed already. Paddy seems to him like a protector now, a guide to life unlimited.

237

'You will note that we are in a taxicab instead of a limo,' Paddy says. 'You'd never get the rock'n'roll guys in a taxicab. They preach power to the people and then they make it their business to avoid meeting the people at all costs. The boybands are working class, the salt of the earth. That's why I love working with them.'

'No Charlie for me, OK?' Freddie says.

'Not using it anyway,' Paddy says.

'Nosebleeds?'

'Oh . . . airport security, all that fucking shit.'

They are on the motorway now, a free run to the airport just before the rush hour. Freddie keeps seeing himself in the rear-view mirror. He is increasingly satisfied with his crewcut.

He is finishing another bottle of champagne as the cab drops them at the departure lounge and Paddy leads the way through the crowds to the more peaceful quarters where the big boys slip aboard their private planes.

The inside of Paddy's jet reminds Freddie of a comfortable little pub. He sits up on a high stool at the small bar. He reaches across for a pint glass and puts it under the Guinness tap.

'You're allowed to go behind the bar,' Paddy says.

Paddy fills the pint and then another for himself. He takes the drinks to one of the long cream-coloured seats that remind Freddie of an upmarket lounge where people sit in a semi-circle on Friday night letting it rip.

'I don't like drink, you know?' he says, starting his new pint.

Paddy splutters. 'Just tell me when you've had enough,' he says.

Paddy gets comfortable on the seat, lying on his side like an emperor about to receive a mouthful of grapes. Freddie tries the lotus position but then sits upright when the pilot slides the door of the cockpit aside.

'Come on, United,' the pilot says.

'This is Neighbour,' Paddy says.

In shirtsleeves and with a strong Dublin accent, Neighbour seems more like a middle-aged taxi driver than an aviator.

'Nice one, Neighbour,' Paddy says. 'Neighbour, this is Freddie. He's looking for the dancing girls. Where the fuck are you hiding them my friend?'

'Short notice,' Neighbour says.

Freddie is mesmerized by the lights of the cockpit.

'You want to sit up with the pilot?' Paddy says.

'No thanks,' Freddie says, embarrassed.

'Neighbour needs watching,' Paddy says. 'The fucker's been running drugs for the fucking CIA all across Latin America. And he still can't arrange a couple of whores for me and my friend.'

He and Neighbour seem almost ecstatic with the banter. Freddie is catching it too.

'Can we bring a couple of them on the way back?' he says. 'A couple of whores?'

Paddy and Neighbour look at him with mock horror. Freddie lights a cigarette.

'Put out that fucking fag first,' Neighbour says.

Paddy gets an ashtray behind the bar. He gives it to Freddie.

'We can only drink on the ground, and take drugs, and fuck. No smoking,' he says.

239

'Come on, United,' Neighbour says, sliding the door shut.

'You'll get the hang of it,' Paddy says.

They are halfway to Manchester when Paddy brings up the whores again. 'You're a horny little bastard, stealing my woman and then looking for whores.'

'Did you . . . did LJ ever go on one of these trips?'

'Did we fuck up here? What do you think?'

'I'll ask her,' Freddie says.

Paddy takes a mobile out of the pocket of his linen jacket and offers it to Freddie.

'Go for it,' he says.

'Don't think so,' Freddie says.

Paddy breaks up laughing. 'Maybe on the way back,' he says.

'Could I really call her from up here?' Freddie says.

Paddy hands him the phone. 'Magic,' he says.

'I do need to check in,' Freddie says.

'Tell her Paddy Lamb is a man of honour. Tell her he's a man who pays his debts,' Paddy says with an aristocratic flourish.

'I was thinking about telling her . . . you know . . . about Nadine and all that. Before Bricks puts it in the fucking paper.'

Paddy laughs again. 'Nice one,' he says.

'I'm serious,' Freddie says.

'Nice one, about Bricks putting it in the paper,' he says.

'Bricks is all over the paper these days. Bringing people out of comas.'

'It wouldn't make any difference if he put it in the paper. LJ doesn't read the papers, as you know.'

'No?'

240

Paddy leans forward and lowers his voice as if others might be listening.

'She can't read, as you know,' he says.

Paddy goes to the bar and selects a bottle of Bushmills. He pours two large glasses and gives one to Freddie.

'She told me,' Freddie says.

He sips the whiskey. It seems to go straight to his brain, turning it to mush.

Paddy inhales his whiskey.

'Amazing woman, to get where she is, not knowing her name on a signpost.'

Freddie feels dizzy. He is swaying backwards and forwards like he is on a ship instead of a plane.

'She told me, as a joke,' he says.

'It's no joke, my friend,' Paddy says.

They are starting the descent to Manchester. Freddie staggers into one of the single seats and fastens his seatbelt. From this point until they reach the hospitality suite at Old Trafford and all through the first half and on through half-time and into the second half, they talk of nothing else in these drunken repetitive patterns except whether LJ is really illiterate, as Paddy says, or whether she just jokes about it, as Freddie insists.

They nearly got run over by a mounted policeman outside the ground but they hardly even acknowledged it, because Freddie, at the time, thought he'd cracked it, remembering how LJ read the Chinese menu the first time they met. Paddy insists in his own pissed way that she was just showing off.

Under the Munich Clock, waiting to be admitted into the VIP enclosure, Freddie thinks he has cracked it. No way would she be able to read the idiot-boards or the autocue or whatever the TV bastards call it, if she couldn't read. Paddy triumphantly reminds him that LJ is the lady who remembers everything, everything except the bad things.

They are seeing only flashes of the game on the closed circuit screen in the hospitality suite. United are winning, which cranks up the mood of all the Irish corporate guys in the suite, making Freddie more demented as he tries to argue with Paddy above the shouting, convinced now that he is on a ship or that he is losing the power of his legs when he attempts to walk to the bathroom.

Guinness, champagne, whiskey and now Man United red wine are churning up inside him. He is smoking incessantly. Paddy is offering him the mobile, saying there's only one way to find out, just ring the woman and ask her the bastard question: *Can you read?*

Freddie sways through the corporate entertainment types who are filling him with all sorts of hate, and across to the corporate bathroom to think about it. He looks at himself in the mirror. He looks like one of them.

He takes the cheque out of his back pocket. Two point seven million pounds only. Sterling. He has a mad urge to flush it down the toilet. But he thinks, no, that would be playing into their hands.

He manoeuvres his way back to Paddy. The crazy debate starts up again. He can't stand it any more. He rings LJ.

She answers straight away. 'Hello?'

'It's Freddie,' he shouts.

A huge roar goes up and subsides before the collective orgasm. United have nearly scored again.

'Call you back,' he says.

In the suite, they are groaning at the action replay.

Freddie takes another gulp of red wine. It seems to be going down and then running straight out his pores. He rubs his forehead. It is wet with sweat. It feels like the alcohol is oozing out of him.

'Do it in the toilet,' Paddy shouts. Paddy is sweating too.

Freddie makes another move to the bathroom. Paddy goes with him.

He rings LJ again.

'Hello, Freddie?' she says.

'I can't talk,' he shouts. 'I'm here in Manchester with Paddy.'

It's quieter in the bathroom, but after shouting for about two hours solid, Freddie can't stop shouting.

'I can hear you,' she says.

'I can't talk,' he shouts. 'Corporate fuckers all round me here. Listen, quick question right? And listen, it doesn't matter to me one way or the other. It's a mad question right? Listen, are you able, as it were, to read?'

There is no reply.

'Hello?' he shouts.

'Yes?' she says.

'Yes, you are able to read?' he shouts.

'No, I am not able to read,' she says.

'You're not?' he shouts.

'No,' she says.

Freddie looks at Paddy, who is going scarlet with the intensity of it. Freddie can't help himself. He gets a fit of laughing. He starts thinking about the dinner party crowd dissing LJ for having no books in her pad. He thinks about all the fuss over *Catch-22*.

The more he tries to say something to LJ, to explain that there's nothing funny about it except that there's some funny aspects to it when you look at it a certain way, the more he is seized by another overwhelming wave until he is helpless, hysterical, weeping with laughter and drink.

'Goodbye, Freddie,' she says.

And she is gone.

Freddie doesn't get to meet Dwight Yorke in the players' lounge. He doesn't get out of the bathroom for the rest of the night. He is still vomiting when it seems impossible that there could be anything else inside him to throw up.

Paddy is drunk but still capable. The drink is working for him. He stays in the bathroom, sacrificing another rap with Dwight to be with Freddie. When he looks in the mirror he sees a nice man, noble after the battle.

He nurses Freddie through it and sits with him all the way back to Dublin, telling him he's rich now, and there will be other women, women with long legs and large breasts.

'We've all been down there,' he keeps saying. 'Some of the best people.'

He takes Freddie back to the Royal Marine Hotel. The porter helps him carry Freddie upstairs, looking like he is mortally wounded. He undresses Freddie, and puts him to bed.

Paddy sees the cheque sticking out of Freddie's back pocket. He has a bad thought, but he thinks about LJ, a free woman again, and he suppresses it. He is already up on the deal.

Chapter 22

Some say there'll be a statue of Bricks Melvin in the front hall. Olivia says it. A lot of the patients are saying it. Even the counsellor is saying it. Nadine is taking this seriously, because the counsellor was pretty cool about everything else. At first she looked like a bit of a nun-type, but she soon started talking about interesting stuff, like loss and low self-esteem and needing space, taking time out from relationships to work on yourself – all of which seem strangely exciting to Nadine, like they must be about someone else with an interesting life.

Today the counsellor took her through it all again, no decisions at this time, or even in the next week, about anything, and definitely not about Bricks, because she felt that Nadine was just too happy to be thinking straight right now. She even told Nadine why she was happy. Something to do with being released from an intense relationship with Freddie, where she was cut off from the world. Something about finding herself in a community at last and being accepted, just someone else trying to get well.

It's a happy community these days, because Bricks

Melvin is wandering the corridors like St Francis of Assisi with better tunes. He is not pressing the flesh, he still refuses to touch another human being, but he is drawing everyone towards him with some inner light, his proven powers of healing.

Nadine forgets sometimes that she is here to be healed. At times she regrets that she didn't get a worse injury, maybe a broken leg that would keep her up here longer. She is even enjoying the hospital food, just the fact that it comes at exactly the same time every day. She likes the routine.

She figures she is feeling together enough to take time out and work on herself. And that Bricks will be cool about it, despite what he says about still wanting her.

Fact is, she feels less tied to him every minute. It's like he belongs to everyone now.

The man who is going to give her all the grief is Freddie. Every minute she is expecting him to march in here and start giving it loads. He leaves a message on the front desk that he'll definitely be up today, like it's taking him twenty-four hours to think up enough shit to throw at her.

Nadine sits on her bed, reading through her leaflets, waiting for him. It's another let-down. She always thought that if she got into some hassle like this, Freddie would be a sweetheart. Instead he starts telling her what to do, like some old bogger.

Freddie comes in around four. He can't be seen behind a huge bunch of flowers. Then he can be seen but it takes almost a full minute for Nadine to accept that this man with the crewcut and the powder-blue suit and the white shirt and the powder-blue tie is her father, Freddie Dowd.

He just sits at the end of the bed, saying nothing. There is nothing to be said.

Freddie, speechless, takes the cheque for two point seven million out of his pocket and hands it to her. She takes it from his trembling hand. She glances at it and hands it back to him quickly like she is afraid of getting an electric shock from it.

He tries to speak. She looks at him intently, watching his lips move, encouraging him to get it out. He starts to cough, a desperate smoker's cough. It seems to bring with it the fumes of alcohol, so strange coming out of Freddie.

The coughing ends and then it looks like he is going to throw up. He retches, but nothing comes out. Nadine wants to get a bedpan but she is transfixed by what she is seeing, and what it might mean.

The retching makes his eyes fill up. He blinks away the tears. She offers him a glass of water form the bedside locker but he shakes his head. Then he speaks, so softly.

'Later for the garbage,' he says.

He moves towards her and gives her a little peck on the cheek before retreating to the end of the bed again in what looks like shame.

'You're . . . eh . . . you're looking well,' she says.

He looks away with a wistful expression, as if he would like to make some comment on his appearance, but the subject is too large, and it is still too soon after the event.

'Sorry . . . about yesterday,' he says.

Nadine nods solemnly. 'OK,' she says.

'You'll have that apartment now,' he says.

'Could I ask you something?' she says.

'Uh-huh,' he says.

'You know the way you look . . .' she says.

'This is me now,' he cuts in. 'This is who I am.'

'It's different,' she says.

'I'm different,' he says, with a little burst of conviction.

They both go silent. Bricks has entered the room. He holds his hands up against his chest, both a greeting and some sort of an apology.

'Bricks,' Freddie whispers.

Bricks stands against the wall, his head bowed. Either he can't bear to look at Freddie out of embarrassment, or because the new Freddie is too much. Nadine can't stand the silence.

'Bricks . . . Bricks is different too,' Nadine says.

Freddie thinks about it. 'I hear great things,' he says.

'Load of shite,' Bricks says.

'Don't let this fool you,' Freddie says, referring to his new suit. 'I still love the old jazz.'

'I'm getting it back, you know,' Bricks says. 'My tone . . .'

Freddie considers this. 'I love what you do,' he says.

'Raising the dead,' Nadine laughs.

'But a man's got to make a living,' Freddie says.

'Yeah,' Bricks says.

Freddie stands up. He brushes a few specks off his powder-blue suit. He goes face to face with Bricks.

'A man's got to ply his trade,' he says quietly.

'Yeah,' Bricks says.

'You need a new direction.'

'Yeah?'

'I've arranged it. With Paddy.'

'Yeah?'

'Jazz is over. The folks won't go there any more.'

Freddie turns and leaves the room with an almost military abruptness. He looks back at Nadine and raises a little fist of solidarity. Skipping down the stairs he thinks he did the right thing, and then he thinks he did the wrong thing. And then he knows it was the only thing to do.

'Ah, that's a shame,' Bricks says. From the window of Nadine's room he can see Freddie driving out the front gate in the powder-blue Mercedes that matches his suit.

Nadine joins him. 'Was that really him?' she says.

'I gave him all the rights. Technically.'

'Freddie is actually ripping you off?'

'Ah, it's a shame,' he says again. He sounds more resigned than angry, like he has heard that some distant relative hasn't long to live.

'You gave him the rights, like, as a present?' she says.

'Ah, he's been through a lot,' Bricks says.

'You reckon he's gone, like, crazy?' she says.

'It's very hard to tell,' Bricks says, almost with admiration.

She squeezes his hand in sympathy. He directs it on to his dick, hard already. She is stunned for a moment. Instinctively she moves her hand away but he tightens his grip and directs it back again. She leaves it there this time.

She hears his voice from last night coming back to her, saying just one time, baby just one time.

'So long, Freddie,' she says.

Bricks forces her down on the bed. Or maybe she is dragging him down. There's nothing much to take off, just a couple of dressing gowns. It seems important to throw

249

them off anyway, to be naked above the sheets in broad daylight. He slips it into her straight away. He puts his hand across her mouth to suppress the moan that he knew would be coming from the first move. He kisses her breasts and then he bites on them, enough to need another hand across her mouth, not enough to draw blood. She reaches back for a big pillow and puts it under her as his grip tightens. They can hear voices down the hall. They speed it up. He humps her frantically, finishing inside her. She doesn't make it.

He slides off the bed. The voices in the hall are getting closer. He puts on his dressing gown and indicates wordlessly that he'd better sneak out. She turns around to watch him tiptoe to the door. He beckons to her to come with him, for a smoke. She whispers no, she's giving them up. He flushes with frustration and asks her again to come with him for a smoke, gesturing like something out of a silent movie, taking out the packet of cigarettes and shaking them, as if the sight of them might weaken her resolve.

She just keeps smiling at him, whispering no. She holds the pillow close to her, like it offers some protection.

The voices in the hall are wearing him down. He holds out his hands in a gesture of helplessness and he is gone.

She lies there for a long time, maybe half-an-hour, drops of Bricks running down her legs whenever she moves.

She can't take it any more. She wants a smoke. She craves a smoke. She needs to have a smoke with Bricks at the old fire escape on the next floor up that the smokers use. A narrow little corridor of guilt tucked away where the good people can't see it.

She puts on her dressing gown and dries the last big stream of Bricks from her legs. She will need to get a move on now, or he could be anywhere.

She sets off, limping as fast as she can. She can smell him now, the way she could smell that other guy for so long. Except the smell of Bricks is stronger than some American soap or oil or spray, it is more like brandy. And if her life is one sweet moment, she has a sudden sense that this moment may be passing.

She sees them but they don't see her. They are having a big laugh about something, Bricks and this doctor at the fire escape, smoking. She comes around the corner and she sees something she knows she shouldn't be seeing. Their backs are still turned to her. She slows down and then she stands still.

Bricks has his arm around the shoulder of this doctor, the one who joked about Bricks and all the institutions he's been in. He is standing there now in his white coat, a very tall, thin man, laughing and smoking. And Bricks is getting a good firm grip on his shoulder, Bricks who doesn't touch people in this way for any reason. Bricks who seems to be suddenly all affectionate to a man in a white coat.

Jesus, she thinks, he's going to . . . he's going to . . . She can see it already, the doctor's body splayed on the tarmac beneath the fire escape, dead the moment he hits the ground. Oh Jesus, she thinks, he's going to do it.

Then she gets it, suddenly she gets it. She has a thousand visions of the truth in about two seconds. The body that she imagines on the ground – it's not the body of the doctor; it's the body of Dorothy. The doctor, he's still here, but Dorothy. . . Dorothy didn't make it. *This* is what happened to Dorothy. She didn't throw herself out the window, she didn't want to die. Dorothy . . . was . . . pushed.

Bricks sees her and he freezes. He knows she has just caught him in what for him is an unnatural act. He knows what it looks like. He knows that she knows.

He takes his hand away from the doctor's shoulder. He smiles at her, a weak effort.

The doctor turns around.

'Joining us?' he says, taking a drag on his cigarette.

He has an extremely courteous manner. For a mad moment Nadine wants to join them. She shakes her head.

'No, actually,' she whispers.

Bricks tries another smile.

'This man is a genius,' he says, putting his arm on the doctor's shoulder again.

'I was telling Bricks I have a tin ear for music,' the doctor says. 'It's the finest of all the art forms, in my opinion.'

He seems to Nadine like such a nice man, she could see herself with a consoling arm on his shoulder. Then he steps back on to the fire escape to stamp out his cigarette, and suddenly he is gone, briskly descending the steps.

Nadine wants to call him back. She wants to scream. She didn't expect him to vanish like that, she didn't think they used the old fire escape any more. She wants to scream, but she remembers Bricks with his hand over her mouth, and it makes her want to puke. She doesn't think she can scream anyway, she feels too weak with fear. Mesmerized, she steps forward, on to the fire escape. She looks down, as if looking will make the doctor somehow reappear. She can't see him anywhere. He's gone and he's not coming back.

She turns to look at Bricks. Did he have sex with Dorothy too before he fucked her out the window? Or did they stand at the window laughing and smoking, like he did with the doctor just now?

'He's a secret smoker,' Bricks says. He sounds completely calm.

Casually, he raises his arm, behind Nadine's body. He leans his hand against the jamb of the fire-escape door. She's trapped here with him, on the metal platform of the fire escape.

Nadine searches deep in her pocket for a packet of Rothmans. She takes them out, her hand trembling, like Freddie's.

She feels it might be easier now to surrender, to let it happen, like she is offering her neck to a vampire, easier to give in than to struggle. She thinks of Freddie hearing the news that she is dead.

She thinks of Freddie too because his mobile is still in her pocket. She can press the button when she puts her packet of Rothmans back in there, but she is pretty sure it will be the last thing she does in this life.

She thinks of the last thing Freddie did, shafting Bricks.

It puts a bit of fight back into her. Through the fear she is suddenly aware of Dorothy, like she is with her in this place, not some scary supernatural presence but something very ordinary. A voice, telling her she's got to come to New York. It was nearly the last thing Dorothy said to her, that she must come to New York. Now the thought of never seeing New York is too much. The thought of dying like this, the way that Dorothy died – it's too much. She will see

New York, whatever it takes. She will not let him take this away from her. The fuck.

She puts a cigarette in her mouth.

'Light?' she says, putting the Rothmans back in her pocket.

She feels the contours of the little silver phone. She touches the buttons until she is certain she has the one she needs, top right. She presses it firmly. She takes the Rothmans out again, and offers them to Bricks. He takes one.

'Here,' he says, producing a cheap lighter.

He lights both of their cigarettes. He leans back nonchalantly. He tries to say something and then he shakes his head in amusement.

That first look said everything, when she caught him out. He knows that she knows.

Freddie answers the call.

'The hot line is open,' he says cheerfully. He is at the bar of the Royal Marine Hotel, trying to drink a Bloody Mary.

He hears Nadine's voice on the line, but in the distance. It sounds like she has knocked the button on by mistake. He is disappointed. Then he hears the voice of Bricks, again in the distance, but clear enough. He realizes that he is eavesdropping and he should leave them to it. But he can't quite bring himself to get off that line.

It's Nadine again.

'You killed Dorothy,' she says, her voice louder than Freddie can recall.

'Blackout,' Bricks says in a softer voice. Something about a blackout. Something else that Freddie doesn't catch.

'You were going to push that guy off the fire escape,' Nadine is saying. 'This fire escape.'

Freddie is stuck to the stool. The barman is wiping the counter.

Freddie has a demented urge to tell him what is happening but he doesn't know how to begin. He can phone the hospital and tell them something terrible is going on at a fire escape. For a split second he is about to use his own phone, cutting off Nadine.

He can run to the public phone or he can drive the three minutes it will take him to get to the hospital. He is halfway to the public phone when he is waylaid by a vision of someone on the switchboard who doesn't understand, fucking it up.

He dashes out to the Merc, straining desperately to hear the voices on the mobile. He starts the car and tears out the gate.

He must drive up a hundred yards to the main street and then just keep going through the traffic until he gets there, going at ninety through the traffic if that's what it takes, like a police car in hot pursuit.

'Will you let me finish my cigarette?' Nadine is saying.

'Ah, it's a shame,' Bricks says.

Freddie hears this clearly. He imagines Bricks is moving in on Nadine. He is boxed in at the traffic lights for twenty seconds, an eternity. He is becoming hysterical. He screams.

'You can do this to me?' she says. She sounds strong.

'These are the breaks,' Bricks says.

The talking stops. Freddie presses the mobile hard against his ear. He is a minute away from the hospital

255

grounds. He is swinging in and out of the traffic, touching sixty on a clear stretch. He knows for sure that someone is going to die.

He presses the phone to his ear until it feels like his brain is bleeding, frantically trying to decipher the sounds coming over the line, the sounds of someone losing their life, the last lonely struggle of Nadine, his baby.

Freddie screeches through the front gate of the hospital. He abandons the Merc in the car park. He runs up to the front desk.

'Fire escape, fire escape, fire escape,' he keeps saying.

The girl at the desk is trying to get his drift.

Olivia comes out of the cafeteria, a vision of salvation.

Freddie goes to her, gasping for breath.

'Fire escape . . . Nadine . . . Bricks . . . please, the fire escape?' he rambles.

Olivia shouts something to the girl at the front desk, a number, a bunch of letters, some sort of signal.

She sets off up the stairs. Freddie follows her. He can sense something in Olivia that he hasn't encountered before. Panic.

He runs and trips and falls after her up two, three, four flights of stairs. Just when he is sure they will never end, he sees Olivia charging through a swing door and down a wide corridor.

He runs after her. He sees her dashing around a corner into a narrow corridor. He follows her in there.

Nadine is sitting with her back to the wall. At a glance she might be a patient who has just been zonked with tranquillizers. She is saying something to Olivia and Olivia is nodding slowly, like she is memorizing a solemn secret.

Nadine sees Freddie. She reaches out to him. He kneels down beside her, holding her hand, just staring at her.

Olivia is at the fire escape. Way down below, she sees a couple of doctors pounding the chest of Bricks Melvin. Then they stop and then they start pounding again.

Then it's over.

Chapter 23

The boat trip brings her out of herself again. Freddie got a bottle of good wine for the trip. They stand at the wheel of the small boat drinking red wine out of plastic cups, Freddie pouring. 'You made it there somehow,' he says.

Then he starts the engine with the aim of taking it very slowly to the top of Dún Laoghaire pier and back. There is little wind on this Sunday afternoon, and anyway it would take a force ten to disturb Freddie's three weeks' growth of fresh fuzz.

Nadine is wearing a pair of blue shades like Gary Oldman as the cool Dracula. They got them earlier at a stall at the Blackrock Market where Freddie goes a lot these days, rummaging through the old books and records, remembering when he was young and had no money. They ate a few fresh doughnuts up there and then Nadine nearly bought a bunch of flowers because the counsellor asked her to look at this, like, it's not a valid position to be opposed to all Nature just because Dorothy liked it.

Go with the flowers thing, she said, go with it, just risk it. Just throw them on the water or something. Say a proper goodbye to Dorothy, who didn't want to die. Just do it.

But Nadine figures she's had enough of the dead. She's pretty sure now that Trayton died too. Looking across at the pier she has no sense of him being out there any more. Even his scent has died, even that.

She's had enough of the counselling too. It did the trick up in the ward, but for real life you need more than this lady asking you to have a look at why you own twenty different shades of red lipstick, like what's that about? Just look at it she says, just look at it, and really there's nothing there to look at, because it's just fucking lipstick, that's all.

For real life you need to have a look at the sort of shit you can only get in Freddie's books. Jack Kerouac, that's what you need to look at. Jack Kerouac's *On the Road*, picked up after a bad, bad, day looking at lipstick, that's all the counselling she'll be wanting for a while. At least until the next time some jazz great fucks her and tries to kill her. Until then . . .

It's the one place she feels totally right in the head these days, reading Freddie's books. So he wasn't wrong about everything.

He was wrong about Dorothy, though. He said she wrote some pretty good poems. In fact, in Nadine's opinion, she wrote some fucking great ones, a bunch written in a jotter just before she went into Stepaside and brought to the house the other night by this sweet-looking young skinhead poet called Stump who wants to publish them. Or who wants Freddie to publish them.

Freddie starts the boat. The sea is calm. The pier is full of Sunday strollers. The wine is going down fast.

Nadine takes off her blue shades and smiles.

'You know I said Dorothy wanted to be buried in the ground?' she says. 'Well, that wasn't totally true.'

'No?'

'She said she'd prefer it but she didn't really give a shit.'

'That sounds right.'

'Sorry.'

'All right.'

Nadine puts on her shades again. Now Freddie needs to own up.

'Confession time,' he says. 'I love about six jazz albums, and that's it.'

Nadine considers this. She looks him up and down like some sort of exhibit.

'You sad motherfucker,' she says.

'Sorry,' he says.

'Do you actually like jazz, like, at all?' she says.

'I love it,' he says. 'I love the guys and I love the clothes and I love the attitudes. I love it. But I don't understand it.'

'Right,' she says.

'I nearly understood it one night . . . with LJ,' he says.

'She's actually back with Paddy Lamb?' she says.

'She's on a journey.'

'Jesus, Freddie, she's going the long way round.'

Freddie laughs. He finishes his beaker of wine.

'She'll get there,' he says.

They can see their new apartments back in Dún Laoghaire. That's why Freddie got the boat, so he might view the property from the water, another of his rich-guy whims. But Freddie still gets his kicks in places like the Blackrock Market, wishing he was young again, seventeen, when he first heard the rumble of blues from a dive on

Baggot Street, seventeen and rummaging through the jazz albums in these flea markets, dreaming of being Miles Davis just for a day, mysterious, beautiful.

He wishes he was young again, seventeen and heavy with longing for something just out of reach, always believing that one day he would hear exactly what Miles Davis hears in the hiss of a hi-hat, that he would understand what he loves.

And now, after all these years searching, he realizes he had it all the time. He understood it perfectly. It was all about the longing, the desire. Charlie Parker didn't really want to find that thing he lost, he just wanted to believe it was out there for him, somewhere in the Harlem night.

That's the deal. And later for the garbage.

Freddie cuts the engine as the boat nears the top of the pier.

'And by the way, why did you go to Man United anyway?' Nadine says.

'Just the vibe,' he says.

'The guys, the clothes and the attitudes?' she says.

'I'm a Forest man,' he says.

'A what?' she says.

'I've always supported Nottingham Forest.'

'But they're shit?'

'They were great once.'

'Once,' she says dismissively.

The boat silently passes the top of the pier. Freddie pours the last of the wine.

'Once is enough,' he says.

He starts the engine for home. Stump the poet is coming over again this evening to talk about publishing Dorothy.

The other night, he said her later work was not just brilliant, it was important. They all drank to that, sitting around the table knocking back the wine and smoking and talking half the night. The poet closed his eyes and said one of Dorothy's poems and it sounded fantastic.

Then Freddie ordered him a taxi.